Totally Bound Publishing books by McKenna Jeffries and Aliyah Burke:

McKingley Volume One
All The Wright Moves
The Best Thing Yet

McKingley Volume Two
Risky Pleasures
Pure Harmony

I0658903

McKINGLEY
Volume Three

Irresistible Forces

Seduction's Dance

McKENNA JEFFRIES and ALIYAH BURKE

McKingley Volume Three
ISBN # 978-1-78184-719-0
©Copyright McKenna Jeffries and Aliyah Burke 2013
Cover Art by Posh Gosh ©Copyright 2013
Interior text design by Claire Siemaszkiewicz
Totally Bound Publishing

Published in 2014 by Totally Bound Publishing, Newland House, The Point, Weaver Road, Lincoln, LN6 3QN, United Kingdom.

Totally Bound Publishing is an imprint of Total-E-Ntwined Limited.

IRRESISTIBLE
FORCES

Dedication

To my brother who, as a police officer, protects and serves, thank you. To my sister thanks for passing on your love of reading and your support.
— McKenna Jeffries

To the men and women who sacrifice so much to protect this country.
Thank you for all you do.
— Aliyah Burke

Chapter One

Leonardo Wright tapped his finger on the steering wheel as he drove toward his destination. Suddenly, a car going way too fast zoomed past him. Leo narrowed his eyes, recognizing the night blue Audi S8 — he flipped on his lights and went after the sporty sedan. From the type of vehicle, he figured the driver had been at business meetings today instead of at her store.

They continued driving above the posted speed limit. Leo knew she saw him, but she was thumbing her nose at him. Suddenly she made a turn and he clenched the wheel tightly, already mumbling the lecture he would be giving her. He followed and drove through the gates that lead to the oasis she had created. The automobile came to a screeching halt between the Sierra 2500HD crew cab and Toyota Land Cruiser, also in blue. The woman he was chasing was partial to blue. Leo parked behind her then turned off his cruiser.

Her car door swung open and one leg appeared, coming to rest on the ground. Leo studied the bare leg from the knee down until he saw the silver, high-heeled sandal. The rest of the woman came into view and he held the wheel, studying the beauty that was Deyon De'clare. She turned to face him, putting her hands on her hips. On her lush lips was a familiar teasing grin, which only made her captivating features even sexier. The face that had graced many runways and magazines—thus making her the most recognized full-figured supermodel in the world—was framed by wild, kinky hair. She wore shades, but Leo didn't need to see her curly lashed, light-gray eyes to know they had the same teasing in them.

Although she wasn't a model anymore—instead now a sought-after designer that catered to full-figured women—Deyon certainly knew how to capture one's attention. She was her own best advertisement that curves were indeed beautiful, sexy and able to bring a man to his knees. As usual, Deyon was dressed stylishly. A dark royal blue with silver patchwork design shirt sloped off one shoulder, highlighting her rich caramel skin. The shorts were the same blue—without the silver—and stopped at her knees. Deyon bent into her car. Leo exited his cruiser before closing the door, gaze locked on her full ass. He clenched and unclenched his fists, aching to touch the round globes. Deyon stood, pushing her hair back with long fingers. She faced him again, holding a purse and briefcase then, using her hip, she closed her car door. Deyon strode toward him—her innate grace, power and all out sensuality of her walk another thing that made her successful as a model. Her movement had a rhythm that made his heart pound and his palms sweat. Leo kept his face contained.

"Leonardo, are you here to return my weapons?" Deyon's melodious voice held playfulness.

Leo knew she was very serious. The question was the same one she had been asking him for a few months, just varied in the way she phrased it. It had begun around the same time she'd started calling him by his full first name instead of the shortened version as she had usually done before. Deyon pushed her shades up onto the top of her hair. She studied him.

"No, I'm holding them until you promise me that you won't pull them on anyone again. When are you going to press charges?" he gave his standard reply.

"Admit it. You're using my weapons. I bet they aren't even at the station but at your house. You're overstepping your authority, Sheriff." Deyon paused, her brow furrowing, then she said, "As I've told you *ad-nauseum*, I only pulled them to defend myself when that fool grabbed me. And for the millionth time I'm not pressing charges. I handled it, and he won't be working for me anymore. Leave it alone, Leonardo." There was a sharp snap to her tone.

It was then that Leo noticed the strain on her face. Deyon might be acting like everything was okay, but clearly something was wrong. He noted the sweat beading on her forehead, her jaw was working and her gaze was slightly unfocused—he knew her well enough to know she wasn't feeling well. For that reason, he'd leave the incident at her house—when a male model she had hired for a show hadn't taken no for an answer—alone for now. Although he knew Deyon would not press charges because she'd handled it by tranqing the overzealous man before calling him, Leo still enjoyed needling her about it. Until that incident, he hadn't realized how much an irate Deyon was a turn on. He focused on her, seeing her wavering where she stood under the unrelenting New Mexico sunlight.

"Come on into the house." He slid his hand around her waist.

It was a testament to how ill Deyon must have been feeling that she didn't resist. She let him lead her to her house. This close to her, the scent of coconut and peaches wafted to him. His member hardened as he imagined tasting every inch of her skin, following the intoxicating aroma. Leo was grateful Deyon, who usually noticed too much, was too distracted to realize his problem—his uniform wasn't made to hide an erection. The fragrance was from the lotion Deyon used, which she had specially made at a store in town. There was so much he knew about Deyon. She was a close friend to his sister Arissa and had, by extension, become a part of the Wright family. Leo saw neither Arissa nor Jackson's cars were parked in their slots to the right of the house. They were staying in the two apartments that made up the second floor of Deyon's home. The place was an architectural vision that suited Deyon very well. She'd created a haven on this land with lots of space between her place and anyone else's.

Deyon fumbled for her keys. Leo moved her hand gently away and slid his fingers into the pocket of her shorts. He bit back a groan at being this close to the curvaceous hips he longed to be buried between. Leo pulled out the keys and efficiently opened the door, keeping his other hand on her waist to steady her. Deyon leaned against him heavily.

"I can't believe you drove and you were feeling like this. Recklessly and fast too."

"I had to get home before it hit," Deyon mumbled.

"You don't get them often but even you know it can be dangerous if the migraine hits and you're behind the wheel of a car." Leo led her inside, kicking the outer door closer with his foot.

He glanced at the key ring and found the correct one. A little away, one on the left and another on the right of the center door, were entrances that led to the apartments upstairs. Leo put the key in the lock of the middle door, pushing it open. The lights came on automatically. Deyon whimpered, pressing her face against the side of his neck. Leo shifted, cradling her, and reached for the lights. He switched them off, darkening the massive living room. Leo lifted Deyon and started toward the master suite.

"If you fall, we'll both have to lay here until someone finds us." Deyon sounded amused by the idea.

"Hush, I know your house as well as I know my own," Leo stated.

"Thank God for that because I really didn't want to be on the ground," Deyon replied in a soft voice.

Leo thought of her driving when she was already feeling the headache. "How'd you plan to get inside if you're already feeling this bad?"

"Walk, and if I fell, crawl until I was at least inside the door. Rissa, Deiter or Jackson should be home soon and they would have gotten me the rest of the way."

Leo tightened his hold. He didn't like hearing that at all. The idea of her lying in the entryway of the house made him furious.

"Calm down, Leo. I've done it before and there has been no one to bring me inside. I just lay there until it was bearable enough for me to get inside. I always make it through fine." Deyon's voice was strained.

"You should have called me or one of the family if you're feeling like this. You don't need to be alone."

"I know, but they hit so suddenly and randomly."

"When was the last time you had one?" Leo pushed open the door with his boot.

"A year."

He carried her across the spacious room to her king-sized bed. Gently, he placed her on top of the quilt. Leo squatted by the bed. He removed her shades and put them on the nightstand then focused on her pushing her hair gently back from her face.

"Where's your medicine?"

"I... It's been so long it's probably expired and I didn't get a refill." Deyon gritted her teeth.

"Deyon—" He growled but cut himself off.

There was nothing to be done about that now. Leo stood and went to the attached bathroom. He got a basin and quickly filled it with cool water while grabbing a cloth. He searched the medicine cabinet and pulled out some over-the-counter pain pills. Returning to her bedroom, he placed the items on the floor by the bed. The pain pills he set on the nightstand. He left rapidly, going back into the hall then down to the living room and making a right into the kitchen. Even in the dark he knew his way as he went to the fridge and grabbed a bottle of water before retracing his steps to the bedroom. Deyon was curled up in a ball, moaning. Leo knelt by the side of the bed, got some pills then opened the water and gently lifted her to give them to her. She moved the water away after just taking enough to swallow the pills. Leo didn't push for any more, knowing she was probably feeling nauseated. He reached for the cloth and wet it before placing it over her eyes.

"Thanks." Her voice was hoarse.

"Shh...no talking. Later we talk," Leo stated.

"Oh shit, that's your lecture voice. What did I do now?" Deyon lifted one end of the cloth, watching him.

Leo stifled a smile. If only she knew how much lately he'd been enjoying their lectures. She would get agitated and start tapping her foot, making her full breasts bob, then she would bite her lip causing them to plump even more enticingly. Finally, when she'd had just enough, she would roll her eyes, shifting around on whatever she was sitting on, moving her body so sensuously he was hard pressed to not push her over and have her right wherever they were.

"Driving. But we'll discuss it later. If I rub your temples will it help or hurt you?" Leo asked.

"It would feel good, but you don't need to do that. You've done enough," Deyon protested.

"Hush, woman."

"Enjoy my not being up to responding to that while you can. Now get to massaging me." She smiled then winked.

"I'll massage you anywhere you want." It was a promise and he stared into her open eye.

Deyon looked startled then speculative. "When I'm feeling better, we're going to definitely talk."

"That's why I was coming to see you," Leo admitted. He'd decided to stop beating around the bush and just make his intentions known.

"Wh—?"

"Shut up, Deyon." He touched her fingers, moving them off the cloth.

Leo smoothed the cloth over her eyes. He rested his fingers on her temples and started massaging. She moaned softly. The sound made his cock even harder. He shifted, trying to get space in his slacks. Leo continued his ministrations then removed the cloth, rubbing along the top of her forehead outwards down to the sides. He alternated the cool water and massaging. A few times he changed the water and kept working on the migraine she was experiencing. Slowly, Deyon relaxed then went lax as she drifted off to sleep. Leo placed the wet cloth in the basin. He leaned over and put his hand on the bed under his chin, studying her face. Asleep, Deyon was even sexier. Her thick lashes fanned out just below her eyes and her lush lips were slightly parted as she breathed deeply.

Suddenly she sat up. "I can't sleep in this."

She went to swing her legs off the bed and Leo stilled her. Deyon blinked, opening her eyes. Her unfocused gaze cleared and she looked at him.

"I'll get it. Stay." He moved her back gently to where she had lain before.

"On the chair."

Leo turned to where she gestured then retrieved the clothing. He shook it open and bit back a groan—it was one of her short, flirty housedresses. This one was burnt orange with dark red flowers. He returned to the bed. Deyon reached for it, but he held it out of her reach.

"You're not undoing all my hard work. Stay there," he snapped.

"No one asked you to. Don't get nasty with me." She mirrored his tone.

Leo smiled. She was starting to feel better. Deyon was very independent and didn't like leaning on anyone.

"Okay. I don't want to argue with you. I'll help you into it." He silently cursed himself for setting himself up for the torture of seeing her almost naked and not being able to touch.

"You just want to get a look at my goodies," Deyon teased.

"Yes, but when you're well enough we can both do something about it," Leo countered.

Deyon's gaze went wide then narrowed. A look of speculation filled her eyes then she smiled, a small twist of lips. Deyon sat up and he helped her. Leo gritted his teeth as he removed her blouse then pants. His hand shook at the first view of her cream colored bra and matching high-cut panties. Both were lacy and looked so tactile. Leo focused on the dress he had to put on her. Quickly he covered her up, breathing a sigh of relief. Deyon ran her cool fingers against the side of his face. He lifted his head, meeting her pale-gray gaze. Leo swallowed at the desire he saw there. He resisted the invitation and slid her back into place on the bed. Deyon shifted on top of the quilt.

"Pull off the quilt," she demanded.

Leo did as she bid, gulping as she moved to the side. He pushed it under her body then she rolled back toward him. The dress hiked up, showing even more of her long legs. Deyon's body pressed against his chest. She moaned, a wanton sound. Leo finished pulling the quilt out then knelt again.

"Sleep."

"I—"

"Do you want the headache to come on stronger? I know it isn't fully gone."

"No, it isn't. It's just lurking in the background waiting to pounce again." Deyon sighed.

"Rest. I'll be here when you wake." He ran his finger down her cheek.

Deyon studied him then spoke, "I'm gonna hold you to that."

"I want you to."

She kept her gaze locked with his before her eyes drifted shut. Leo kept watch as her breathing deepened and she went back to sleep. When he was sure she was out, he went into the other room to make a call. Once finished, Leo returned then lifted the chair he'd retrieved the housedress from and carried it to the bedside. Sitting, he crossed his arms over his stomach and observed the woman who had gotten under his skin. They'd have to talk about what to do about it once she woke. Leo pulled off his boots and socks. Removing his gun belt, he stood then placed it on a table by where he knew she kept a gun safe behind the picture on the wall. He relaxed against the high-back chair, shifting to get comfy. The sound of Deyon's soft breathing filled the room.

* * * *

Deyon blinked, stretching as she woke. She was thankful the migraine had gone. Mentally she made a note to get her prescription filled. She rarely got migraines, but when she did, and didn't take her medicine, they lasted longer than they should. This time it hadn't and she knew why. Deyon turned her head and a smile curled her lips as she spotted his large feet. They were propped against the bed. Leonardo had sexy feet— all manly, big and looking so touchable. Not that she had ever touched them, but she'd fantasized about it. About a lot of things she'd like to do to Leonardo Wright. Until recently, she might have called him Leo out loud, but in her head he had always been Leonardo. His name matched the man—a compelling face that made her pulse race and panties get wet. All those things were Leonardo.

Deyon raised her gaze, studying those long, muscular legs in his uniform. The sheriff uniform he wore should be listed as its own lethal weapon. It was hell on the pulse and made her want to rip it off. His broad chest was showcased in his shirt, but it was better viewed bare as she had seen it at various times when they were around his family. His dark sienna skin offset his light brown eyes. Rugged, masculine features and a short haircut matched his strong, confident and straightforward personality. The combination of his traits was what had got him elected as Sheriff of McKingley and made him the man who awakened things inside her that she'd not pursued in a long time. She'd known him a long time and had been studying to gauge what was in his psyche. She still hadn't figured him out and wanted to get deep within the layers of who Leonardo Wright was.

She could have approached him before but hadn't for two reasons. One, he was the older brother of her friend Arissa, which would create problems if they didn't work out. Deyon knew when it came to relationships, she was passionate and went all in with no holds barred. She expected the same from her partner. Which led to her second reason—with Leonardo she already knew she would accept nothing less than a relationship. But seeing the way the man had his pick of women and how he'd dated some of them for a short time, she was not about to be another notch on his belt. She wouldn't call Leonardo a player by any means—women loved him and if he was interested he accepted their advances, but for some reason his interest in the ladies he dated didn't seem to last long. That was the one thing she couldn't figure out. What kept his interest? Leonardo was a complex man and she wanted to figure out what made him tick, then make him hers. Deyon remembered what he had intimated earlier—seemed as if he wished to be hers. But she wasn't one to pussyfoot around—she needed what he expected to be laid out clearly. They would make it clear what they each expected.

Deyon slid out of the other side of the bed and stood. She looked once more at the big man sprawled in the chair then strode out of the room. In the darkened hallway, she made her way to the living room then toward the kitchen. Inside she turned the dimmer switch on at a low setting. She noted it was already after ten p.m. No wonder she was feeling hungry—she'd been asleep for hours and she'd missed lunch. She'd arrived home a little after five o'clock, later than she usually did on a Friday. Fridays at her store were her early day, and she usually left at twelve to start her weekend. Unless there was something pressing, she didn't work on the weekends anymore—the perks of being the boss. A sound caught her attention and Deyon headed toward the living room. Hearing it again, she realized it was a knock on the door. Deyon went to it, wondering why they hadn't rung the bell. It could only be one of three people who were knocking directly. Anyone else would have pressed the bell outside the building, which would have come through the intercom and they would have to be let in. Deyon opened the door.

"Shouldn't you be in bed?" Arissa Wright, one of her best friends, scowled.

"Why?"

"Migraine. Leo called me to get this." She handed her a pharmacy bag.

Deyon took it and hugged her. "Thanks, I didn't get it refilled."

Deyon spotted the man waiting on Arissa. She released Arissa and waved at Deiter, Arissa's fiancé. He'd moved in with Arissa upstairs for now while they looked for a place of their own. Deiter nodded at her, smiling before turning his attention to Arissa. Deyon noted the possessive look on his face.

I want someone to look at me like that.

Arissa spoke again, capturing her attention. "You should know better than letting it run out."

"I know. I know. Won't happen again."

"It better not, I had your doctor add refills on it so you have no excuse," Arissa said.

Arissa was a doctor at the hospital. Deyon figured Arissa had contacted her doctor to have them call in the prescription.

"Thanks again."

"Thank Leo." Arissa craned her neck as if trying to see inside. "Where is he anyway?"

"Sleeping. He watched over me," Deyon said.

Arissa focused on her, her gaze questioning. Deyon shrugged, not saying anything. Until they talked, there was nothing to tell.

"Listen to his lecture and actually do as he says," Arissa said.

Deiter laughed behind her. Deyon glared at the big German. He smirked. Everyone knew of Leo and his lectures. He was an equal opportunity lecturer— anyone he viewed as family or friend might be made to sit through what he called 'a talk'. Deyon swore the man took too much joy in lecturing her. Deyon glanced at Arissa.

"I was making something to eat. Do you all wanna join me?"

"Nah. I'm beat and going to get an early night." Arissa walked over to Deiter, sliding her hand around his waist.

He rested his arm over her shoulder. "Make sure you take care of yourself, we all care about you. Feel better, Deyon."

Arissa waved and they headed to their apartment. Deyon leaned against the entryway and watched as they disappeared inside. She stepped back, closing the door then turning. Deyon gasped as she hit a solid body. His manly scent surrounded her as he steadied her. His large hands rested on her cloth-clad hips as he held her in place. She wished he were touching bare skin. Deyon raised her head and met his light brown gaze. Leonardo's lids were practically lowered over his eyes.

"Deiter was correct. We care about you. You need to take better care of yourself, Deyon." His deep voice rumbled out of his chest.

The broad expanse was pressed against her breasts making them tingle. Deyon shifted her legs, almost straddling his thigh. Leonardo's hands tightened on her hips. Deyon licked her lips wanting a taste. He followed the motion then dipped his head.

Yes. Kiss me. Make it hard and good.

Chapter Two

Deyon closed her eyelids and opened her lips, waiting for the press of his. None came, making her frown. She blinked, opened her eyes and stared into his—Leonardo's gaze was intense and she could see the desire, but he didn't make any further move to close the distance.

"I want to taste you, Deyon."

"What are you waiting for then?" She licked her lips again.

Again he followed the action then met her gaze. "We need to get some things straight first. I want to date you and work up to more. I can't—"

"Won't."

He shook his head. "Can't taste you until you're ready. When I do taste you for the first time, I won't be able to stop."

"No one is asking you to stop. And I'm ready. More than ready." Deyon moved her hips, rocking against his thigh between hers.

She was soaking wet and prepared to take whatever he had. One touch and she was willing to throw caution to the wind and have Leonardo in her bed, making her go out of her mind with pleasure. Yet he was resisting and she was ready to jump him. Rip his clothes off, take his cock inside her body and ride him until they both were spent.

He inhaled then breathed out before speaking. "If it was sex I wanted, I'd already have you on the bed with me buried deep in your body. Fucking you so hard that you'd be screaming until you were hoarse." He paused and a slow, arrogant grin curled his lips. "If that was all I wanted."

Deyon's breath caught and her heart started to race. "What do you want, Leonardo?"

"You, Deyon. I want to date you and get to know you better. I don't want just sex, but more. What makes you happy? What do you like to do in your spare time? I want to know everything a man finds out about a woman who has captured his interest." He moved his head closer but still didn't kiss her.

"But...you know these things about me already," she protested, not sure what else he wanted to find out.

"I know some of the things about you as a friend, but not as a man who wants to be buried inside you. Not as a lover."

"For Christ's sakes, Leonardo, why do you pick now to decide to be a gentleman?" She blew out a breath.

"You're always so impatient. Slow is very good and it heightens the pleasure."

"You can go as slow as you want in bed," she stated slowly.

"Dating first, then we'll work our way there. Be patient, believe me I only have patience to be a gentleman for so long." Wicked laughter fell from his plump lips.

Deyon moved her head closer to his. He moved his back.

"Bastard. You're getting some perverse pleasure out of torturing me."

"Now, now. You know my parents were married before they had me, and anyway, you shouldn't be using such nasty words."

"Humph, you know that isn't as nasty as my mouth can get. I'm being nice, but you are taxing my good nature," Deyon growled.

He put his head back and laughed loud and long. Deyon pushed out of his arms, but Leonardo caught her again, holding her easily. There were tears of mirth in his eyes.

"You're funny."

Deyon focused on the main point of the conversation. "So let's get this straight—you want to date me but no kissing until you decide we can go to the next step."

"Yes."

"Okay, I can go along with that." Deyon moved out of his embrace and passed by him.

She reached out and caressed his firm ass as she went by then smacked him on the butt.

Leonardo jumped then glared at her. "Deyon," he said warningly.

She put up her hand, walking backwards. "You didn't say anything about touching."

"And that's your idea of going along." Leonardo stalked after her.

"Leonardo, that's my way of going along. I didn't say that I wouldn't try to convince you to give up your stupidity and move things along." Deyon stopped.

He kept coming, crowding her back against the doorway that led into the kitchen.

"I like hearing you say my name."

"You do, huh? I'll have to say it often then, Leonardo." She'd lowered her voice, making it huskier.

His eyes darkened. "You're going to make this hard."

"I don't think you need help there." She rocked against his erection, pressed against her belly.

Leonardo groaned then stepped away. "Uh-uh. You can touch, but not that. Above the waist."

"Now there are restrictions. You so know how to challenge a girl. But I'm really adaptable. Above the waist has so many interesting places to touch." Deyon reached up and stroked down from the top of his ear to the bottom, playing with the lobe.

"Don't forget that touching goes both ways." He stroked his fingers along her lips, top then bottom.

Deyon followed it with her tongue, whimpering when he removed his touch. "You *are* so wrong. Damn you, Leonardo."

"Patience will do you some good." He sobered then said, "Now about your reckless driving—"

She groaned then interjected. "If you're going to lecture me, I need to at least get something to eat."

She turned and entered the kitchen. Deyon finished pulling fixings for a sandwich out of the fridge.

"You need to be more careful how you drive. I know you were trying to get home fast, but it was dangerous how you were driving. Hell, you shouldn't have even been doing that when you were getting a migraine. Promise me you'll call me next time if you feel like one is coming on."

Hearing the concern in his tone, Deyon stopped making the sandwich and went to him.

"I promise I will." She hugged him, looking at his face.

He nodded. "Good. Now let's talk about vehicular safety."

Deyon rolled her eyes and released him, returning to her sandwich. She didn't even listen to him as he continued his lecture. After making her sandwich, she made one for Leonardo. She left off the cheese, since he didn't like it on turkey—any other cold cut and he had it but not turkey. She put everything away then retrieved each of them a bottle of iced tea. Grabbing a bag of potato chips, she turned, placing it and the drinks on the island before getting the sandwiches. She put hers down by the stool she was planning to use and slid the other across the counter to him. He caught the plate and reached for the bag of chips.

Leonardo didn't even pause in his lecture as he finished fixing his plate. Deyon went back to the fridge to grab some pickles. She placed the jar on the counter then sat again on her swivel counter stool. Deyon leaned against the back of the stool, relaxing as she ate. Between bites, he continued his lecture. Deyon lowered her head, rolling her eyes again. She ate her food as he spoke in that tone that she only admitted to herself made her hot. It was authoritative and firm, making her want to stick her tongue between his lips. Hell, if she was truthful, everything he did made her want to kiss him. But he wanted her to wait and expected it of her. He didn't know her well if he thought that was happening—she was very good at finding ways around things that blocked her path. Leonardo's need to date and be a gentleman was just another obstacle she would conquer then she would have him anyway she wanted him.

"Deyon." His sharp call made her glance up.

"Huh?"

"You're not listening to me." Leonardo crossed his arms over his chest, leaning back on his stool.

Seeing he was finished, and since she was too, she retrieved his plate then her own. She scraped off the remains of their meal into the trash then faced him. She moved to the stool beside him, leaning on the counter by where he sat.

"I never listen. Lecturing is for you to vent, so I wait until you wind down."

He barked out a laugh then said, "What am I going to do with you?"

"Date me then let me in your pants," Deyon replied.

"Sassy woman," he said fondly as he ran a finger down her cheek. "I know you don't work tomorrow, but do you have anything planned?"

"Nothing that can't wait."

"Good. I'll pick you up tomorrow at two o'clock." He slid off the stool, brushing against her body as he stepped away.

Deyon followed him as he strode out of the room and through the darkened living room beyond. Leonardo opened the door, stepping outside before turning to her. Deyon leaned against the doorjamb, crossing her arms over her chest. He moved closer and placed his hand on her upper thigh, just below the hem of her housedress. Deyon moaned softly.

"Tomorrow." He stroked his thumb on her thigh.

"No below the waist. That's your rule, unless you want to change it." Deyon lowered her gaze, taking in all she wanted to touch below his waist.

She would start with his bulging shaft. Deyon clenched her fists, shifting her stance. He gripped her thigh to keep her in place. She widened her legs, willing him to move his touch up. As if hearing her fevered entreaty, he moved his hand up below her hem.

"That's the rule for you. Didn't say it was for me."

"Ah...so we have different rules. Am I going to know what these rules are?" Deyon clenched her pussy as it flooded even more.

"Nope. I need some advantage in dealing with you. Tomorrow at two o'clock." He released her before pivoting and heading for the door.

"What sort of date starts at two o'clock in the afternoon?" she called.

"One you will enjoy," he replied not turning.

"No hint so I can know how to dress?"

"Not fooling me into telling you. Dress as you usually do."

"How?"

"To drive me wild." Leonardo glanced over his shoulder from the open front door and winked.

Shadowed in the recess lighting she kept outside, he looked like a mythical warrior. He exited into the dark night. Deyon straightened, stepping back inside. She closed the door and moved back into the house.

I'm going on a date with Leonardo and there will be no kissing or sex. At least not yet. Lord have mercy on me not to jump the man.

* * * *

The next day Deyon opened the door and repeated the prayer as she viewed the tall, dark and handsome man at her door. In uniform, Leonardo was authoritative and attractive but out of it he was devastatingly sensual and predatory. The rich, hunter-green button down shirt he wore had three buttons open at the neck and the hem rested mid-thigh on his slacks, which were dark gray. On his feet were a pair of open toed sandals. Deyon glanced down at her own outfit. She had on the same color but in reverse — her shirt was gray and bottoms green.

She raised her head and laughed. "People are going to think we planned to dress alike."

"Just good taste," he replied.

On him, it indeed was. Deyon retrieved her bag and stepped outside. Together they headed to his vehicle. Once inside, Deyon relaxed against the buttery-soft leather as he got them on their way. They drove for a few minutes, the silence comfortable.

"I'm surprised you have no questions about where we're going."

"You're not going to tell me anyway. So why ask." Deyon shrugged.

"But your asking is the fun part." He pouted.

Deyon chuckled. "The look on you doesn't work on me. Not falling for it."

Leonardo winked then turned on the car radio. He pushed in a CD then skipped some songs before leaving one to play. Deyon recognized Hemingway's Whiskey by Kenny Chesney. She hummed along as it played, followed by a few of the other of the songs on the CD. By the time they arrived at their destination, she knew without going inside where they were. The area came into view and excitement filled Deyon. Leonardo found parking then exited the vehicle before coming around to open her door. He led her to the hood of the truck and she viewed the sign 'Clarington Weapons Expo'. She turned to Leonardo and smiled.

"If I was allowed to kiss you, I would give you a big fat one with tongue. This will have to do instead." She groped his ass, pulling him against her and whispered, "You sure do know the way to a girl's heart." She got another squeeze in then released him. "Come on, let's go check out some weapons."

Leonardo put his hand against her back, escorting Deyon into the expo. He was thankful his shirt was long enough to cover his hardness. If it were any other woman but Deyon he wouldn't have taken them to the expo—they wouldn't have appreciated it as much as she would. She was more into weapons than he was. Deyon had even had a whole room specially made for her collection. Leonardo could admit that seeing her holding a gun did a lot of things to him. She was a crack shot and could take a gun apart and put it back together in a time that could almost beat his. Deyon was also partial to knives and swords and one of her most recent acquisitions was a pistol crossbow. When she had sighted down the barrel and shot he'd almost come in his jeans. Yeah, he was a weird man to enjoy watching her go gooey over weapons.

He stood back as Deyon started to speak with the man selling various guns. She paused and waved. Leo glanced to see who she was hailing and spotted Rhianna De'clare—Deyon's younger sister—and stifled a chuckle. Like Deyon, her sister had an affinity for weapons, although Rhianna preferred to collect swords and knives. Leo lifted his hand and Rhianna returned his gesture with a smile then went back to conversing with one of the vendors. From where Leo stood, he could see the man Rhianna was talking with had many sorts of blades. Leo focused on Deyon and the gun vendor. At first, the man looked at Leo, then he focused on Deyon, and from the expression on the vendor's face it was clear he wondered why she was the one doing the talking. Soon the man's expression changed and he got that star struck look men got around Deyon. When Leonardo crossed his arms over his chest and cleared his throat, the man glanced at him then inclined his head.

Deyon turned and patted his arm. "I'll be a moment."

She went back to talking with the man. The other men in the vicinity came closer and soon they surrounded them, chatting with Deyon. He didn't move his stance, staring down the men to let them know she was his. Deyon reached back and slid her hand into his. She pulled him closer, pointing out the gun she was thinking of buying. He shared his opinion and she nodded then started discussing price. The men who had surrounded them started to disperse.

"Lucky man," one whispered as he departed.

Leonardo smiled smugly—he knew he was. Once Deyon got the price she wanted and had made arrangements, she gripped his hand and dragged him off to another table. They spent hours at the expo—Deyon and he even tried out a few weapons in the exhibition. Leonardo held her bag as she matched off with a man with a sword. Deyon kicked off her high-heeled sandals in his direction. He picked them up by the straps. She smiled then blew him a kiss. Deyon focused on her opponent and moved slowly as they circled each other. He looked like he was humoring her. Leonardo shook his head—that was a big mistake. Deyon moved in and in a dazzlingly display of swordsmanship she disarmed the supposed expert. He looked stupefied then he laughed. The group around them joined in. Deyon took a bow then lowered her head closer to the one who was speaking to her—Leonardo was too far away to hear what was being said. She shook her head, gesturing toward Leo. The man glared at him then raised Deyon's hand to his lips. He kissed it and she chuckled before removing her hand and strolling toward Leo.

He viewed the men watching her. They were as captivated by her strut as he usually was. Deyon stopped before him and smiled widely.

"This has been a fun day. If could kiss you, I would show my appreciation." She smiled a sassy grin.

He stifled a groan. Him and his stupid rule. Deyon thought he was torturing her, but in reality he was tormenting himself. Deyon pulled him along and he followed her to another exhibit.

* * * *

Leonardo relaxed in the booth at Morrow's after their scrumptious dinner. Deyon rested against his shoulder as she listened to the live band the supper club had playing. She hummed under her breath, swaying to the music. It was driving him crazy. Deyon had a dreamy smile on her face. She turned to him, cupping his cheek and moving close to him so he could hear her.

"You having a good time?"

"Yes. I'm enjoying being with you," he whispered against the side of her face.

"It would be better if we could kiss. But your rule, at least until you break it, says no. So I'll settle for this." Deyon scraped her nails gently inside the open neck of his shirt.

He groaned, putting his hand over hers. Raising her hand, he squeezed it and slid out of the booth. He helped Deyon out then intertwined their fingers, guiding her through the aisle toward the exit. He was glad he had already paid the bill because he couldn't have waited for it. Outside in the slightly cool night, Leonardo led her to his brown F-150 King Ranch SuperCrew truck. He helped her in then looped around the hood to the driver's side. Inside the cab, he started the truck and got them on their way. She was silent leaning against the seat as they went toward her home. Leonardo gripped the wheel of his truck.

Be strong. You can resist stripping her and having her.

He repeated the words to himself in the forty-five minutes it took him to get to her house. In her driveway, he parked then got out and opened her door. Placing his hand at the small of her back, he stifled a groan as he touched bare skin. The dark gray halter-top shirt she wore dipped low, stopping just above the swell of her ass. Her dark green pants flared at the bottom to her ankles offsetting her high-heeled sandals that were the same color as her shirt. He figured the entire ensemble was from her shop, Deyon's. They had everything from accessories, clothing and even shoes. Their lingerie was also spectacular — Leo moaned at the thought. Leo was impressed that Deyon created all the clothing and some of everything else that she carried in her store. The bulk of the rest of the things were done by designers she employed.

Leonardo couldn't resist smoothing his thumb over her naked back. She shivered, pressing against his frame. He kept them going toward the house, quickly. Her chuckle was wanton and beckoned his raging libido. He took the key, opening the door before herding her inside. Leonardo unlocked her front door then stepped back as Deyon entered. He placed her key on the table she kept by the entry way and walked rapidly to the outer door.

"Bowling tomorrow. Six o'clock. Night," he said, beating a hasty retreat.

"Leonardo."

He ignored her surprised call and got out of there. In his truck, he spun the wheel and drove off.

Why are you leaving? She wants you. Follow nature and get on with it.

"You need to keep control, old man." He didn't know if he could, but he was determined to try.

Chapter Three

"Control," Leonardo repeated what had become his mantra in the month he'd been dating Deyon.

Every time he saw her, it was getting harder to resist the temptation that was Deyon De'clare.

Then why are you resisting, you ass? A voice that sounded suspiciously like his older brother Dimitri Wright came in his thoughts.

It was exactly what Dimitri and his other brother Jonathon had said in varying ways. Their family was close and he hadn't even made it home from his first date with Deyon before he'd had calls about what was going on. He'd admitted they were dating and had told everyone to mind their own business. Leonardo knew it was useless to say so, but he had tried. His siblings had interjected in his business until their parents had put a stop to it. Leonardo knew that was a reprieve. His parents were also curious, but more patient in waiting to see what would happen. Eventually they would ask outright, but for now, he was grateful for their holding everyone else off.

Leonardo focused back on the building that housed Deyon's—the business had the same name as the woman who had gotten under his skin. He rolled his shoulders then exited the vehicle. As he strolled to the door, he exchanged greetings with various residents of McKingley.

"Afternoon, Sheriff."

"Afternoon, Miss Sadie. How's the hip feeling? I'm expecting that dance on Saturday." He slid his hand under her elbow, steadying the woman as she walked beside him.

"You'll get that dance if you want it, young man. However I think your dance card might be filled with a certain young lady." Her smile was wide and knowing.

Leonardo didn't question how she knew—Miss Sadie, who was the third oldest resident of McKingley, seemed to know everything that was going on. For a woman who was ninety, she was spritely. They had all worried when she had hurt her hip but from how she was walking she was doing much better. Nothing slowed her down.

"Since we are heading the same way, may I escort you?" Leonardo took off his hat, holding it over his heart.

"You're such a charmer. You're my favorite Wright man." Miss Sadie glanced around then put her hand by her mouth. "Tell any of the other men in your family and I'll deny it."

Leonardo laughed. Miss Sadie told all of them that. She was a flirt.

"I won't. And you're my best girl." He opened the door for her.

"Now lying to an old woman is a sin. Here comes your best girl. I'll settle for second and if she's stupid enough to dump you then you're all mine." Miss Sadie winked.

"Trying to steal my man, Miss Sadie. Don't make me take out your other hip." Deyon kissed the woman on her cheek then turned to Leonardo.

He steeled himself for her touch. Deyon groped his butt—something she did regularly since they hadn't kissed. It was within his rules, and she took pleasure in telling him so often. Deyon smiled. Leo focused on Rhianna who had walked up with Deyon.

"Hi, Rhianna."

"Hey, Leo." Rhianna was dressed as was her norm in jeans and T-shirt.

She preferred to be more casual than Deyon. Leo studied the woman whose features looked a lot like her sister's. She studied him with light gray eyes and with a grin on her face that Leo knew meant she was up to something.

"Give me a few minutes while I get Miss Sadie's things." Deyon led the woman away.

Leonardo watched the two of them talking as they moved deeper into the store.

"Is his ass as firm as it looks?" He clearly heard Miss Sadie ask.

"Firmer. You should give it a squeeze sometime."

"I just might, since the owner of the ass is giving me permission. I might give him a heart attack though, they think I am a stuffy old lady." There was teasing in Miss Sadie's tone.

"Now, Miss Sadie, lying so blatantly is a major sin." Deyon laughed, a rich sound.

"Don't tell Pastor. He's been trying to pick me up for ages. I've been having to turn him down telling him I'm an innocent woman. Poor man is heartbroken," Miss Sadie replied.

Leonardo stifled a laugh. No one in town bought that big fib. Miss Sadie was irreverent and loved by everyone. Thinking of the older residents of the town, Leonardo made a mental note to check in on the others. He did it regularly to make sure they were okay and didn't need anything.

"Ogling her butt in public. Shame on you, Leo."

Leo started, forgetting Rhianna was standing beside him. He glanced at her and didn't reply.

"How are things at the center?"

Rhianna was second-in-charge at Oasis, the community center owned by his sister Katiya, which helped lots of residents by offering classes and other social functions.

"Things are well." Rhianna brushed her short, curly dark brown hair from her face then placed her arm in the crook of his elbow and led him toward the exit. "Don't hurt my sister, Leo, or I'll have to hunt you down."

She patted his hand and continued alone toward the door. Leo stared after her. Rhianna, just like her sister, made an impression as she walked to the door—the sisters made the simple act of walking so graceful and sensual. To Leo, Rhianna's movements were more reserved while Deyon's were all power and passion.

Leo went to sit in one of the chairs in the sitting area that was closest to the door. He noted the one on the other side had a few people there too. He inclined his head to those he recognized. The one he didn't stared at him. Leonardo knew it was the uniform—he'd been told he could be intimidating in his sheriff uniform. He amused himself by looking out of the plate glass window that had the name of the store scrawled across it with the logo of the shop. The people on the sidewalk most of the time paused, glancing in. He turned his head, studying the eye-catching displays Deyon kept by the windows. He returned his attention to the passing pedestrians.

"Ready," Deyon spoke, capturing his attention.

Leonardo stood, joining her. He did what had become a normal thing when he was around her—he placed his hand on the small of her back as he led her to the door. As they went by, he observed the looks they were getting. If there was anyone in McKingley who didn't know about them, they would before the day was done. Outside, he lowered his hand and they intertwined their fingers as they strolled toward where they were going to lunch.

"It was a nice surprise that you called to go for lunch. A quickie would be good too," she teased.

Leonardo tightened his hold on her fingers then relaxed. "Wicked woman."

"I try. So, how's your day going?" she asked.

"I had to go by the Conner place again."

Deyon started laughing not even asking what had happened.

"I swear, if I have to go out there one more time I'm going to arrest him. I don't know why he doesn't give up on shooting that damn rooster. It's too evil to die."

"Was he naked again?" Deyon wiped her eyes with her fingers.

"Yes. His willy all out to see as he chased that damn, demented rooster." Leonardo chuckled as he thought of the sight.

James Conner was new to town and had bought a parcel of land close to where Deyon was located. What no one had told him was that he'd inherited Sigmund the rooster with the land. No one knew when Sigmund had become part of the ranch—he just was. Sigmund would be all-sweet between certain times, but he was ornery when the clock hit two-seventeen a.m. At that time, every day, he crowed incessantly until six seventeen a.m. James hadn't been told that little quirk and had thought it was nice at first. Now the man was determined to shoot that 'damn singing fucker', as he called it. Sigmund was wily and couldn't be shot or caught. Lots of folks had tried, but Leo had to give James an 'A' for being determined.

"Who called you?" Deyon asked because no local would call. It had become funny how determined James was. Even though people were starting to think of him as a local now, they were still amused by his determination and had bets on who would win. Sigmund was in the lead for coming out on top.

"Another tourist who was driving in the area heard the gunshot."

The same thing had happened four times in the last week.

"I'm tempted to have a sign made to put out there that says 'Ignore the gunshots—lunatic chasing a rooster ahead'." Leonardo smiled, imagining trying to get that approved by the city council.

Deyon laughed again then wiped her eyes once more. "I could imagine a vote for it. Yay to vote to appease crazy. No to enjoy him running around after the ornery rooster."

"Or..."

They made teasing jokes of different votes as they had their lunch. Later Leonardo escorted her back to her store, holding her hand. He followed her inside and waited patiently as she talked to a few employees and customers as she went. They passed into the back and she led him into her office before closing the door. Deyon released her hold on his hand. Leonardo opened the door before going farther into the room.

"You don't trust me to be alone behind closed doors?" She leaned against the desk.

He knew why she thought that — he'd avoided being alone with her in any room. There was only so much control he had. Leonardo moved between her legs and stifled a groan when she widened her stance. He enjoyed these moments of teasing after they'd been out. Today was the first time they'd had lunch together during their workday, and he wasn't about to leave without it. He placed his hands on the desk on either side of her hips.

"Myself. Don't trust myself," he replied.

"Hmmm…good to know. Note to self — get Leonardo behind closed doors alone." She slid her hands up and down his forearms.

Leonardo braced himself harder on the desk. When he had made the rule that touching was okay, he'd forgotten how tactile Deyon was. He'd seen her many times stroking weapons and fabrics with the same sensual way. On his skin, it only made him even hornier. He stepped back, touching the brim of his hat.

"I'll call you later," he stated.

"I'll be waiting." Deyon lowered her lids, running her hands down the front of her short skirt.

Leonardo swallowed, knowing what that meant. Since she couldn't kiss him or touch him where she wanted, Deyon used her creative mind to tell in detail what she wanted to do. Their nightly conversations had become another form of torture. He pivoted then left.

Why am I resisting again? That's right. I want more than just sex.

* * * *

Deyon stabbed the needle through the hem of the housedress she was making. The jersey fabric was a variety of blues in a geometric pattern and she'd fallen in love with it. It was soft on her skin and she was just finishing the hem before she added it to her collection of housedresses. She liked making them—short, flirty dresses in various fabric and colors that were comfortable to wear at home. She poked the needle through again.

"What did that fabric ever do to you?" Arissa's amused voice came across to her.

"She thinks it's going to run away and scream for help." Rhianna laughed.

It was then that Deyon realized the music had been turned off. Deyon lifted her head, studying them where they were sprawled on another couch, facing her. Deyon wiggled her toes on the low center table between them. She'd left work early. After her lunch date with Leonardo, she'd been too hot, bothered and out of sorts to stay. At home, she'd turned her music on high and started working on the housedress. By the time she had it finished and was hemming she was calmer. Rhianna had come by for their usual weekly dinner and when Arissa had knocked they'd asked her to join them. Arissa and Rhianna'd reclined on the couch listening to the music and chatting as Deyon worked.

"Nothing," she replied, lowering her head to continue sewing.

"Come on, Deyon. Talk to me." Arissa sat beside her.

"She's being very evasive about Leo."

Deyon didn't think she could very well tell Arissa her older brother wouldn't lose his control enough to let her have her way with him. She stopped, then thought about it. Hell if she couldn't.

"As soon as I get your brother alone in a room, I'm going to jump him. Won't let him out until we both can't walk." She pulled the needle through the fabric then met her gaze.

Arissa knew her so well, she didn't even look surprised at her words. Instead her brow was furrowed. Rhianna just laughed, placing her hands over her belly.

"Wow. I'm surprised you all haven't yet." Arissa put her hand on Deyon's forehead. "Are you feeling okay?"

"I was wondering the same thing." Rhianna touched Deyon's head too.

"Knock it off." Deyon chuckled, smacking at their hands.

"Well it isn't like you to let anyone dictate what you want." Arissa picked up a pillow and hugged it, leaning beside her.

Rhianna nodded in agreement.

Deyon stopped sewing. And that was what was bugging her. Arissa was exactly right. No matter if Leonardo said he wanted to date and wait—normally she would have already found a way to make him lose control. They would have been fucking like bunnies and she'd not be wound so tight.

"What are you waiting for?"

Deyon thought about it then shook her head. "Nothing. Your brother is just being difficult. Stubborn man." She went back to hemming her dress.

"Says Miss Obstinate. Use your Deyon mind and outmanoeuvre him." Arissa poked her in the shoulder.

"You're acting very unlike yourself," Rhianna said.

Deyon glared and threw a pillow at her. Rhianna caught it and put it behind her back.

"I wonder what your brother would say if he knew you were helping me plot his downfall." Deyon lifted her gaze to hers.

"He'd think you're corrupting me again." Arissa blinked innocently.

"If only he knew. You're the troublemaker." Deyon snorted.

"Hey, I learnt from the best." Arissa pushed against her shoulder.

"I'm glad you moved back home. I missed you. You've been so busy we haven't had time to hang out. We need to make some plans. You, I and Jackie," Deyon said referring to their other friend Jackson Carlyle.

"Sounds like a plan. How about we just veg out here, cook, laugh and watch movies. That sounds really good right now. Don't have to get dressed, just chill."

"That sounds like a plan. We'll have to check you and Jackie's schedule and see what time you all have free together." Deyon pulled through the last stitch for the hem.

She stood and shook out the dress. Holding it to her body, Deyon moved from side to side. "You like?"

"Beautiful," someone with a deep voice said behind her.

Deyon turned, meeting light brown eyes. Leonardo strode inside the open door.

"You shouldn't leave the front entrance open."

"That was me, I was bringing in something from my car but got distracted chilling with Deyon. Let me get to it now." Arissa stood.

"Sit, where are your keys?"

"In my bag on the table." Arissa gestured to the table by the door.

Leonardo nodded as he came toward Deyon. He ran his finger over her lips—something she had come to think of as his version of a kiss. He turned then headed back outside, pausing on the way to retrieve the keys. Deyon clenched her hands in the garment she held before lowering it then shifting it to one hand. She stared at his ass in his uniform pants.

"Stop drooling." Arissa smacked her bare thigh.

"Ow." She rubbed, still staring.

Rhianna laughed then stood. "I'm heading out."

"But we haven't eaten yet," Deyon protested.

Rhianna kissed her on the cheek then left. Deyon flopped on the couch and glanced through the doorway after her, watching as Leonardo passed back and forth taking the things from Arissa's car up to her apartment. After a few minutes, there was a thump as the door closed, then Leonardo returned.

"What are you doing here?" Arissa asked what Deyon had been thinking.

"Came by since I was in the area and my shift was done. I went to the Conner place again. He's gotten it in his head if he caught Sigmund when he wasn't crowing he'd be easier to shoot. I think it's become a game between them." Leonardo chuckled.

Arissa joined in. Leonardo sat on the couch, beside Deyon. He placed his hand on her upper thigh, starting a maddening caress with his thumb. The siblings chatted, but Deyon didn't really listen to what was being said. Deyon glanced at him and noted he wasn't even aware of what he was doing. She inhaled, smelling the fresh scent she equated with him.

"I'm heading out too, see you later, Deyon. I'll check with Jackson and get back to you with a date." Arissa squeezed her shoulder then rose and left, closing the door behind her.

Deyon moved to stand. Leonardo tightened his grip on her upper thigh. She turned her head to meet his gaze. He was watching her mouth then lifted his eyes—need burned in them. Leonardo moved closer. Deyon licked her lips, anticipating the press of his on hers, but Leonardo stopped before they touched.

"Damn it, Leonardo. Kiss me," Deyon said.

"I'm planning on it. But just wanted to point out we're alone and you didn't plan it."

Deyon glanced at the door then back at him. "What changed? Why now, after a month, can you kiss me?"

"It was stupid of me to keep us both waiting for what we obviously want." Leonardo's breath tickled her lips.

"Stupid man. Don't make me wait again." She placed her hand on his chest.

"Don't plan on it." Leonardo closed the distance between them.

Deyon moaned as his lips covered hers. He took her mouth as if he owned it. His tongue moved along each part inside, making her shake. Deyon gripped his shirt. Leonardo's growl reverberated and he held her tight against him, pinning her hand between their bodies. He deepened the kiss, thrusting in and out, mimicking what she hoped he would do to her body. Deyon pressed closer to him, taking all he could give. Leonardo gentled his sensual invasion then pulled away, still holding her close. After rising from the couch, he lifted her in his arms before taking her to the bedroom.

Leo put her down on her feet next to the bed and divested her of her clothing. He reached for his shirt, but Deyon knocked his hands away removing it herself, revealing his chest, running her fingertips over the hard planes of his silken sienna skin. The muscles felt even better than they looked and Leonardo moaned at her touch. She got to work on his pants and once she had it open, she slid her hand in the sides of his pants and underwear pushing them both off. He toed off the loafers he was wearing. After viewing all the delectable skin she'd uncovered, Deyon pressed kisses along his collarbone, licking it then biting gently. His big hands cupped the back of her head loosely not guiding her but holding her.

Deyon moved her hand between them, gripping his erection and rubbing her thumb over the spongy head leaking pre-cum. Leonardo thrust into her hand then pulled back.

"No...I want inside of you." He moved back, lifting her again then placing her on the mattress.

Finally I'm going to feel him inside me. Deyon widened her legs, cradling his bulky frame as he blanketed her body.

"Deyon." He hissed as their skin touched.

"Leonardo." She whimpered moving against his heated body.

Deyon lifted her head, seeking his lips. Leonardo met them, kissing her in a carnal demand. Wetness gushed from her as she readied for his taking.

Chapter Four

Leo had no control left. He'd been waiting for too long to get Deyon where he had her right now. Below him. Ready and waiting for him. Poised at her moist entrance, he hesitated as the final thread of common sense penetrated the haze of pleasure surrounding him.

Condom, it said.

Shit. He was always so careful to insure there were no accidents. But the incredible woman beneath him took away everything but his need to be buried to the hilt within her.

"Wait," he croaked.

Deyon narrowed her eyes at him. "Now?" she growled. "Why?"

He climbed off her luscious figure and grabbed desperately at his pants. "Protection." He sighed in a relief when he located one in his wallet. Turning back to the bed, he found her propped up on her elbows, her eyes transfixed upon his groin.

He tore open the packet then fisted himself as he stared at her breasts as they rose and fell with each breath she took. Tearing his gaze from them, he scanned her. Every inch of her was made to be loved. And he planned to do it. He didn't take long in sheathing himself and he was back over her, pressing her into the mattress.

"Deyon," he whispered.

"Leonardo."

He bit his lower lip when she gripped his shaft and placed the head at her entrance. With a deep breath, he flexed his hips and drove home with a single stroke.

"Ahh!" Her moan was music to his ears.

He had no way of speaking. She held him so tight, he was ready to come already. He withdrew until just his head remained then slid back in.

Another groan from Deyon. Oh yeah, he liked this. A lot. Leaning down, he flicked his tongue over her lips and began to move. In and out.

Deyon met him thrust for thrust. She drew him closer as they kissed. She dug her nails into his shoulders as she nipped at his tongue. He trailed one hand down her side to her leg. When he reached her knee, he lifted it, slid his arm under, and raised it higher.

"Oh yeah." Her response was pure guttural pleasure.

He couldn't have said it any better. The deeper penetration had his balls drawing up, warning him of his rapidly nearing release. He clenched his jaw and moved faster, determined to go as long as he could.

"Leo...I... Shit...more!"

Deyon babbled beneath him—her eyes had drifted closed, her skin was flushed and sweat dotted her. Her internal muscles rippled as she flexed them around his cock. Dear Lord, if he was to die now it would be with a smile on his face. Nothing had ever felt so right.

He thrust, she undulated. He withdrew, she drew him back in as they worked in a harmonic blend. She was getting close, he could tell for Deyon's moans had become higher and had changed into little mewling pants. She'd captured her plump lower lip in her teeth and her pussy held him even tighter.

Repositioning his face by her head, he put them nose to nose and worked his hips faster, feeling his own release hounding him. Harder and deeper he stroked, reveling in each sound she made, the sound of their bodies joining.

"Come for me, Deyon," he murmured. "Open those beautiful eyes so I can watch you."

The reaction was instantaneous. Her amazing brown eyes opened and she tightened around him, back bowing, and a scream rent from her throat. Her nails digging into his skin tore deep, and he grunted as the sting, combined with the feel of her slit milking him, threw him over the edge. He powered fast twice more before he came with such force it astounded him.

Releasing her leg, he slid both arms under her shoulders and cupped her head before capturing her mouth with his. Shaking and a bit lightheaded, he moved with small strokes as his mimicked the action in her mouth with his tongue.

Bit by bit, his heart slowed down to its normal cadence. He remained inside her the entire time, unwilling to leave the haven he'd found. She moved her hands up and down his back, rubbing and scoring him with her nails.

"Again," she said against his lips.

"Yes."

He couldn't agree more. It had been far too fast. He needed to take his time and indulge. It had just been too strong of an urge the first time—the need to rush and feel her around him—but it had taken the edge off.

She rolled them so she was on top then took off the used protection. Deyon placed on a new one before smiling wickedly then straddling him and taking him back in. His cock went fully erect within her at the image of her body seated upon his, her full breasts right there for him to cup, suckle and play with while she rode him.

Oh yeah, again was just right. Although, more would have worked just fine for him as well. The first time she rotated her hips nothing else mattered but the two of them. All his attention and focus went right back to the woman in bed with him.

* * * *

When he woke it was dark out. The soft body pressed to his brought a smile to his face. For a moment there, he'd been afraid it was nothing but another dream in which he'd finally got to sleep with Deyon only to wake and learn it wasn't true. Now he knew. Her head rested on his shoulder and she had one arm draped over his midsection.

Her body moved with each deep breath she took. He skimmed his hand up and down her upper arm and brushed a kiss over her head. Closing his eyes, he allowed himself to be taken back into the world of slumber.

A faint beeping brought him back to consciousness. He blinked a few times before it registered. His pager was going off. With a grunt, he disentangled himself from Deyon's body and climbed out of bed, reaching for his pants, which still lay in a heap on the floor.

Just as he got there, his cell went off. He grabbed it and put it to his ear.

"Yeah?"

"Sorry to bother you, Sheriff, but we've got a situation."

Terri's no nonsense voice wiped away the remaining visages of sleep. The dispatcher was extremely effective. She and her sister Trina were two of his favorite ones to work with. Nothing ever rattled them. They didn't panic and they didn't mess up calls. Hell, sometimes he wondered if they weren't robots for all the emotion they put into it. He didn't care—all that mattered was they were good. Damn good.

He was shoving into his clothes even as he listened to her give the details. Some kind of explosion at the university. "Thanks. On my way." He hung up and sat, grabbing for his footwear.

Buckling his belt, he made his way back to the bed and the goddess sleeping there. He turned on one of her bedside lights and the soft glow filled the room. Lust rocketed into him as he stared at her.

"Deyon," he called out softly.

She rolled toward him, sheet dropping enough to show him one nipple and he bit back a groan. Forcing his eyes to remain on her face, he crouched down beside her.

"What are you doing up?" she croaked, her voice heavy with sleep.

"I have to go."

Her lids flew open and she watched him with a mix of disbelief and uncertainty. "What?"

"I got called to work. I have to go and I woke you so you didn't think I just ran off. I'll see you later." He didn't say anything else—he had nothing else to tell her—so he kissed her quickly, shut off the light then left. It may have been a bit harsh, but he didn't have time to wait until she completely woke up.

He drove to his destination fast, the scanner on giving him bits and pieces of what he could expect to find. Lights flashing and siren wailing, he whipped into the parking lot and stared up at the smoldering remains of part of a building. He hopped out then strode up to the police tape barricade.

The officer who was there immediately lifted it and he ducked to pass under. He could see the news trucks gathering and pressed on. Those would be dealt with later.

"What do we have?"

"Part of the science lab blew. A few injuries but thankfully zero casualties."

He took a deep breath and shook his head. "Thanks." He glanced at the officer by him and gave her a smile. "Evening, Deputy Conner."

Her return smile was fleeting and he didn't begrudge her that. She was all about her job. Part of which made her so damn good at it.

"Sheriff." She cleared her throat and touched the side of her cheek. "You…umm…lipstick."

Damn. He rubbed it with the back of his hand until she nodded it was no longer there. Anyone else would have pressed him for who he'd been with. Not Conner. She didn't pry.

He opened his mouth to say something else when another explosion rocked the area. Flames shot out of the hole and a few more windows shattered with the force of the heat and projectiles that hit them.

"Get down, get down!" he hollered, shielding his eyes from the flare. "Get those people back, goddamnit!"

He ran toward the building to a man whose leg was on fire and helped put it out. Sirens pierced the night as more trucks rolled in to help combat the flames.

"Come on, Thom!" a feminine voice came from the building and he turned in time to see his sister, his *baby* sister, hauling a stretcher down the ramp. Smoke billowed out after her and he pointed the man with him in the direction of medical and headed for his sister.

Her face had streaks of soot on it and drywall dust seemed to fly off her with every step she took. Firefighters raced up past her, but he paid them no mind. Shoving through people, he made his way to her.

"Lis!"

She lifted her head and looked around. A ghost of a smile lifted her lips when she spied him.

"Hey, Leo," she said. They never slowed and he pivoted to keep pace with her. "Quite a mess wouldn't you say?"

"What are you doing in there?" He nodded at Thom who was rattling off stats into his radio.

"My job." They veered around a large chunk of concrete, which had blown out earlier.

"We don't even know what kind of chemicals are burning in there."

"And I can't sit around and let injured people suffer because of that." She touched his arm before opening the door to the ambulance. "I don't need you to bandage my knees anymore, Leo. I'll be okay." She and Thom shared a look and lifted on their silent count. They'd worked together for so long they didn't need verbal communication. Thom climbed in the back with the burns victim and she shut the doors. "Stay safe, okay?" She squeezed his arm then ran around to the front. Seconds later the ambulance had driven off.

She was right—he couldn't protect her. Didn't mean he would stop trying, but he'd been hovering more than usual ever since their cousin, Justin, had been shot on her lawn. They all looked after Lis, though—she'd been so sick as a baby, they hadn't known if she would make it. She'd done more than just make it. She'd surpassed anything they could have hoped for.

"Sheriff!"

Snapping his head around, he spied Deputy Conner waving at him. He jogged over to her side and the man she was talking to. Rolling his shoulders, he sighed in disappointment. This was going to take a long while. So much for getting back to the warm, willing woman he'd left in bed.

* * * *

Deyon couldn't go back to sleep after Leo had left. She'd thought about it but fell short of reaching the actual goal of slumber. She stretched and yawned before rolling out of bed and snapping on a light. Almost three in the morning. He'd been gone for all of fifteen minutes.

"What the hell happened to get him out of bed so early?"

She slipped on some silk pajamas and padded barefoot to her living room. As she reached for another light switch, she noticed lights coming on over by Arissa and Jackson's outside doors. Sure enough, soon they both exited. Arissa stopped to kiss Deiter before hastening after Jackson.

Deyon hurried to the door and opened it. "What's going on, Arissa?" she called out.

"Explosion at the university. What are you doing up?"

Shit. "Leonardo just left a few minutes ago, so I was up."

"Ohhh, I see how it is," she said in a teasing voice. "We'll see you later, Deyon." And just like that, the doctors left, both climbing in their vehicles and racing off to the hospital.

Uncertainty filled her and she wanted to call him and find out what was going on. Shaking her head at the emotion streaming through her, she scoffed at herself. *What the hell is wrong with me? I sleep with him once and all of a sudden, I need to know he's okay every second of the day? That's pathetic.*

Despite the mental derision, she continued to worry. Turning on the news, she curled up on the corner of her couch. She didn't have to look far for information—the local news had put up a special report on the incident.

"...and we still don't know the cause of the explosion. All we know right now is that it occurred in the science wing of the building. The police are keeping a perimeter around the area as hazmat sweeps the area to insure there are no toxic fumes floating around. In addition, since the fire has yet to be extinguished, there is still the potential for another explosion. We've seen two already. The ambulances have been coming and going constantly. We'll keep you updated with more information as we get it. I just want to reiterate, at this moment we have been told zero casualties. Lots of injuries but so far there has been no loss of life in this horrific incident."

It switched back to the news anchors in the studio and she captured her lower lip in her teeth and gnawed on it. Two explosions already. She wasn't a science geek by any means, but even she knew that there were plenty of things that could go boom in that vicinity.

Her heart pounded harder and she shifted on the couch, unable to tear her eyes away from the screen. She got flashes as they showed more live shots. She even recognized some people, but still no sign of Leo.

The reporter on the scene was giving another update when a large explosion rocked the location. A blaze of light and a plume of dust rolled from the left. The woman ducked and turned panicked eyes in that direction.

The camera operator zoomed in and Deyon whimpered as she saw more of the destruction. It looked horrible. Where was he? The camera continued to roll and she saw him step through the dust, tall and strong, as he continued to deliver orders and direct people. She couldn't explain the relief she felt at that image. He was dirty and covered in dust but alive.

She lingered in front of the TV even after the section had been deemed secure and the news crews had begun to leave. When all that remained were smoldering embers and firefighters, her gaze continued to be transfixed upon the television screen. She reached for the phone numerous times only to draw her hand back. Now was not the time to call him.

Damn it though, she wanted to hear his deep voice. Just to assure herself he was okay and seeing him hadn't been a figment of her imagination. Only when she had to get moving so she wouldn't be late for work did she move from that spot. She ate a light breakfast, watching for any more updates, which might come down the pipes.

Nervous, she drove to work and got ready for the day. Her employees and customers were talking about the incident and while she wanted to yell at them to stop, she kept it buried. They had the right to do so.

She was up front when the door opened and she looked up with a forced smile on her face. One which changed to a real one the moment her brain registered who had just walked through.

Leonardo. He was out of uniform, in jeans and a T-shirt, and appeared exhausted but she didn't care—he was here. He was alive and well. She skirted out from around the counter and walked toward him.

He stared at her with those killer brown eyes of his and she swallowed at the wealth of emotions that assailed her. He meant so much to her it almost scared her.

"Hey," he said softly, eyes remaining locked on hers.

"Hey yourself." She swallowed and reached out almost hesitantly to touch him. "You okay?"

He didn't answer, just pulled her close and kissed her. She melted into him immediately. This was what she'd needed. Physical confirmation. To be held and kissed by him. Shown he was truly all right. Entwining her arms around his neck, she pressed closer.

When the kiss ended, she fought back a whimper of disappointment. She wanted it to continue. Leo backed off a bit and cupped her face with his large hands. The calluses on his fingertips teased her skin.

"I'm sorry I had to run out like that on you. It's not what I had envisioned for our first night together." His voice was low and for her ears only. "Or rather, morning after."

"I'm just glad you're okay."

"Can you leave?"

"Yes," she said without hesitation. "Let me get my things and I'll be ready."

Another kiss and he walked out without a look back. It didn't take long to tell her workers she was leaving before she was out of the door after him. She found him leaning against the passenger door of her vehicle.

Once they were on their way back to her place, she asked, "How did you get to the store?"

"Conner dropped me off."

She didn't know Conner but assumed it was someone he worked with. "Do you want to stop for anything?"

"Hell no. You have what I want."

His directness made her smile. "Good to know." She wanted to speed, get him home quickly, but she stuck to the speed limit, especially when she looked at him and found him asleep. His thick lashes rested upon his cheeks as he took deep breaths. When they reached her house, he woke as she waited for the gate to open.

"Sorry."

"For what? You're exhausted."

They walked inside together and she shoved him toward the bedroom. "Go."

He captured her wrist and drew her near. "What about you?"

"I'll be right in."

He took another breath-robbing kiss before walking off. Hell, even as tired as he appeared to be, there was just no stopping that inherent swagger he had about him. She licked her lips and watched until he vanished from view.

She took about fifteen minutes to pull out and fill up her slow cooker. Turning it on low, she allowed the chicken a la king to begin cooking. Then she followed in the direction Leo had gone.

He was sleeping when she got there. After stripping down she climbed in beside his naked body and pressed close. He didn't wake, but he did wrap his arms around her, holding her tight.

She closed her eyes and drifted off to sleep, tired as well. She felt safe in his arms and let the gods of sleep and dreams dictate to her.

Waves of pleasure woke her as an orgasm crashed over her. Opening her eyes, she allowed them to close again at the sight of Leo with his head between her legs. *It's not a dream.* He continued his assault on her slit. The flat of his tongue lapping and stroking against her clit sent tremors through her. He slid two fingers within her, adding more stimulation.

"Shit!" she cried as he wriggled his fingers inside her.

He turned his head and pressed a kiss to the inside of her thigh. "Good evening," he muttered.

Grabbing the back of his head, she redirected him where she wanted him. Mouth on her. Pleasuring her. His chuckle vibrated through her pussy and she thrust against him, wanting more. He didn't disappoint. She came twice more before he left her wetness and moved up her body. He licked and laved his way, taking his time, ratcheting up her desire even more.

"Leo," she panted.

"Deyon," he replied, nipping the skin on one breast.

Her back bowed when he drew the nipple in his mouth. Christ, she couldn't take much more of this. Her body was already aflame. Back and forth he moved between her breasts, loving them both. Tossing her head on the bed, she gripped his shoulders and urged him up even farther.

Finally, he covered her mouth with his and thrust his tongue in deep. She purred in pleasure and reveled in the combination of their tastes. More, she wanted more. Undulating against him, she widened her legs in silent invitation. He didn't make her wait, just slid deep with one stroke.

"Yes," she hissed.

"Been waiting for you to wake up, sweetheart," he murmured in her ear as he set a fast past.

Feet planted on the mattress, she worked her hips in time with his thrusts. A wicked glint in his eyes made her shiver in pleasure. He took her hands and captured them in his before dragging them up over her head and holding them there.

He filled her so full she could barely keep her eyes on him. All she wanted to do was close them and ride the sensations bombarding her. She watched him turn his attention from her face to the way her breasts moved with each powerful piston of his hips.

In and out he drove. Back and forth. She lost all track of time as pleasure swarmed her. His gaze had grabbed hers and wouldn't let go. No matter how much she wanted to shut hers, she found she couldn't. She stared at him—at the way his jaw clenched, the sweat, which beaded along his head and began running down.

"Don't hold back," she panted, wanting all of him.

He rose up, releasing her hands, and gripped her hips. Angling her, he began to slam into her. The entire bed shook with the force of his thrusts and she arched up to meet each stroke, desperate for more. This was what she wanted. What she needed. To feel him so deep inside her until she wasn't entirely sure where she ended and he began. Surge after surge of pleasure broke over her and she embraced the oncoming orgasm. It exploded and she saw stars.

"Shit!" he swore as he pumped faster. Harder. Deeper. A low roar left him as he stiffened and she could feel his cock pulse as he released his seed. For a moment, she wanted to know what it would be like without protection. Protection he must have had on before she even woke up. He *had* been waiting.

Leo fell toward her, catching the brunt of his weight at the last minute and rolling off her. She watched him stride from the bed and back after he'd disposed of the condom. He wasn't ashamed of his body and he had no reason to be — the man was a work of art.

"I see you've woken up now," she said as he climbed back in the bed.

"Oh yeah."

"Well we have about two hours before dinner is ready." She trailed her hand down his chest and curved her fingers around his semi-erect cock. "Still tired? Or..."

He covered her bare pussy with his hand and slipped two fingers inside her without releasing her gaze. "Or is right. Let's make good use of these two hours."

She smiled even as a moan left her. She couldn't have said it better herself.

Chapter Five

Leo strode through the station only to pause when he saw who waited for him in his office. A smile lifted his lips as he altered his course and headed there.

"Hey, stranger," he said, stepping in.

His brother Jonathon sat there, looking totally impeccable as usual. Leo would admit that since Jonathon had met Harmony Oshiro, he'd learnt to relax a lot. Hell, the man even got dirty on occasion now — not often, but he would. "Hey, brother." Jonathon stood and they embraced briefly.

Leo couldn't hide the smirk when his sibling's first move after was to straighten his suit. Perching on the edge of his desk, he crossed his arms over his chest. "What can I do for you?"

"Can you get Mom off my back?"

His lips twitched and he tried to hide this one. "She getting bad with you as well?"

"Our mother showed up at my office with bridal magazines. *Bridal.* To my office. I'm not Warwick, I don't want to be all up in the business here. I don't know how to tell her to back off."

Leo didn't laugh at that one. Jonathon and Harmony had recently gotten engaged. Leo shook his head at the coincidence that his siblings, one after the other, had started falling in love and were getting ready to walk down the aisle. Jon had started dating Harmony after Leo had Deyon, yet here Jon was preparing to get hitched — another of the Wright children ready to commit. Their mom couldn't be happier with the way things were turning out. Jon's concern was very well founded. Their mother was a force to be reckoned with. Moreover, she had it in her mind that she needed to plan huge, lavish weddings for each of her children. And even though Jonathon was the first of her boys to be engaged, she didn't back off — she'd gone all out and had a wedding planner folder for him as well. Hell, for all he knew, she had one for him and Dimitri also, and was just keeping them hidden until they announced their engagements.

Deyon's image flashed before him and he imagined what she would look like dressed in a white dress walking down the aisle toward him. The vision caught him so off guard he almost fell over. Clearing his throat, he righted himself and focused on his brother again.

Damn. He really looks distraught.

"Look, maybe Dad can tell her it's not her job to plan for the male as well."

"Thought of that already," he said, shaking his head. "Dad doesn't stand up to her. We both know this."

"Why'd you come to me? Why not the sisters?"

"Katiya is enjoying this more than I ever thought she would. Arissa is too busy for Mom to bother her and for some reason she leaves Deiter alone. We both know Warwick is definitely way too into this and Lis, well, you know her. She's already told Mom to back off and dismisses just about everything she says, but Mom doesn't stop. Harmony is getting a bit overwhelmed."

"She's not liking it?"

"Not really. She's worried about upsetting Mom and ignoring what she wants for her wedding, which isn't lavish at all."

Leo sighed. "Where is she?"

"Who? Mom or Harmony?"

"Harmony."

"Out gallivanting around with Lis." Finally, a smile appeared on his brother's face. "She just couldn't take it anymore so Lis showed up this morning and said they were going out into the mesas for a day of hiking and whatnot." He blew out a breath. "You should have seen the gratefulness on her face, Leo. I'm worried if Mom keeps up like this, by the actual day of the wedding Harmony isn't going to want to marry me."

"You need to talk to her."

"I've tried. I actually just came from attempting to do just that. She patted my hand and said, 'I'll have a chat with Harmony when I take her to try on some more dresses'. It's not working." He scowled and muttered, "We should just do what Lis and Archer did."

Leo leaned forward. "What? What did Lis and Archer do?"

Jonathon paused and ran a hand down his face and Leo recognized the 'oh shit' look filling his expression. His brother must really be rattled, for normally the all-to-together Jonathon Wright barely made a mistake. "You can't tell anyone, Leo. Not *anyone*. Not even Deyon."

"Did they elope?" he asked, leaning forward.

"Yes."

"No shit. When did they do that? And why didn't she tell us?"

Jonathon gave him a look and he realized why. Lis didn't like pomp and circumstance. She'd had enough attention on her when she was the sick baby sister. "Who else knows?"

"Harmony."

"But I can't tell Deyon?" He didn't like that.

"No. Lis told us both, Leo. I should have been more careful with what I said here, but I told her I wouldn't say anything."

"Deyon won't—"

"No, Leo. She's friends with Arissa. I don't want it to get back to Mom before she has a chance to tell her."

He understood, he truly did, but he also felt a bit hurt by it. "Have they had a party or anything like that?"

Jonathon shook his head. "Don't even think about it."

"I feel bad. We haven't celebrated it."

"This is what they want. Please don't tell anyone. And when Mom calls, because we both know she will, tell her you haven't seen me."

Leo nodded. "Okay, so what else can I do for you?"

His brother's expression grew serious and as he began talking, Leo moved around to sit behind his desk. Two hours later, he was alone in his office when a knock came to his door. Glancing up from his computer, he grinned at the woman who leaned against the frame.

"Knock, knock," Deyon said. Dangling from two fingers was a bag. "Have time for a meal?"

He pushed to his feet and walked to her where he paused for a kiss of welcome. "I always have time for you."

Once she sat across from him and the food was set up between them, he paused. "What brings you by?"

"Is it a problem?"

"Not at all," he replied immediately.

"Good." She peeled the cover off her chopsticks and lifted some beef pancit into her mouth.

He figured it out—it was just a visit. So he began to eat as well. There was little talk as they filled up on the food. Only when they got to the fortune cookies did he pause and look at her again. Lord help him, he wanted to lower the shades on the windows, lock the door to his office and have his way with her.

Deyon watched Leo as he stared at her. Hungrily. Heat pooled in her belly and she shifted against the seat. He really was just too damn handsome. She paused as she reached for her cookie. "Is everything okay?"

"How are the wedding plans coming for Katiya and Arissa?"

"Katiya's are fine. She has shown up for fittings and all that. Arissa, well I know where to find her when I need something. Lis"—she shook her head—"just shakes her head and says no to everything. That girl is frustrating. And now with Harmony, I just don't know."

"She's overwhelmed. Jonathon was just in here before you. Mom's pushing her too hard."

"She does seem like a very soft girl." She had met Harmony a few times and found her to be very quiet, keeping to herself.

He shook his head. "She's not soft. She's had a hell of a life, but Mom, well, you know how she is."

A twinge hit her at the pride in his voice when he spoke of Harmony. "I don't know her that well. All I know is that after I came with the clothing, she's been reserved with me."

"She is quiet." He spun the cookie around on his desk. "Jonathon is afraid she's going to want to call off the wedding."

"I don't think she'd do that. I've seen the way she looks at your brother. Maybe she needs a girls' day."

He opened the cookie and broke it, withdrawing the fortune. "She's on one with Lis. They're out getting dirty."

Deyon smiled. That sounded like Lis. "Okay. Don't worry about it. Jonathon is a smart man, he'll figure something out. Hell, he should go to Lis and ask her what she's done. That woman can't be pinned down for anything at all. Your mom was complaining about that the other day at the shop with Katiya." She shook her head. "I don't know how she has any energy planning all of these weddings."

"That's our mother. Master multitasker."

Deyon opened her cookie and read her fortune, smiling at the message.

"What's yours say?" he asked.

"Isn't it bad luck to read them aloud?"

"No."

"Humph. Fine, it says 'Sometimes the truth is right before you'. Now, what does yours say?"

He smirked. "I agree with yours." He opened the piece of paper and cleared his throat causing her to laugh. "Mine says, 'Love isn't handed to you, you have to go reach for it'. I think this one is true as well."

His eyes gleamed with a passion that made her shift on the seat. She shook off her increasing desire and focused on why she'd arrived. "I had a real purpose for coming here."

"Do tell."

"A woman I used to work with when I was modeling is getting married."

He didn't move, didn't speak, just stared at her unflinchingly. Damn him, he was going to make her ask him instead of accepting. "Congratulations to her."

"I'm going, she asked me to, and I wanted to know if you would be interested in coming along with me as my date."

His smile made her insides melt. He popped half his cookie and chewed it. "When and where is this occurring?"

Now came the potential problem. "Two months away and it's in New York City."

He leaned back in his chair and smiled. "It would be my utmost pleasure to escort you to this wedding, Deyon De'clare."

"Thank you."

"No, thank you." He leaned forward, ate the last bit of his cookie then sent her another wicked grin. "I just need to know the exact dates so I can set up time in the books."

Reaching into her pocket, she pulled out a folded sheet of paper. "Here you go."

"She comes prepared. I like that in a woman."

She laughed. "You like a lot of things in a woman."

His gaze twinkled as he winked at her. "You would know."

She flushed and shook her head. It didn't matter how confident she'd become in her life—all it took was a look and wink from Leonardo Wright and she felt like blushing as if she were still a schoolgirl.

They'd left for work this morning from his place. She was tired for they definitely hadn't got much sleep. "Okay. I have to get back to the shop. Have to deal with some crazy people who want wedding dresses, bridesmaid dresses and all that."

He stood and gathered the empty containers. "You know you could say no."

"You have a crazy family, Leonardo, but I love them." She brushed it off. "Besides, I just have to get a bit ahead before the wedding." She got to her feet and walked around to where he stood. Turning his face toward hers, she traced a finger along his lower lip then kissed him. "I'll see you later."

On her way out of the station, she waved at some of the people she knew. She was trying to get past the fear she'd felt the other week when the explosion had happened at the university. Up until that point, she'd never really understood the extent of the danger cops faced. And it wasn't only cops who faced it, but she was only interested in one. Leonardo Wright. And that incident had scared the crap out of her.

After blowing out a breath, she made her way to her car then slid behind the wheel. Lunch had been a spur of the moment decision on her part—she'd really just wanted to see him again. So she had. And now she had a job to return to.

When she arrived at her shop, she got back into the flow of things and worked with her employees. They were busy—busier than usual with the addition of the Wright women's approaching nuptials. Sitting at her desk, she flipped through her calendar and jotted down some notes.

* * * *

Later that night, she was at her place. Leo had to work late so she'd gone home. Music played as she sat on the couch sewing another housedress while her food cooked. A knock at the door had her going to answer it.

She opened it to find Arissa standing there. "Hey there." She stepped back and Arissa walked in.

"Hey yourself. You busy?"

"Nope. Waiting on dinner." She held up the sewing. "Just passing the time. What about you?"

"I came to talk to you."

She looked at her friend. Arissa still wore her scrubs and her light brown eyes looked tired. Her hair had begun to grow out so she no longer had the pixie cut she'd sported upon her return to McKingley. It still was the same color, however, and the reddish-gold worked really well with her skin tone.

"Have you eaten?"

"Not yet, just got home."

"Can you stay?"

There was a slight hesitation before she nodded. "Sure."

Deyon led the way back to the living room. "It'll be ready in a few. Want something to drink while we wait?"

"I'm fine." Arissa perched on the edge of a chair.

"So, what's up?"

"I wanted you to know from me before someone in the family blabbed it. Deiter and I are moving out. We found a house."

She grinned despite the pain she felt. "How wonderful. I'm so happy for the both of you. Where is this house?"

"Nearer to Lis than I am now. We closed on it this afternoon. Tomorrow we will tell the others but since you so graciously opened your place to us, I wanted to make sure you didn't hear it from someone else, since you know damn well this family can't keep secrets."

Deyon smiled at her statement. Her heart was saddened though—she'd gotten used to her and Deiter being near. "Well, what can I do to help?"

Arissa shook her head. "Nothing at all, but thank you." She rolled her shoulders and leaned back against the couch. "We've been packing up our things already. So it's all in boxes. I set up for the movers to come after we closed today, so we're having someone else do it. The two of us just don't have the time right now. We're short staffed at the moment and Deiter is about to leave for the some huge summit meeting which is being held in Switzerland. We figured it would be easier this way, I'll be able to unpack at my convenience."

Deyon put down her sewing. "Wait, Deiter is leaving for Switzerland? Why didn't you say anything?"

"Couldn't, we weren't positive on that. He found that out a week ago."

"So you couldn't tell me then?"

Arissa lifted an eyebrow. "You've been shackin' up with my brother. I barely see you now unless he's latched onto you, or you on him."

Deyon calmed herself. It was true—ever since she and Leonardo had first had sex, they'd been going at it like rabbits. Other things got neglected. And she was taking her frustration out on Arissa.

"Sorry."

"Nothing to apologize for." Arissa stifled a yawn. "Excuse me."

"When did you last get some sleep?"

"Too long."

"Go. Get some sleep."

Arissa stood and walked to her. Bending down, she brushed a kiss along her cheek. "Thanks for everything, Deyon."

"I'll check on you tomorrow. And you know if you need me to do anything just let me know."

"I know. Thanks." With a wave, Arissa left.

Deyon sat there, sewing untouched on her lap and thought about it all. She still hadn't had the movie night with Arissa and Jackie like they'd talked about. Now this. With Arissa moving out—granted it wasn't like when she'd moved to Chicago—there would be less time together. And it saddened her. At least Jackson was still here. But, for how long? Surely some woman would be snatching him up as well.

She set her work to the side and got to her feet. Once in the kitchen, she poured herself a glass of Chianti. After drinking it, she refilled and blew out a breath. *Why are you so surprised?* Her brain queried. *She's getting married. Surely you didn't expect her to stay here forever.*

That was the problem. Part of her *had* expected that. Everyone was moving on around her. *I have to give myself a break. I'm surrounded by people getting married, it's logical that I feel a bit left behind.* Marriage hadn't ever been foremost on her mind—she'd had her modeling career and now she had this life. She sighed and lowered her head, rubbing the back of her neck.

"What's wrong?" Leo's deep voice reached her.

She jumped and lifted her head to find him standing there looking all too gorgeous in his uniform. "You scared me," she said, placing her drink down on the counter.

"Sorry. What's wrong?" He approached and lowered his mouth to hers for a kiss, which had her toes curling inside her slippers.

"Nothing."

"Why do you think I'm ever going to let that bullshit answer fly?" he asked, cupping her ass and squeezing.

She moaned and flexed her hips, loving the feel of his hard length against her. It would be better for it to be inside her and she reached for his belt just as the timer went off on her oven.

"Damn it," she muttered.

He laughed and kissed her again before letting her by. The moment she pulled the dish out of the oven, he was right there beside her. Rubbing against her, enticing her.

"How long does it have to cool?" he whispered.

Grabbing his belt, she headed for the bedroom. "Long enough."

Chapter Six

Leo stood in a shooters stance and took aim at his target. He emptied his clip into the paper silhouette. After ejecting it, he set it down then hit the switch to move the target forward. Unclipping it from the clasp, he stared down at it and sighed.

"Used to be two holes, little brother, not clusters. What's going on? You seem to be losing your touch. Could it be true? The great Leo has lost his touch?"

He turned his head and glared at the speaker of the unwanted and definite sarcastic commentary. The eldest of the Wright siblings stood there. Dimitri wore a suit and a half grin. Removing his ear protection, he sighed when Dimitri did the same.

"What brings you here?"

"Can't I just visit my brother?"

Leo snorted. "Not if you're here to criticize my shooting."

"Not criticising. Commenting. Perhaps you need that bloodthirsty woman of yours to teach you a bit more."

He flipped his brother off then crumpled up the target. "Such an ass." Although the idea of going shooting with Deyon held a lot of promise.

"Well thank you. I'm fond of it myself."

There were just some days when he wanted to be an only child. This was turning into one of them. "What do you want, Dimitri?"

"Just came to talk to you about the findings from the university fire."

All joking aside, he immediately sobered. "What do you got?"

Dimitri gave him a look he understood and before long he'd cleaned up his area, shoved his gun back in his holster and was leading the way to his office. As the door shut behind them, he watched his brother sit before he made his way around the desk.

Seated, he laced his fingers and leaned forward, giving Dimitri all his attention. "From the seriousness in your expression and the fact you didn't just send over a report, I'm going to assume it's arson."

"Yes. Sorry man. But I looked over it all and I can't come to any other conclusion."

"Shit."

Leo rubbed the bridge of his nose and exhaled loudly as he digested the facts. He didn't like the implications this had.

"What possible reason could someone have for blowing up that part of the university?"

Dimitri didn't answer, but then Leo didn't expect to get one. Leo knew his brother understood he was just talking through things out loud. He reached for the receiver then made a brief call asking for the file.

One of his officers knocked a short time later and dropped it off for him. "Thanks, Murphy," he said.

"You're welcome, sir." The man left as silently as he'd arrived.

Leo flipped the file open and stared down at all the notes on it. He really didn't want to believe the worst in people, but it happened occasionally that the crap came to the light and made its presence known.

"Before you get into that, let me ask you something."

"Yes. I think you're uptight and anal." Leo leaned back in his chair and watched his brother.

Dimitri narrowed his eyes and flipped him off. "Very funny, little brother."

"You do know I'm not really little, right? We're actually the same height."

A smirk filled his face. "You'll always be my little brother."

Leo muttered under his breath and rolled his eyes. "Fine. What did you need to ask?"

"Have you noticed anything strange going on with Jonathon?"

Leo picked up a pen and twirled it in his fingers. This was a problem with a larger family — there always seemed to be something going on with someone in it. He didn't usually mind. "Um, you do realize he's just weird anyway so your comment needs to be a bit more specific before I can address it one way or another. Why?"

"No reason. You know he was at the university when the explosions went off."

He nodded. "Yes. Not in that building though."

Dimitri sat forward. "No, but Harmony had been."

That was information he hadn't known as he'd not seen the completed report yet. "She wasn't hurt was she?" He mimicked his brother's action and rested his elbows on his desktop.

"No. I think it rattled him a bit more than he would like to face."

"It would have any of us. I damn near freaked out when I saw Lis coming out from inside covered from head to foot by the plaster dust falling everywhere."

"She's our baby sister. Of course you would be worried." A slight pause. "She is fine, right?"

He gave a sharp nod — as if he would have let her go back in had she not been okay! "Not what she said to me. Told me to let her do her damn job basically." He shook his head. "I'll see if he's doing all right or not."

"I know they come to you more than me, so let me know if he needs anything."

"They'd come to you if you quit trying to be their father and more of a brother."

Dimitri got to his feet and arched a brow at him. "Tell me again, how'd it go again with you and Lis?"

"Not about me, brother."

"Convenient that, don't you think?" Dimitri waved then walked out of the room.

Leo turned his attention back to the case before him. Not much later, he headed off to talk to some of the witnesses. Now that it had been determined as arson, he had to look for a suspect and see what he could do in order to get someone brought to justice for this.

His day was long and not productive in solving the university explosion. It definitely perked up however, when he pulled into his driveway and saw Deyon's car parked there.

He walked inside and set his bag down by the door. The television was on and he heard some fashion show, which made him shake his head in amusement. Moving silently, he walked through, searching for his target. Pushing open the door to his bedroom, his cock leaped in his pants as he recognized the sound of his shower running.

Stripping quickly out of his uniform, Leo made his way to the bathroom door. He paused outside the shower and just watched her through the frosted glass. Her full figure moved with sensual grace as she washed herself. He gripped himself and stroked slowly as desire ran roughshod over him.

He released his cock and slid open the door. She had her back to him and he ogled the view of her ass. He slipped in behind her, wrapping his arms around her.

"Hello, gorgeous."

She jumped but immediately calmed against him. "You scared me."

"I must say, Deyon, this is an amazing thing to come home from a day of work to."

She directed his hands to her breasts where he eagerly began massaging her flesh. He tugged on her nipples until they hardened and she expelled little panting moans.

"So how was your day?" she asked.

"Busy." He smoothed one hand down her belly and over her bare pussy, slicked by both water and soap.

"Good busy or bad busy?" Her voice went up a notch as he dipped a finger inside her wetness.

"Just busy."

In and out he stroked her with one finger. She widened her legs and he added another. He moved his wrist in a continuous motion, using the heel of his palm to toy with her clit, his cock pressing insistently into her back.

"Anything I can do?"

"You're doing it, Deyon." He rolled one nipple and pinched as he grazed along her neck with his teeth, delivering a swift bite.

"Fuck!" she screamed, her hips bucking against his hand.

"I'm going to do exactly that to you."

"Talk is cheap, Leonardo." She pushed back into him, silently asking for more.

He rumbled low in his throat as he withdrew his fingers and returned them to his cock. The hot water poured down around them as he guided his shaft home and sank fully into her pussy with a single, forceful stroke.

So tight and hot. She gripped him and his legs wobbled. Her gasp of pleasure made him grin. Then he began to move. Her moans turned to screams as he pounded hard and unrelentingly inside her. Her breasts were flattened against the wall of his shower as he thrust.

"How cheap?" he asked.

Water mixed with sweat and washed it away as he continued to work his length inside her. She reared back to meet each of his forward moves, encouraging him deeper. Harder. Faster.

Grabbing her hands, he laced their fingers and placed her arms out high over her head, making her go up on tiptoes. He sucked on the side of her neck as he moved. The intensity and need built up quickly between them. This wasn't any sort of slow, taking their time, kind of loving.

"Uh...oh...fu...Leo..." she babbled as her body tightened around him and she came in a rush.

Christ, he could feel her muscles clamping down and rippling on his shaft. Her warm cream covering him made him groan low in pleasure. It also reminded him he wasn't wearing protection. With the last little bit of control, he pulled free and came against the small of her back, his seed vanishing with the water, which continued to pulse around them.

Exhausted, he sank against her warm body. Her breathing was rapid and he was a bit lightheaded. He reached around her for the loofah and lathered it up before he washed her clean. They were silent for the remainder of the shower.

After they had dried and dressed, he grabbed her hand as she went to move by him. Tugging her close to his chest, he wrapped his arms around her.

"What?" she asked.

"Thank you," he murmured against her lips. He dipped his head and stole a kiss. Lord, he could kiss this woman forever. She tasted so amazing, it was like a drug he couldn't ever get enough of.

"Humph. I think you should make us some dinner."

"I think you're right. You go back to watching you fashion show and I'll whip it up."

"Fashion show?"

"The television was playing some kind of fashion thing when I got home."

"Ah, well I honestly have no clue. I hadn't planned on watching anything, just turned it on for the noise."

He nodded. "Okay." Another kiss. "I'll be in the kitchen."

He stood in the middle, unsure of what to make. Opening his freezer, he nodded at the sight of some frozen pizza. It had been a while since he'd had that and it would do. Once he'd turned on the oven, he pulled out the pizza and placed it on a cookie sheet.

While waiting for it to heat, he went and set the table.

"Dining on the fine china, I see," Deyon spoke from the doorway.

He looked at the paper plates sitting on the table and nodded. "You got it. Nothing but the best for my girl."

She wrapped her arms around him. "Is that what I am, Leonardo? Your girl?"

He rotated so they were face to face. "Have I not made that clear yet?"

She gave him a sassy grin. "Sometimes we like to hear it more than once."

"Noted."

They watched *Jeopardy!* as they ate, having forgone the table to eat on the couch. They played along with the contestants on the TV. Leo won in the end but only because he'd wagered more on final than she had.

"You're ruthless," she said.

Readjusting himself on the couch so he could see more of her, he swirled the rest of his wine in the glass before drinking it. "Yes. I can admit it. I like to win."

She pointed a finger at him. "So do I, just so you know. Don't get used to it."

He grinned at the challenge and said, "We'll see."

She sipped her own drink then shrugged. "We'll see how well you do when the stakes are higher. Like strip Jeopardy."

He almost choked. "Strip Jeopardy?"

"Sure. What you've never played?"

"You have?" One eyebrow rose when he asked that question.

"My turn to ask the questions, Sheriff. Besides, you can turn any game into strip whatever, so long as you have the requirements."

"And those would be?"

She leaned closer and swiped her tongue over her lips. "Willing participants." Deyon moved back to her original spot. "And I think we have those, unless I'm mistaken."

God, she was a tease. "Oh no. We have willing participants."

"Good. Then that's all we need."

Christ, he was ready now. "So, tell me. *Have* you played it before?"

She got to her feet and flashed him a sexy smile. "Wouldn't you like to know?"

Yes, he would. She went to the kitchen and came back with a plate of cookies.

"Deyon?"

"Hmm?" She bit into one and moaned in bliss, which nearly derailed his thought.

"Answer me."

Deyon watched Leo as she chewed on the chocolate chunk and macadamia nut cookie. He was so fun to rile. She'd seen that spark of jealousy when he'd asked her the first time.

She shook her head and took another bite. If she were honest with herself, she liked seeing it. He crossed his arms and glared. She licked a final bit of chocolate from her thumb and smirked at the answering flare of heat in his eyes.

"No."

"No you haven't played?"

"No, I'm not answering you." A low rumble escaped him and she grinned. "Are you going to handcuff me and have your wicked way until I break?" She batted her eyes and held out her hands, wrists together. "Be gentle."

"No, you'd like that too much." The corners of his mouth twitched as he tried to hold back his smile.

"Damn straight."

"How about I take away your weapons?"

She narrowed her eyes at him, suddenly no longer so amused. "Sheriff or not, that wouldn't be in your best interest to attempt."

"So protective of your weapons."

She reached for another cookie. "Like you're protective of your family jewels. Take mine, and I'll take yours."

She would swear his face went a few shades lighter and he shifted his weight on the couch to protect his balls—it had to be instinctive. "Why do I think you aren't joking?"

"Because I don't joke about my weapons."

"Anyone tell you, you are a bit too obsessed with weapons?"

She just waved him off. "Whatever. A girl has to have a hobby, you know."

"Collecting weapons like you do isn't a hobby."

"Would it be so strange if it was a man's collection?"

He thought about it and shook his head. "Probably not. I'm just saying, Deyon, one doesn't meet many famous models who love weapons as you do."

"That's because I'm unique. And I'm not a model anymore."

He nodded. "That's true. Although some would say you were special."

She crossed her arms and sneered. "Why doesn't it sound like a good thing when you say it?"

Leo batted his eyes at her and shrugged with innocence she didn't buy for a second. "No clue."

"Whatever."

She watched him eat a cookie and found herself mesmerized by the working of his throat when he swallowed. The silence, which lingered between them, was comfortable and neither of them rushed to fill it. That was another reason she liked Leonardo so much—they didn't *have* to have conversation going. They were relaxed enough with one another to have silence.

"Want to watch a movie after we clean up?" he asked a while later.

"What'd you have in mind?" She got up from the couch and took the cookies while he got the remaining dishes from dinner.

"I don't know. Something mindless that I don't have to think on. So no drama or documentaries."

While he loaded the few items that actually had to be washed in the dishwasher, she returned to the living room and opened his television stand to see what movies he had that she wanted to see.

She settled on one of the *Lethal Weapon* movies and soon they were cuddled on the couch watching Sergeants Murtoch and Riggs as they worked their jobs. Leo fell asleep and she covered him with a blanket before she left. She would have loved to stay with him, but she had a buyer coming in early in the morning and wanted to get home, since she didn't have her outfit here.

She drove home then. As she parked her car and headed for the front door, she glanced over to where Arissa used to live. It was completely dark there and she sighed heavily. She missed her friend. She didn't even bother looking at Jackson's side—he was working the overnight shift at the hospital this week.

She focused back on Arissa's apartment door. She'd not seen her friend since she'd told her she was moving. Deyon shook her head. She'd been so busy with work or with Leonardo, nothing else had seemed to matter. Something she needed to rectify.

Inside, she ran herself a bath and groaned in ecstasy when she submerged in the hot water. With a glass of wine beside her and some soft music playing in the background, she relaxed then got out when she began to doze.

She slept well that night and was up before her alarm went off. After a light breakfast, she made her way to her Audi and slipped behind the wheel. She drove to her business and let herself in. Not much later, another worker joined her and they got everything set up for when the buyer arrived.

It went well and she was happy despite being tired. Meeting with a buyer always stressed her and made her a bit exhausted. The unknown, the worry, it all played a part. Thankfully, this one went off without a hitch.

"Thanks for all your help, Susanna," Deyon said as she and her employee put things away in the storage area. Sounds from the front filtered back, alerting her to the fact her store was again busy. She loved that noise.

"It was my pleasure. I'm so glad it went well."

Susanna was a larger woman who had started running the register to help make ends meet. That was five years ago. Now she could do anything in the store and had people who would come in just to talk to her.

Deyon squeezed her shoulder as she walked by with some fabric bolts. It didn't take them long and the back room was back to the organized chaos she was used to seeing.

"Let's go to lunch," she said.

Susanna looked at her. "Us?"

Deyon nodded. "Yes. We've been here all day and I don't know about you, but I could use some food."

"Okay."

They grabbed their purses then walked outside. The day was cooler than normal for the time of year but still extremely comfortable. "Where to? Milton's?"

"Sounds good to me. I haven't been there in a while."

Milton's was a nice family restaurant, which had good food and friendly staff. Two must-haves, in her estimation. It was within walking distance of her shop and was one of the oldest establishments in town.

The women walked and chatted. They entered Milton's and Deyon smiled in contentment—she loved it here. They had bread bowls to die for, huge hamburgers and pasta that made her wonder if she hadn't taken a left and ended up in Italy. That wasn't even getting her started on the desserts.

* * * *

Things went along smoothly for the next two weeks. She finally tracked down Arissa and was now on her way over to see her friend. Just the two of them, no Jackson, no Leo and since Deiter was still overseas, no him.

She pulled into the drive of her friend's new home and nodded her head as she took it in. A typical, southwest, adobe style home. Nothing overstated. Just a very nice one story. After shutting off the engine, she climbed out and headed for the door.

"Hey, stranger," Arissa said swinging the door open after she'd knocked. "Come on in. Have to forgive the mess, I'm still unpacking. Work hours seemed to have doubled recently."

"Here"—Deyon thrust the basket at her—"a housewarming gift."

"You didn't have to do that, but thank you. Come on, I'll give you a tour."

After she'd taken a tour of the four-bedroom home, they sat at the dining room table and ate fajitas accompanied by some of the wine she'd brought.

"So tell me how you and Leo are doing?"

"Good, we're good."

"I'm glad to see you two together. Always thought you would be a good match for him."

"Really? Why's that?"

"You're good for him. He's happy with you, and some days I'd wondered if he would ever allow himself to be."

She smiled softly at Arissa's candid answer. "Now Dimitri needs to get a woman." She shrugged. "Or a man."

Arissa choked on her wine. "Oh…wow, yeah, no. He'd be after women."

"He's not settled down."

"You hadn't either, until Leo. Didn't mean you wanted another woman."

That was true. "Point taken." They ate in silence until she finished. "So, how is Deiter doing over there?"

A wistful look crossed Arissa's face. "He's doing good. I miss him, but hopefully he should be home soon."

"Do you get to talk to him every day?"

"No. We try, but it's not working out that way."

She could hear the hurt in her friend's voice. Reaching out, she squeezed her hand. "I'm so sorry."

She shrugged. "It's okay. Better than when we separated after the cruise and I knew nothing. At least I get text messages from him and phone calls, even if we can't coordinate enough to be on Skype. I just hope he comes home soon." She took a deep breath. "But this isn't supposed to be about me and my moping about. I want to know more about you and my big brother."

"Want the sordid details?" she teased.

"Eww, no. I don't even want to think of my brother doing such things. Has he gotten you any weapons?"

She laughed. "Are you kidding? Your brother wants to take my collection from me. Says they're too dangerous to have in the house. Well, too dangerous for me, anyway."

Arissa rolled her eyes. "Don't let him fool you. He's really very impressed by the collection."

"Really?"

"Oh yes. I've heard him talking about it for a long time. Somehow he even knows when you get new pieces."

She leaned back and crossed her arms. "Has he now? Hmmm, I think I'll have to check on that next time I see him."

"Just don't tell him you heard it from me."

Deyon laughed again. "Right, I'll tell him Dimitri told me." She got up from the table and said, "Put me to work. What can I do to help?"

"No dessert?"

"Yes, just not yet. I have to let this settle first."

Arissa got up as well and waved to her. They headed to the farthest room to the left—one she assumed would be a guest room.

"The boxes marked 'curio' all have to be unloaded into the cabinets throughout the house. Those two boxes are for the one by the picture window in the living room."

"I'll take those. You want them how they were set up in your apartment?"

"Yes, please."

The women worked until all the cabinets had been filled and the boxes broken down and piled near the door to go out with recycling. Then they headed to the kitchen again and heated up some brownies, topped them with French vanilla ice cream and a drizzle of fudge.

"Thanks for stopping by, Deyon," Arissa said around a bite of her brownie.

"You're my friend and I've missed you."

She was about half done when her cell rang and she got up to answer it. "Hello?"

"Hey, beautiful."

Leo. Her heart picked up its pace.

"Hey, yourself. What are you doing?"

"Well I came to your house to see you. Where are you? Are you still working this late?"

"No. I'm with your sister."

"Arissa?"

"Yes. We had dinner, put some things away and are eating dessert now."

"Okay. Have fun. I'll be here waiting for you." A short pause. "Naked."

He ended the call and she did too, a bit out of breath at the visual he'd left her with. Arissa was chuckling when she sat back down.

"What?"

"Go," she said.

"Go?"

"Leo called you and probably said something dirty. I see the lust in your eyes. Go."

"We've not had much time together," she protested lightly.

"We can do this again. At least one of us should be getting some."

Deyon shook her head, determined to spend time with her friend. "Nope, I'm fine. He just wanted to know where I was at."

Amusement lingered in her friend's eyes. "Ahh, making sure you weren't out past curfew?"

She glared and stuck her tongue out. "Well, yes. That and he wants to fuck me before bed."

"Ohhh crap, Deyon, I don't want to hear that. This is my *brother* you're talking about."

"You are such a prude. When did this happen?" she teased.

"I'm not a prude. I just don't want to know about my brother's sex life."

She blinked innocently. "I thought we were talking about mine."

"You are such an evil bitch. New topic."

With a wicked grin, Deyon allowed her to change to something else. All the while, her mind continually drifted back to the thought of the man sitting at her house, waiting for her. Naked.

Chapter Seven

Leo walked down the steps from the house of the couple he'd just delivered the news to. Damn it all, there were some days he hated this job. This counted as one of those days. The couple's daughter, Aslynn, had been riding her bike back from school, as she'd done every day, when a reckless driver had hit her. She'd died on the way to the hospital.

He blew out a sigh as he opened the door to his vehicle. The mother's wailing could still be heard and it was like a knife to his heart. The child had been their only one and now…they had none. Normally people were asked to come to the morgue for identification, but he'd said no to that. Her face had been so badly mangled it wasn't recognizable. Her school bag had been beside her and they'd also run a dental on her to get positive identification. No parent should have that image of their child as the last one. They needed to remember her as the vibrant girl she had been.

He stopped for a coffee at a small diner, needing a moment to decompress. Climbing out, he noticed a familiar, mostly dirty, green and dented Jeep parked in the lot. He entered the diner and scanned the area. Finding who he looked for, he made his way there.

"Hey, Sheriff," the server greeted him.

"Candy."

"Coffee?"

"Please." He paused by the booth and stared down at the woman there. "Hey, Lis."

"Hey, bro. Grab a seat."

He did and nodded his thanks when Candy dropped off his drink. "How you doing?"

She shrugged. "Some days are harder than others, you know?"

"I do. I just got done with telling Aslynn's parents. I convinced them not to go down for a look."

Her eyes glistened with unshed tears. "I tried, Leo. I really did."

He reached across the table and squeezed her hand. "It wasn't your fault, Lis. You always do your best."

"Doesn't make it any easier. I'll be playing the 'what if' game in my head for a while."

He nodded and grabbed for her plate, dragging it closer to him. Helping himself to her fries, he glanced at her ringless left hand.

"You know you can ask me. Jonathon told me he slipped up and mentioned it to you." The plate moved back out of his reach. "And you can get your own fries."

"Candy," he called out. "An order like Lis has, please."

"Coming right up, Sheriff."

He turned his attention back to his sister. "Why?"

She lifted one eyebrow and he read the question before she voiced it. "Really?" She ate a bite of her hamburger. "Have you *not* seen the insanity Mom's doing for these weddings? I'm not going to be a part of that. Besides, I don't do girly. I have *no* desire to be put through all of that craziness."

"What about pictures?"

"We had some taken."

"Why didn't you tell me?"

"I wasn't going to tell Jonathon, but I didn't return his car to him the next day. You know how he is about his vehicles anyway. This was his new one. His *baby*. So when we got back he demanded to know why. He had Harmony with him to drive one vehicle for him so we told them both."

"That's not an answer."

She blew out an exasperated breath. "Fine, because you blab. And you're dating Deyon. She would blab to Arissa, which would get it back to Mom." She shrugged. "I'm going to tell them. Eventually. Perhaps after Katiya and Arissa get married."

Why did he doubt that? His sibling had absolutely no desire to tell their mother. Or the rest of the family. "What about all the work Deyon is doing for you?" he asked, not at all liking the fact all her hard work and dedication would be for naught.

"She's not doing anything for me."

"The dresses?" He scowled at his baby sister. "How is that nothing? And her employees."

"Damn, Leo. I had no idea you thought I would be so callous. I've not told her anything other than 'no' and 'I have to think on it before I make a decision' so nothing has been started for me."

"She's a friend of the family."

"She is. Yours and Arissa's, mostly."

He ate some more fries. "Are you saying you don't like her?"

Lis threw up her hands in exasperation. "Oh, for goodness sakes, Leo. That didn't even remotely come out of my mouth. I like Deyon fine. But she's Arissa's close friend and you, well, it's obvious you two are fucking. I don't need my business all over McKingley before I'm ready for it to be. I grew up with everyone watching my life through a microscope."

"So you really didn't tell Arissa?"

"God no! I love her, but she's so likely to blurt it out. Same with you and Deyon." She pointed a finger at him. "Which is why I mean it, Leo. She doesn't get told."

"I'm not going to keep secrets from her."

"You're not. She would have no reason to ask so long as you don't mention anything about it. And you're keeping *my* secret."

He began to shake his head when he stared into her chocolate mousse brown eyes. They shined with unshed tears. Her lower lip trembled slightly.

Shit. Archer will kill me if he finds out I made her cry. It didn't matter—he knew she was about to leak crocodile tears. Delicia was the baby in the family and he hated to see her crying. Not to mention Archer Bennett, her *husband*, wouldn't be happy. The man was damn protective of her. Moreover, he wasn't a slouch by any means. It wouldn't be a pleasant discussion if Archer found out Lis had been crying because one of her brothers.

"Okay, okay," he said. Hands out in a placating gesture. "Just don't cry. I won't tell anyone until you give me your go ahead."

Just that fast the tears vanished and a brilliant smile lifted her lips. "Love you, Leo." She leaned over the table and kissed his cheek.

"I didn't stand a chance, did I?"

"No, not really."

He chuckled. She was good — he had to give her that. It wasn't something she did often for Lis didn't like people who pretended to be upset to get their way.

"What happened to not liking women who use their feminine wiles to get away with things?"

"I'm not using feminine wiles with you."

"Sheriff," squawked the radio at his side. "As soon as you have time can you please come back to the station, over."

"I'm on my way, Trina." Pinning his gaze back on his sister, who'd fallen silent the second the call came across, he asked, "What do you call it then?"

She gave him a Cheshire cat grin. "Candy, put these on my bill will you, please?" The waitress waved her acknowledgment. "For you, Leo, it's all baby sister wiles. And I get to use those at my discretion." She leaned close. "In case you wondered, no I have absolutely no qualms about doing that to you or anyone else in this family."

She slipped away to pay the bill while he laughed. He leaned back against the booth and watched Lis stride to the door, glance at him then wave. He returned it and continued observing her as she jogged down the steps to hop in her rugged and dirty vehicle.

I am a lucky man. He knew this. His family was a large one and they all loved each other.

"Trina?" he radioed back to dispatch.

"Go ahead, Sheriff."

"Is it important what I come back for or can it wait a bit?"

"No rush, just have a message for you from another officer." Her tone, like her sister's was nothing but professional.

"Great. I'm off to speak to someone else from the university incident. Then I'll be along to the station."

"Very good, sir."

He continued eating his meal and tossed some bills down to cover the tip, although he was pretty sure Lis had as well. With a wave, he was on his way out then slid behind the wheel of his cruiser. He started the powerful engine then headed off in the direction of the college campus. He wanted to learn who had set the fire and what the reason was for it.

After work, he would go find his woman and see what fun they could get into. He also needed to double check the dates for the wedding she'd asked him to attend with her up in New York. He was actually looking forward to that. Being away with Deyon. A hotel room, room service. His cock stirred and he shifted, hoping to ease his arousal before he got to his destination. It wouldn't be easy. Especially when all he could think of was having Deyon all to himself in a hotel room for a few days, away from every day issues which got in the way.

* * * *

Deyon dropped the bolt of cobalt blue fabric she held as a piercing pain infiltrated her head. *Oh, shit this hurts.* She knew what it meant. Another of her debilitating headaches was right on its way. Based on past experience, she had very little time to make it home before she would be worthless. At least the shop was closed so she didn't have to worry about having someone cover for her, or trying to get the patrons out.

Swiping her purse, she headed at as fast as pace as she could manage for her car. She unlocked it and slid behind the wheel as another one hit. Tears formed behind her eyes and she stared blurrily through them as she revved the engine and tore out of the lot.

She wove in and out of traffic as if it stood still, doing her damnedest to get home before her world went black. A yellow traffic light before her almost had her slowing, but she pressed down on the accelerator, shooting through at the last minute.

By the time she made it home she was shaking and sweat had begun to run as she fought to stay upright and get inside. She dropped items as she fought through the ferocious pain and stumbled to her bedroom.

"Close shades," she slurred as she stripped out of her attire she'd worn to work.

Even the faint whir of the motor doing as she'd ordered seemed too damn loud and she winced. But blissfully her room became encased in total darkness. With her final bit of waning energy, she flopped on the bed and dragged a coverlet over her before succumbing to the world of darkness.

* * * *

She stirred and moaned slightly. Sitting up slowly, Deyon reached to her bedside table and her touch lamp, triggering it to the lowest setting. The faint glow made her squint regardless, but it wasn't as bad as it could have been. She found her pills and a bottle of water where she always had them. She popped a pill then washed it down with a swig of the tepid liquid.

Again, she'd forgotten to take her pills out with her. This time she'd changed purses yesterday and hadn't put the item in the new bag. Swinging her legs over the edge of the bed, she took several deep breaths before she got to her feet and made her way gingerly to the bathroom.

A hot shower was just what the doctor ordered and she felt better after. With no energy to dress, she merely slipped on her robe and walked out of her bedroom. The setting sun shined through the windows of her living room and it took a few moments for her eyes to adjust.

Shit, I was out longer than I thought. At least it was the start of the weekend as well and she had nothing planned so she didn't have to explain anything to anyone about missing an outing. Or so she thought. *I'll check my calendar later.*

In the kitchen, she stared at the array of things before her. She wasn't that hungry, but she knew she had to eat something. So she reached for a can of vegetable beef soup. While it heated on the stovetop, she leaned against the counter and toyed with the spoon.

She'd just turned the heat off and ladled some into the bowl when her front door slammed shut. A smile lifted the corners of her mouth—Leo had a key. She loved spending time with him and after the day she'd had, it would be so lovely to have him rub her temples and hold her close.

She replaced the pot on the stove and turned to the doorway. Her smile faded when she saw the anger flashing in his eyes.

"I'd say hi," she began. "But I think you'd bite my head off. Did you have a rough day?"

Not even a hint of a smile at that comment. In fact, his gaze hardened more. *I will go with yes, he had a bad day.*

"I can't believe you!" he spit. "What the hell were you thinking?"

She arched an eyebrow and crossed her arms. *Okay, not the greeting I was expecting.* "Don't you come in here and yell at me. I had another of my headaches. I didn't think we had anything planned. If I missed it, then I'm sorry. We both know I'm not going to listen to any 'lecture' you give, so just skip it."

He scoffed. "Really? You think that I'm mad over the possibility you missed something with me? This angry?"

"Then what?" She shifted her weight. "What happened?" It had to have been something—he was almost over the edge with his anger. Not to mention he didn't even comment on her saying she wouldn't listen to his lecture.

"You, Deyon. You happened."

She shook her head, not following. "Care to explain that anymore?" Her own voice had begun to rise.

"Another headache."

"What, you're mad because I didn't tell you I had one?"

"Get over yourself." The anger in his tone set her back. He no longer had a raised voice, but there was no mistaking the fury radiating from him.

"Excuse me?"

"Listen to me, Deyon De'clare, and listen well. And I'm not kidding, this isn't something you just ignore me on. You do that again and you'll answer to me."

"Do what?" Lord, he was furious.

"Drive like you did. You're reckless and stupid to do such a thing. If you think you being who you are should give you a free pass then move to some big city where that works. But not here, not in my town. Your ridiculous, *selfish* actions could have killed someone. You know what my day was like? I just finished telling some parents their child was dead because of a reckless driver only to find out you were out not much later than that, doing the exact same thing."

"I had a headache," she said, defending herself. "I wanted to get home. I've done it before, you know this."

"I don't fucking care if you did have a headache. I know you've done it before and it was my stupidity and my obsession with you that allowed you to get away with it. You have friends you can call and one of us would have come gotten you no problem. You know that. But this...hell no, not anymore. Not in *my* town. Do it again and I'll take your license and lock you up."

How dare he? "Fuck you, Leonardo."

His eyes were unforgiving and alive with flames of rage. "Do *not* push me on this, Deyon. You're lucky I don't take it now. Don't test me. I've told all my officers as well. You drive like that again and that piece of plastic will be gone so fast it'll make your head spin."

He whirled around and stalked off, anger evident in every inch of him. She jerked when the door slammed behind him. The sound of gravel spraying made her wince again.

She sank to a seat, her appetite all gone, and wavered between anger and shock. What had just happened? She'd never seen him that upset before. Never. Sure, they'd had arguments before – they were both passionate people. But this. No kiss. No hug. No anything other than anger.

She stomped back to her bedroom and flopped down, upset with him. *Bastard.* Who did he think he was to reprimand her like that? And why the hell did she feel so terrible?

Chapter Eight

Deyon stood on her back porch watching as the sun rose the next morning. Leo hadn't come back or even called. The bed had been empty without him and all night she'd cursed herself for getting used to him being by her side. The terrible feeling had only increased as she thought about what he'd said and finding out what had happened yesterday. The accident had been on the news and from what Leo had roared when he was yelling at her, he'd been the one to tell the parents. She could only imagine how he had been feeling. Leo didn't say much about his job, but she knew when he had bad days and tried to ease him and not to pry. From the reports, it was no wonder he'd been so furious when he came by.

"It still doesn't give him the right to curse at me, but I get it," Deyon said.

She sighed, rolling her shoulders. If she wanted to salvage her weekend off, she'd have to track Leo down. First, she had to make a stop in her store to get the presentation she had planned to do a little work on this weekend. With the way her head had been hurting, she'd left it. After, she'd find Leo—she already knew he was probably in his house since it was also his weekend off, and after a day like yesterday he'd not want to be around too many people. Deyon straightened and took her mug back into the kitchen then went to get dressed.

Ten minutes later, she was in her vehicle. Deyon drove out onto her road then onto the main one. A sound from her cell in the holder caught her attention. The tone she recognized as the security system at her store then it was followed by another sequence of notes that she didn't recognize. Frowning, she started to reach for it but stopped—driving and looking at her cell was a bad idea. A flash out of the windshield caught her eyes and Deyon gasped, jerking the car hard. She slammed on the brake but nothing happened. Gripping the wheel, she glanced wide-eyed as the tree she was heading for seemed to keep getting bigger and bigger. At the last moment, she jammed the car into neutral then hunched herself over the wheel, bracing for the impact. The car jolted and Deyon grunted as the belt dug into her and her head hit the steering wheel. The vehicle stopped and Deyon breathed out, realizing that she was fine.

The door opened and a frantic male voice called, "Miss Deyon, are you okay?"

Deyon lifted her head, blinking and seeing the tree. She turned then winced before focusing on the concerned teenager looking at her.

"I'm fine, Carlton." She fumbled with her seat belt, getting it off and turning to get out of the car. "Are you okay? I didn't hit you, did I?" She stumbled as she stood.

Carlton Rawlings held her up and shook his head. "No, Miss Deyon. I'm sorry I was speeding and didn't see you."

Deyon stifled an ironic laugh. She only sped when she was trying to beat her migraine, but other than that she drove within the speed limit. Yes she did drive at the higher end of the posted limit, but since she was being mindful of what Leo had said, she'd been driving slower.

Yeah the damn bastard is going to love it when I tell him this.

Deyon brought her attention back on Carlton—he was the brother of one of her neighbors. The area they lived in didn't have houses close to each other, but everyone in the area knew their fellow neighbors—there was a yearly get together held either at Carlton's or at her home where they invited every neighbor.

"It's okay, Carlton." Deyon pulled gently away from his hold now she had her bearings. "I see Kenton finally let you ride his bike."

Kenton was Carlton's older brother and his guardian. Kenton also owned a custom bike shop.

"It's mine. He made it for me as a graduation present. This is my first solo ride. He's going to kill me for running you off the road." Carlton smiled ruefully.

"You didn't run me off the road. There is something wrong with my brakes." Deyon stepped from behind the open door then closed it glancing at the front and was relieved to see there wasn't too much damage. "Which is weird. I just had it serviced at Bennett's."

"You're very lucky, Miss Deyon. You didn't hit the tree too hard," Carlton said. "When the cops get here I am so dead. Maybe that'll save me from Kenton's lecture."

Deyon turned back to him, noticing the young man was anxious. "Hush now, it will be fine. There is no need for the cops to know. I'll speak with Kenton to calm him down."

Carlton was already shaking his head before she even finished speaking. "I already called them on my cell."

"Bu—"

The sound of a vehicle pulling up caught her attention. Deyon frowned at the police Jeep pulling in.

"Let me handle this, Carlton. Call Kenton," Deyon told him.

"I should—"

"You can't avoid it. You, *his brother*, were in the accident too. He needs to know." Deyon stared at the young man until he nodded.

As Carlton moved away slightly to talk on the cell, Deyon remembered hers and the security noise. She turned, opening the car and retrieving her cell and purse before facing the officer. Deyon studied the woman who already stood waiting for attention. She didn't recognize the caramel skinned officer who was watching her. Wire-rimmed glasses covered her dark brown eyes with thick lashes. The cop's hair was neatly pulled back from her face and she was sans cap.

"Deputy—"

"Conner, Miss De'clare."

Deyon waited for her to continue and it took her a moment to realize she wasn't.

"There is no need for the police. We'll—"

"I've been ordered to take you in, ma'am."

Deyon stared, unsure she had heard her correctly then sputtered, "Excuse me?"

"Sheriff Wright ordered you be arrested for speeding."

"But, how did—" Deyon stopped, realizing that Leo *had* given orders to his deputies after he left concerning her.

"You can't arrest her. It was my fault, I was speeding. She swerved to avoid me." Carlton came abreast to her.

Deputy Conner looked between her and Carlton then said, "Explain what happened."

Carlton did. Deyon didn't pay attention, anger slowly filling her. Leo had gone too far. She glanced at her cell, pushing a button then reading the screen. Fear gripped her and she glanced up at the Deputy.

"I need to go—"

"You can't. I have to call the sheriff." Deputy Conner turned and walked away, talking softly on her radio.

Deyon stood, waiting impatiently for her to come back. Her hands shook and she tried to be still.

It'll be okay. Breathe, Deyon. She inhaled then exhaled.

"Are you okay, Miss Deyon?"

"Yes. Did you reach Kenton?"

"Yes. He's home today and will be here in a few moments."

Deputy Conner returned. "I'm taking you in, Miss De'clare. You'll have to straighten things out with the sheriff at the station."

"What?"

"It's my fault," Carlton protested.

"I know that. But the sheriff didn't let me explain and ordered Miss De'clare be brought in." Deputy Conner's face was composed.

Deyon tried to gauge what she was thinking.

"Bu—"

"It's okay, Carlton. Stay here and wait for Kenton. If you don't mind, can you and he stay and wait for the tow truck?" Deyon looked at the deputy. "Can I place a call?"

She fought to stay polite. It wasn't the deputy's fault. It was all that hard-headed Leonardo Wright and she would deal with him directly. The deputy nodded and moved away to give her some space.

Deyon patted Carlton's arm then dialed. She didn't wait when it was picked up. "I'm being arrested for speeding." She quickly explained what had happened and about the security signal then finished. "No, I'm not injured. Can you also get a tow truck to retrieve my car?"

Once she'd hung up, Deyon strode over to the deputy and glared. "I could just deck you and go on my way."

"You could try, but then I'll have to put you down. Taser you then the charge for resisting arrest and assault on an officer will make your arrest a reality instead of a bogus one." Deputy Conner spoke in a firm, succinct and no nonsense manner.

Deyon lips twitched. "You don't say much, do you?"

"No."

"If you know this is bogus, then why are you arresting me?" Deyon was more curious than anything else.

In the brief time in the deputy's presence she suspected the woman followed the rules.

"Following some of the sheriff's orders."

"What other orders are there?"

"I'm to cuff you and put you in the back seat then in a jail cell. Cuffs in my opinion are not necessary. Unless you plan to try to deck me that is, then I'll have to put you down on the ground." Deputy Conner's face was serious.

Deyon gritted her teeth. Leo was going to get it for putting her through this.

"Let's go, Deputy Conner." Deyon strode toward the car.

The cop opened the back and Deyon slid in, placing her bag on the seat beside her then dropping her cell on the top. Deyon clasped her hands in her lap, looking straight ahead as the door closed. In moments, the officer got in and got them on their way. As they drove, Deyon's mind started to race with what was happening at her store. To get her mind off thinking about it, she looked at Conner through the panel separating them. She remembered Leo mentioning a Conner before, but she'd assumed it was a man with the first name Conner. The possible relevance of the name finally dawned.

"Are you related to Conner from the Sigmund's ranch?"

"Yes."

That was all and Deyon waited again then said, "Talking to you is like conversing with a rock."

"Not really. Rocks don't talk."

Deyon laughed. "Don't be literal. You know what I mean."

There was no reply. Deyon tried not to think of her shop.

"What type of gun do you carry?"

"Why?" Deputy Conner made a turn.

"I like guns. I have a collection of them as well as other weapons."

"What sorts of weapons?"

Deyon noted the interest on her face. She recognized the look of someone who enjoyed the same thing she did.

"Since this is a bogus arrest can we make a stop?" Deyon glanced out of the window at the way her store was. She couldn't see anything, but could imagine the chaos going on.

"No."

"I need to go to my store." The desperation in her voice pissed her off.

If it wasn't for Leo she'd be there.

"Why?"

Conner's one-word answers were aggravating her even more.

"I'd like to be there to see if all I built will be burnt to the ground." Deyon blinked, not going to cry.

She would not show weakness. She didn't know how big the fire was that the notice from her security at the store had sent her—the alarm had never been triggered before. The idea of losing everything was filling her but no matter what, she'd rebuild if she had to. But she'd like to be there to do something. The feeling of being helpless did not sit well with her.

"It mustn't be too bad or we'd have heard of the fire on the ra—"

The radio in the dash came on and the dispatch asked for officers to report to the fire to help the fire department. Closing her eyes, Deyon gripped her hands tighter as they talked in codes she didn't know while referring to her business.

"Tears are useless. Tell me about your weapons."

"I'm not going to cry." Deyon opened her eyes then met dark brown, wire-rimmed eyes in the rear-view mirror. "I have this sweet piece I bought a few weeks ago while at a gun show with L—" Deyon cut herself off, frowning as she thought of the man who had her here instead of where she needed to be.

"He's not thinking. Which is unlike him. Emotions cloud your judgment, making you stupid."

Deyon focused on Conner. "From your tone, I can tell you think being emotional is a bad thing."

"Yes. Practical thinking makes you avoid shit like what Sheriff is doing now."

"I think you and I'll get along real well, Conner." Deyon laughed until tears rolled down her face.

Conner didn't reply. Deyon calmed and they rode on toward the station. When they arrived, Conner parked close to the door then turned to her, placing her hand on the seat while looking back at Deyon. Absently, Deyon noted her nails were short, neatly clipped with a natural color.

"The sheriff told me to walk you through as any other perp, but I won't be fingerprinting you, taking your picture or anything else like that. I'll call a medic to fix the right side just above your right eyebrow while you wait in his office."

"What—" Deyon stopped speaking as she touched where Conner stated and felt the stickiness.

She lowered her hand, shocked to see she was bleeding. Quickly she pulled off the scarf she had and dropped it on her bag.

"The scarf would be better on your cut than on the seat."

"No, it was given to me by my mom," Deyon stated, then asked in disbelief, "He wants me treated like a criminal?"

"He's emotional." Deputy Conner shrugged.

"Emotional my ass. I'll show him emotional." Deyon muttered a few curse words in various languages, not even registering what she was saying, then focused on Conner. "I don't want to be in his office. Put me in a cell."

"I won't."

"Fine, I'll do it myself." Deyon reached for the door.

"Wait."

She did and Deputy Conner exited and opened her door. Deyon got out, head held high. It was early enough in the morning that there wasn't anyone around. She strode into the station, her high-heeled sandals clicking on the floor with each step. The dispatcher's gaze widened when she saw her.

"Dey—"

"I've been arrested, Trina. Show me to my accommodations please," Deyon stated.

Trina glanced behind her.

"Mix up. I'll put her in a cell."

"I thought you weren't going to?" Deyon snapped.

"You want to go, I'll put you there. Your bag and cell phone stay here." Deputy Conner shrugged.

Deyon bit her lip, holding in what she wanted to yell, then handed over the items. Conner handed it to the dispatcher then she led Deyon to a cell. Conner put her in then left. Deyon paced, fuming at Leo and his bullshit.

"Deyon."

She stopped turning, spotting Lis. "Hey, Lis."

"I'm even afraid to ask why Leo put you in jail."

"It says a lot that you know he had me put here," Deyon pointed out.

"Sit. Let me look at your head." Lis efficiently herded her to sit.

She placed her bag down and started working on her head. "This is a small cut, but they bleed badly."

Deyon held still as she wiped it. Lis reached for something else in her bag.

"When are you finally going to pick something for your wedding? You'd think you're avoiding it because you're already married or something."

Lis stopped. "Fuck, Leo told you I'm married."

"Excuse me?" Deyon blinked then shook her head. "Leo didn't tell me anything. You mean to tell me you're married and none of you told me?"

"No one but Leo and Jon know." Lis frowned. "And well, now you."

The way she said it made Deyon wonder why it seemed as if that was a bad thing. "Why didn't you want me to know? Hell, why didn't you tell everyone instead of making your mother plan your wedding when you're already married?"

"You'll blab to Rissa." Lis got a stubborn look on her face. "And I'll tell everyone when I'm ready. No one asked any of you to plan anything for me. You all need to stop treating me like a child. I—"

"Whoa. Stop the fuck right there." Deyon held up her hand, moving away from her and standing. She kept a tight hold on her emotions. She would not fall apart—not here and not now. "I've never once treated you like a child, Lis. I know your family is over protective of you, but *I* am not like that. Am I?"

Lis shook her head grudgingly.

"As for my telling Rissa. If you told me not to I wouldn't. You know this. All the times you've come to me and we talked. Have I ever broken your confidences to anyone?"

Lis moved her head side to side again.

"You know what." Deyon rubbed along the bridge of her nose then lowered her hand. "Grow a pair and fucking deal with your mama and your family shit on your own. Patch me up and get the hell out."

"Deyon, I'm sorry. I was feeling so cornered with everything I—"

"You should be fucking sorry. But right now I have enough crap going on, I don't have time to give a boo fucking hoo." Deyon sat down and said in a hard tone, "Do your job then go."

Lis recognized her tone and did as she'd asked then repacked her things, putting her bag over her shoulder. "De—"

"Go."

Lis went, not saying anything further. Deyon scooted back against the bed and placed her head against the wall closing her eyes. Steps came toward her and the bed dipped.

"Lis, for fuck's sake." Deyon opened her eyes.

She was startled to see the deputy beside her. Conner held out a bottle of water which she took. Conner sat beside her.

"Don't you have other innocent folks to arrest?"

"You're not officially under arrest."

"So?"

"It's a liability for us if you pass out from your injury."

"I'm not going to sue you or anyone here for this." Deyon laughed bitterly. "I'll take it out of Leo's ass."

"That's your prerogative."

Deyon glared at the composed woman. "Doesn't anything get to you?"

Conner didn't answer.

Deyon sighed then said, "You should come check out my weapons sometime."

"Nope. Don't like people."

"I'm with you on that one today." Deyon chuckled. "I'm not people. I'm Deyon. Let me see if I can entice you. My favorite weapon in my collection is my crossbow. I had it specially made. I—"

Conner interrupted, "You are a strange woman."

"Ditto, Conner. Ditto." Deyon squirmed on the bed settling in to talk about one of her favorite subjects—guns.

* * * *

Leo strode into the station, wincing as he noted the time. It had been over three hours since he'd got the call from Deputy Conner about Deyon. His fists clenched as he thought of her recklessness. Speeding, after what he'd told her yesterday. It was blatant defiance. He'd been headed to the station right away when James had called to remind him about their plans. Leo had planned to take Deyon over to meet James, who had become a friend since Leo went on so many calls to the ranch. He knew Deyon would enjoy visiting James to see some of the weapons he had. The man's collection was more extensive than Deyon's. Leo hadn't got a chance to tell her because of yesterday. Leo'd decided to go over briefly to visit the man. It would give Deyon time to be processed at the station and some time in the cell then he'd talk with her. Maybe then she'd have more sense. He should have figured James would prod him into some hand to hand, as they had been doing recently whenever he went by. Leo had got so caught up he hadn't realized so much time had passed.

Leo noted that there wasn't anyone at the front desk. He paused before the impeccably dressed man sitting with two others.

"I should have figured she'd call you, Jon." Leo glanced at the other two. "Kenton and Carlton, are you bein—"

"You arrested Miss Deyon for nothing." Carlton stood, his fists clenched.

Leo stared at the young man in surprise. Kenton and Leo had grown up together. Their families were close, and when the elder Rawlings had died, leaving Kenton as Carlton's guardian, many of McKingley's residents had helped Kenton while he'd figured out how to raise a kid. Kenton had done a great job— Carlton was very respectful and bordered on quiet. Confused, Leo looked at Jon and Kenton. Kenton smiled that playfully wicked grin that made Leo know that he was about to get him into trouble.

"Let's explain," Jon said.

Leo nodded then listened as Jon explained. Carlton interjected as he told the story. Leo realized he'd made an error. He glared at Kenton who still had that damn grin.

"You're always getting me in trouble."

"*Me*. I'm not the one who arrested the woman I'm dating and left her in a cell for hours." Kenton whistled. "You're losing it, buddy."

"Christ, she's making me crazy." Leo gestured to Carlton. "It is your fault, Kenton, for giving him his own bike." Leo warmed to the idea. "Yes, your fault indeed. Isn't he a little young for a bike?"

"I'm eighteen," Carlton stated with attitude.

"You are?" Leo looked at him surprised. "God, I'm old. Too old to deal with irritating women." Leo sat in the chair beside Kenton.

"You're the one who wanted her." Kenton pushed at his shoulder. "Now go and play nice."

Leo frowned. "Conner knew all this, but why did she put her in a cell?"

"She asked," a quiet voice stated.

Leo looked up and spotted Conner.

"Just like her." He shook his head and rose. "Let's get her out and give her our apologies."

"Your apology." Conner turned on her heel and left.

Although her tone was respectful and she didn't expand, Leo heard the censure behind it. From the few months Conner had been on the force, Leo had come to appreciate her being such a steady cop and he knew it had to have grated on her to arrest Deyon for a false charge. He hadn't listened, which was unlike him. Leo knew he had to apologize to her, but first he had to see Deyon. He headed to the cells, frowning at Jon when he joined him.

"You don't need to come."

"I need to insure that my client is being treated fairly."

"And you're mad at me too." Leo shrugged, not caring either way.

"My feelings are irrelevant in this case." Jon's tone was silky. "At least your deputy was smart enough to get her injuries taken care of."

"What? She was injured?" Leo hurried to the cell before opening it.

He studied Deyon, whose legs were crossed as she sat with her back braced against the wall. Leo spotted the bandage just over her head. He went to her, reaching out.

"Don't." Her tone was a clear warning and she never opened her eyes.

Leo stopped, hand in the air.

"Jon."

"Everything is fine. Lots of water damage, but nothing other than that."

Deyon released a shuddering breath then opened her pale-gray eyes. "Am I free to go, Sheriff?"

There was no emotion in her tone. Leo was ready for her to be furious and scream at him, but this he wasn't sure what to do with this unemotional reaction.

"You shouldn't have been here."

Deyon didn't say another word. She slid forward then stood, her body almost touching his. She studied him deliberately then Deyon pushed past him. Leo grabbed her on the shoulder. Deyon shrugged him off and went outside to Jon.

"Thanks, I was worried about the store."

"Why are you worried about the store?" Leo could tell he was missing something.

Deyon didn't answer him focused on Jon.

"I took care of your car and they will check the brakes. Kenton is waiting to give you a ride to the store."

"I'll ta—" His words stalled as Deyon glanced over her shoulder.

Leo shivered at the coldness in her pale-gray gaze then she turned her head, deliberately dismissing him. He took a step toward her, but she was already heading out of sight. Outside the cell, he watched as she sauntered down the hall, her dark red dress moving seductively with each sway of her hips.

"You're an ass," Jon said conversationally.

"I know." Leo sighed. "I'll talk to her and work it out. What happened at her store and to her car?" His attention was still on Deyon as she stopped to accept her things from Conner who came to meet her in the hall.

"What? You don't know?"

Leo glanced at Jon. "Know what?"

"Someone tried to burn down her store and from what she said with the car, her brakes might have been tampered with."

"I'm off duty today." Leo looked back to Deyon and didn't see her. "She's in danger and you just let her go by herself?"

Leo started down the hall the way she had went.

"That's why Kenton is with her." Jon hurried behind him. "You know if I tell her, she'll refuse anyone watching her."

Leo cursed then quickened his footsteps.

"Sheriff, there's been another fire," a voice yelled behind him.

Leo almost told them he wasn't on duty but thought of the store fire and that many of his officers would be there, limiting the response time to any other emergencies.

"What the hell? We've been getting a lot of fires in McKingley lately," Jon commented.

Leo didn't say anything to that since it was true. "Make sure someone keeps an eye on her and I'll be there as soon as I can."

He didn't wait for a reply, knowing his brother would insure Deyon was protected. Leo turned, heading the way he came to get the details on the fire before going out. Hours later Leo went home instead of to Deyon's since it was too late to disturb her.

That hasn't stopped you before. Leo ignored his inner voice. They were both wrung out from today and he was not in a good frame of mind to talk.

* * * *

He spent the next day convincing himself of that as he puttered around his house, not really getting much of anything done. Finally, he couldn't take any more and went to see her. Instead of using his key, he knocked then waited.

The door opened and Deyon leaned against the doorjamb, no expression on her face. Leo pushed his hands into his pant pockets.

"How are things at Deyon's?"

"I've made arrangements to get things fixed. Nothing much to do until then." Deyon studied her nails.

Leo opened his mouth then closed it, thinking about what to say before he just blurted out, "I'm sorry, Deyon."

She lifted her head, causing her hair to slide along the sides of her face.

Deyon raised an eyebrow. "Exactly what are you sorry for?"

"What do you mean?" He scowled, not sure what she wanted.

"It's simple. Are you sorry you assumed I was speeding? Sorry that you had me arrested? Sorry that Conner didn't do everything you ordered and give me the whole treatment including cuffs? Or possibly is it that I was there for hours? What exactly is it you're sorry for?" Deyon's voice was still devoid of anything he could use to gauge what she was feeling.

Leo was at a lost what to say.

"Maybe it's that neither you nor Lis trusted me enough to keep the secret of her marriage."

Leo gulped. "I wanted to tell you, Deyon, but I pro—"

"I get it, Leo. You promised to not tell me, Deyon, the flighty woman who can't be trusted. The woman who you could fuck but not give credit enough to listen to you." Deyon lifted her hand then ticked off on her fingers. "One—you and Lis not telling me are separate issues. I don't blame you for that. It's all Lis. You should have kept your promise to her. That was right."

"Dey—"

"I'm not done," she stated then continued as if he hadn't interrupted, "Two—I broke my promise that I would call you or someone when I got a migraine instead of speeding. For that, I'm sorry."

Leo breathed out, hope filling him that she would listen to him.

"Three—I'm not alone in this mess, Leo. Until you can tell me exactly what you are sorry for, don't come back to my door." Deyon stepped back, going to close the door.

"Deyon, don't be mad. I'm sorry."

She paused, looking at him surprised. "Mad. Oh, no, I'm not mad." Deyon's smile was sad and bitter. "I'm disappointed that you're sorry. Sorry don't get you anything if you don't know why. Goodbye, Leo."

She closed the door. Leo stood there stupefied. Every instinct filled him to burst down her door and demand she tell him what she wanted. Deyon was a complex woman and he enjoyed that about her, but now, trying to get into the way she was thinking—it worked against him. The angry woman he could deal with but what could he do about the woman whose hurt smile made him feel like shit? Leo turned and left.

Chapter Nine

Deyon stood before the door, watching on the monitor as Leo turned and left. She clenched her fists, not going after him. The stubborn idiot might be sorry, but unless he knew for what, it was a useless apology.

"Damn you, Leo. Get your head out of your ass." She pounded her fist on the door.

Deyon crossed her arms over her chest, cursing Leo for making her feel this way. She should have left well enough alone, but hadn't and now she had to deal with him. Deyon blinked, refusing to cry. She'd give the lunk head-time then if he didn't come to her, she'd hunt him down and tranq his ass. Deyon laughed, thinking of doing just that. A ringing caught her attention. Deyon reached into the pocket of her housedress and pulled out her cell. She saw the number on the display and was surprised. She pressed the answer button, before putting the phone to her ear.

"Hey, Queen. You haven't called me in a long time, you heifer."

The melodious smoky laugh came over the line, making Deyon laugh.

"You don't know how to say hello like normal people, Diva," Kendrix 'Queen' Brandon said. "I've missed you, my friend."

"You know it," Deyon replied, sitting on the chair by the entryway table. "I've missed you too. But I've sure seen your face all over the fashion mags and runways."

"A girl's gotta work." Queen laughed.

"And you're doing it showing those youngsters how it's done." Deyon smiled.

"I have to. You left me alone to school them," Queen accused in the same way she did whenever they spoke.

"It's been years, get over it already," Deyon gave her standard reply.

"Yeah."

Deyon became concerned at the tiredness in her tone. "What wrong, Kendrix?"

"You're one of the two people who call me that anymore. To everyone, I'm Queen."

"Humph, we started the business together when we were nothing but Deyon and Kendrix before all the fame and shit. So when we're serious, it's Kendrix. Now spill."

"You know me so well." Kendrix sighed. "Is your offer still open for me to come full-time to design for your shop and line?"

Deyon blinked, startled. "Of course. The few pieces you have done are a big hit. I was going to call and get you to design something new for the store."

"Please. You were trying to entice me to move to McKingley and work for you."

"That too." Deyon laughed then sobered. "What's wrong?"

"It's not been announced yet, but I'm retiring from the business."

"What? Why?" Deyon sat up straight, shocked.

"I'm getting too old to put up with this shit." Kendrix blew out a breath and the frustration in the sound came clearly over the cell line. "No, that's not true. I just want to get out. So I'm in Milan doing my last show. My big send off. Or at least, that's what it's supposed to be."

"For God's sakes, spit it out already." Deyon rolled her eyes. "I swear if I was there I would yank your hair and poke you in the side."

"And you're rolling your eyes at me. Don't do it." Kendrix laughed. "God, we know each other too well."

Deyon chuckled. "We do."

"The show will be off because the other model pulled out. Saying she wasn't going to be second fiddle to anyone." Kendrix laughed. "She was intimidated by me. Can you believe it?"

Deyon rested back in the chair. She could believe it. Queen was fierce on the runway and everyone took notice. They assumed that because of her beauty she was a stuck up bitch. When Deyon got to know her, she realized she was the sweetest person and although she knew she was good, she helped others who modeled with her. Just as Deyon had done when she'd worked — you had to pay it forward to survive long in the modeling business.

"Tell them the bitch is on the way," Deyon said.

"What... Deyon, you're retired?" Kendrix said.

"I'll come for this once. *For you*." Deyon stood, already thinking about what she needed to do. "If you had told me you were retiring I would have come for your show. That we will discuss when I get there. Oh, whose show is it?"

"God, Deyon, only you would come just for me and not know whose show you are modeling in. It's René, by the way."

"That pompous little man with his Napoleon complex." Deyon groaned then warned, "You better tell him I'll cut off his hands if he gets grabby."

"After the last show you did with him, I don't think I need to tell him. He still talks fondly about you. That lovely, luscious woman who makes his heart beat like no other." Kendrix laughed. "He's going to shit a brick when he hears you're coming."

"Yeah, yeah. I'll book a flight and get there. I'll send my measurements so he can get his staff to work on fixing the dresses to fit me." Deyon entered her bedroom and went to her closet. "And you better start planning your packing, because you're coming back with me to McKingley."

"I need time to go to my home in Paris to get things situated," Kendrix protested.

"Fine, we'll go there after the show. How long will it take for you to get everything done so we can get you moved here?"

"Ummm…two months."

"Three weeks." Deyon pulled out some clothing, putting it on her bed. "That's how long I'm giving you."

"God damn bossy woman. Fine." Kendrix paused then said softly, "It's been so long since I lived in the US. And I've only visited McKingley. Am I crazy to uproot my life and move there?"

"Nope, you finally got some sanity getting out of the business."

"You're right." Kendrix sounded surer. "Okay. I'm doing this. Wait…don't book a flight—I just remembered Chandler is flying in today on his private jet. I'll see if he can stop in McKingley to get you."

"Okay," Deyon said absently, heading to her storage room for her suitcase. "Call me back and let me know what's what."

"Okay. Thanks, Deyon," Kendrix said.

"Don't make me hurt you."

"I know, I know you don't like being thanked. I'm going to hug you so tight when I see you," Kendrix promised.

"That I'll take. See you soon, Queen." She hung up.

Deyon pulled out her suitcase and quickly packed. She stood then thought of what was left undone and went to make some calls and send out some notes.

* * * *

Hours later, Deyon exited the private plane, yawning. She walked down the stairs and hefted her carryon over her shoulder. Since she and Queen were the same size and had the same taste in clothing, she didn't walk with much.

"Diva," Queen called sensually.

Deyon dropped her bag and struck a pose. Kendrix came beside her and mirrored her. Then they looked at each other before they started to strut. The rhythm of the movement came back to Deyon and she slid into her walk that made her one of the most famous plus-sized super models. She and Kendrix stopped, pivoted then walked back to Chandler. They leaned against him, Kendrix on his left and Deyon on his right. Chandler, knowing his part, slid his hand around their waists and kissed the side of each of their cheeks. His husky chuckle filled Deyon's ear.

"The Diva, Queen and Prince are back." Chandler Brooks led them along.

Chandler was the male counterpart of their three-person team. They used to work together in various shows. His devastatingly handsome, sun-kissed good looks had made him very sought after until he too had retired.

"Now that you're coming stateside, Kendrix, I might just have to spend more time in McKingley," Chandler said.

"Maybe instead of gallivanting all over the world you'll settle down there," Deyon suggested. "Come on board with my store and line and create a male line."

"Oh, God. Give it a rest, Deyon. I've been hearing this for hours." Chandler squeezed her waist. "I said I'll think about it."

"You already have a house you rarely use. It's a waste of good space. McKingley is beautiful and a great town to live in," Deyon said.

The two of them laughed and ignored her joking, filling each other in on what they were doing. Queen grabbed her, hugging her tight as she'd promised then they got into the limo waiting.

"Humph, I see René is feeling generous." Deyon knew it was he who'd sent them a car—Kendrix wouldn't have wanted the attention it brought.

"He insisted." Kendrix leaned back against the seat, a glint in her golden gaze. "He did have a fit when he heard you were coming. By now, the press knows that the three of us are going to be together on the runway."

"Oh for… Damn little man," Deyon said.

"He was excited I was coming, but with you added, yeah his head probably did a spin around his shoulders." Chandler laughed.

"See, see I knew it. He's possessed. Maybe we can get the driver to stop for some holy water." Deyon crossed her arms, sliding down on the seat.

"He'll calm down once you growl at him," Kendrix said.

"Yeah, you're so fierce when you get all Diva." Chandler put his hand over her shoulders.

"Don't patronise me, you two." Deyon kissed Chandler on the cheek then leaned forward and did the same to Kendrix. "Leave me be while I get into my mode."

She sat back and they conversed among themselves, leaving her to her thoughts. They knew this was how she got ready for any assignment. A sexy, roguish face filled her mind and the ache she felt intensified. She missed Leo and it hadn't even been a full day. Leaving things the way they were between then didn't sit well with her, but she couldn't turn her back on Queen. She hadn't asked, but Deyon would not let her last show before retirement be anything but fabulous. Deyon slid out the picture she had in her inner pocket of her sweats, looking at her and Leo. It was of their date at the gun show. The car slowed and Deyon looked up—they had arrived at what she assumed was René's. She pushed the picture back in her pocket then put on her Diva face.

When the car stopped, she exited and strode behind Kendrix and Chandler as they went to the huge house. Inside, Deyon noted the beehive of activity then it stopped and they all looked at her.

"The Diva is here." She threw her arms out and then placed her hands on her hips and posed.

Everyone laughed and rushed toward her. René hugged her and she pushed him away when he grabbed her ass. She showed him her fist and he chuckled, stepping back. She recognized many of the faces around her and chatted with them while her thoughts were back in McKingley with a certain stubborn sheriff.

* * * *

Deyon's body relaxed as her feet touched the ground. She breathed in the scents of home for the first time in over three weeks.

"Are you sure I can't give you a ride home?" René asked.

Deyon turned to him and smiled. He was a pompous ass when he was in show mode, but outside he was a nicer man. Not easy to take, but better than when he was showing.

"Nope. I've got a ride. I'll see you at my store in the morning."

"I don't know how you convinced me to come to this place and work on a few items for your shop." René smiled ruefully.

"I'm charming," Deyon said dryly.

"You are my Diva." René laughed lifting her hand and kissing it.

"Deyon. I'm retired and will stay that way," Deyon warned.

"I know that, Deyon. But as per our quid pro quo you, Kendrix and Chandler will model some ads for me."

Deyon nodded. She had agreed with the others to do that. Some professional shots for René, and in turn she got his style for some items for her store that she could mass produce.

"Are you sure this photographer can do the job? I can still send the jet to get a professional one."

"You saw Lis' work. She'll do it." Deyon thought of how excited Lis had been when she'd called her. "Tomorrow we'll go to my store then scope out some places to shoot. And get it done this week."

René nodded. "I'm off to my hotel."

Deyon watched as René and his entourage walked to the SUVs he had waiting. She shook her head, imagining how busy the next few days would be.

"I wonder if Leo knows he has competition," someone with a deep voice said behind her.

Deyon turned. "Jackie." Then she looked at the man with him. "Tarak, what are you doing here?"

"He was sitting on the curb looking all lonely and someone needed to take him home," Jackson Carlyle answered with a devilish grin on his face.

"More like I was coming out of the airport and ran into him." Tarak Brady snorted, pointing at Jackson. "And he begged me to come help him get you and all the luggage you probably had." Tarak glanced at the pile of suitcases then her. "And he was right."

Deyon laughed. "I couldn't not shop while I was away. It's for the store."

"Sure, all of it is for the store." Jackson walked over and picked up a suitcase.

Tarak joined him. Deyon frowned then went after him, stopping him from picking up anything.

"Your leg is bothering you."

"Leave it, Deyon." Tarak's lips pulled in a tight line. His thick, curly lashes framed icy green eyes, and his face showed strain.

"Not working on me. If you try to pick up one bag I will make you regret it. And you're not going to your house, you are coming home with me for me to take care of you," Deyon stated.

"Dey—"

"Shut up." Deyon looked at Jackson who was biting his lips. "What are you waiting for? The suitcases won't move themselves to your truck. Get moving. I need to get Tarak home."

"For God's sakes, Deyon. Stop," Tarak protested.

"That growl won't work on me." Deyon led him to the car, putting her hand around his waist. "It's either me or I'll call Rissa or Lis."

"Damn you." Tarak growled. "I'm not an invalid."

"I didn't say you were. Now be a good boy and get in the truck." Deyon opened the back door. "Lay out to prop up your leg."

"Leo is a lucky man," Tarak said, kissing her cheek.

"He is, although he's an idiot," Deyon said.

Tarak nodded then got in the vehicle as she'd said. Deyon closed the door before going to help Jackson with her things.

He went to protest. "I've got—"

"You want a piece of me too?" Deyon stared him down.

"Not at all, Divalicious." Jackson put his hands up and let her do as she wished.

They got her bags and went on their way to her home. Deyon watched out of the windows, longing to see Leo.

* * * *

Leo held his cell, listening again as he had for the last three weeks. Deyon's voice came from his cell's voicemail.

"Oh…I thought I would get you but…that doesn't matter. I'm going out of town for a few weeks. I have to do a favor for a friend." She paused then said, "Think about what I said, Leo. We'll talk when I get back." Another silence then, "That is if you get your head out of your ass." She hung up.

Leo clicked on the phone, thinking again how even in her message she sounded so cold. Over three weeks and the only time he'd heard her voice was from her voicemail, where she'd called him an ass. Well, telling him to get his head out of it meant he was being an ass, any way he worded it. He couldn't say Deyon hadn't kept in touch — she'd emailed him often to let him know what she was up to. The messages, however, had nothing to do with them. Leo sat back on the couch, placing his cell beside him. He picked up his remote and keyed the TV to the program he had taped. Deyon flashed on the screen.

Her one-time only return to the runway to model had created a frenzy. Leo watched as she moved down the runway in the strut that had made her famous. The woman known as Queen came after her in a regal movement that made her seem haughty. Leo's hand clenched on the remote as the tall Caucasian man stopped, waiting for them. The women posed together at the end of the runway then the man strolled up behind them. The media said this man they called Prince — his real name was Chandler — strode with a sleek grace, but all Leo saw was a man who was heading to his woman.

Yes, Deyon was his. The joker came between the women and slid his hand along Queen's ribcage, pulling her against his left side then inhaling deeply and pressing a kiss on her cheek. Leo tensed even more.

"Don't you do it," he growled.

Prince — or Chandler or whatever the hell he was called — of course couldn't hear him. He moved his hand in the same position on Deyon. Leo stared at his hand on Deyon's bare skin then grunted as he pulled Deyon into his right side. Chandler inhaled, nuzzling the side of Deyon's face. It seemed so intimate and personal. Chandler looked between the two women, all his attention on them. The threesome standing on stage weren't looking at the audience, just each other — capitalizing on it being just about them. Then in unison they lifted their heads and watched out. Even through the camera, Leo could feel the sizzling sexuality between them. He hated the look on Deyon's face out there for anyone to see. The only thing that calmed him was that he knew what she looked like in the throes of passion and that wasn't it. Leo clicked the remote to pause when the camera panned to her, freezing her on the TV screen. A ping made him look at his cell then pick it up.

I'm at my house and going to bed. Deyon.

That was all the text said. He hadn't even known she was returning McKingley — if he had, he would have picked her up at the airport. Leo stood, cutting off the TV, already moving toward the door. He slid his feet into his sandals and went to his vehicle. Later, when he walked to her door, he thought of what he would tell her. Leo paused, pulling out his key then put it back knocking on the door.

Moments later it jerked open. "Shh…Tarak is sleeping."

"What? What's he do—"

"Keep your voice down," Deyon said, taking the same stance she had weeks earlier by the door. "What do you want, Leo?"

The fury he'd had bottled up for three weeks exploded. "Is that all you have to say to me? You've been gone weeks and no call, Deyon."

"I emailed you. The phone works both ways."

Leo paused, conceding he hadn't tried calling either. "Fine, but come on, Deyon, you just left when we were—"

"You were acting as you are now. Like an asshole," she stated. "If all you came here for is to yell at me and wake my house guest then good night."

She slammed the door in his face. Leo stood there shocked. He heard the locks being turned then the alarm arm. In disbelief he stared at the door.

"Go home, Leo," her voice came over the intercom.

Leo glared at it, knowing she could see. He turned on his heels and walked away. Outside he stopped then went back. Using his key, he opened the door then disarmed the alarm before reactivating it again. Leo turned to face Deyon who stood across the room.

"Look, Leo, I'm tired. I had a long ass trip and I don't want to deal with this now." Deyon put her hand on her hip.

Leo closed the distance between them, getting into her space. "Fine. But I'm not sleeping alone. I'm used to being with you and I'm staying."

Deyon studied him then stomped toward her bedroom. Leo watched her then went to the opposite side of the house—he figured she'd put Tarak in one of the bedrooms there. He pushed open the only door that was partially closed and stood in the doorway. He saw Tarak sprawled in the center of the bed with his hand under his pillow.

"No need to get the knife. It's only me," Leo called.

"I knew it was." Tarak turned onto his back, watching him. "Sorry, it's automatic."

Leo studied the man who had been adopted by his family in every way but on paper. "You need to take better care of your leg." He figured that was why Deyon had brought him home.

"God, all of you are a pain in the ass. Especially your woman." Tarak sighed. "I wanted to get home and pushed to get here. Since I've moved back, I don't like being away from McKingley. And my leg is sore because of it. I'll be fine."

"Make sure you work out to loosen it."

"Deyon already said so." Tarak smiled.

"And she lent you a knife, since I know you couldn't have taken one with you on the plane."

"She did and showed me her new weapons. Damn, I love a woman who knows her weapons." Tarak laughed.

"Did she show you the gun?"

"Uh-huh. I'm going to have to come back to try it out." Tarak studied him. "You know, women tend to react better to sweet words than yelling."

Leo winced. Tarak with his sensitive hearing would of course have heard them, even though he hadn't been near the door.

"Hardy ha ha. You are so funny." Leo stepped back. "Get some rest. See you in the morning."

"Fix it, Leo, or you won't like the repercussions."

"Don't threaten me, Tarak," Leo replied good-naturedly. "It'll be okay."

Leo knew it was Tarak's way to be protective of those he loved. And from the silence on the subject of him and Deyon in family emails, he knew the rest were waiting to see what happened. Their family was close but knew when to back off. In this case, what had happened between him and Deyon wasn't their business until it was sorted out. He put the door as he had found it then went to Deyon's bedroom. The lights were off except for one lamp, on what he had come to think of as his side of the bed. He went there and undressed then slid between the cool sheets. Leo turned off the light then looked at Deyon's back. He moved closer then pressed against her back and put his hand over her belly, cuddling her. She tensed then relaxed.

"I'm sorry, Deyon."

"For what?"

This time he had the answer. "For all what you said. Also for being an ass and taking out my frustration on you."

Deyon turned to face him. In the light coming in from the windows, Leo could see her clearly.

"I don't have a problem with you taking out your frustrations or snapping at me, Leo." With her pale-gray eyes she studied him and she said softly, "But next time, and there will be many, don't you ever leave like you did."

"I won't," Leo promised.

"Good. Because your deputy told me harming a cop could get me arrested." Deyon turned away, moving back against his chest. "Although tasing you might be worth it."

"I missed you whispering sweet nothings to me," Leo teased.

Deyon yawned then said sleepily, "Just you wait, buddy. I have an earful for you."

Leo grinned. He couldn't wait to hear them. He pressed against her — he was hard, but he'd wait until morning. Let her say what she needed to then he'd make love to her. His cock hardened further as he thought of sinking into her heated core. He listened to her breathing slow as he held her.

Chapter Ten

Leo rolled over, reaching for Deyon. He frowned when his hand meet cool sheets. Opening his eyes, he sat up and glanced around the empty bedroom. Noting the time, he got out of the bed and pulled on his pajama bottoms she had left out for him on the chair then headed out to the hall. At the cusp of the hall to the living room, he saw the TV was on.

"Deyon."

"She's left for work," Tarak said.

Leo approached the couch, coming to stand behind it and looking at Tarak where he was slouched on the cushions.

"So early."

"I guess. I don't know when she usually leaves."

"Okay. I don't have any clean uniforms here so I'm heading home to get ready for work. Do you want me to give you a lift?"

"I can't leave. Deyon told me to stay here." Tarak chuckled.

"No one can keep you where you don't want to be," Leo countered.

"True. Although it would be delightful if Deyon tracked me down and tied me up. Then brought me back here and she threatened me, I'm staying until she gets back. I'm not pulling one of my hocus pocus now you see me and then you don't shenanigans." Tarak rolled his eyes. "Deyon has a colorful way of putting things."

"That sounds like something Deyon would say. Hell, she'd do it too." Leo laughed. "So I'll leave you to it. Do you need me to bring you anything from your house?"

"Nope. I'm good. Deyon already retrieved my e-reader." Tarak pointed to the center table. "And anything else I need."

Leo knew he was obsessed with the thing—Tarak loved to read. "What historical romance are you reading?"

"I don't know what you are referring to? I don't read such things." Tarak shifted lower on the seat.

"You're such a liar." Leo headed back to the bedroom, shaking his head.

"They're good reading. I'm learning about history," Tarak called.

Leo didn't answer. He got dressed then left Tarak in the house. Outside he was surprised to see Tarak's truck. He wondered how Deyon had retrieved it without someone to help. He'd ask her later.

* * * *

Later that day, Leo entered Deyon's, glancing around. He hadn't had a chance to come by since the fire. Heck, he hadn't wanted to come by with Deyon not there. Everything looked fine now and the shop was busy. He went in search of Deyon.

"She's in her fitting room," the store manager told him as she hurried past.

Leo changed his course and went the way she stated. As he got closer, he was curious at the crowd that was in doorway of the fitting room.

"What going on?"

The people looked at him but none answered. They returned their attention to whatever was going on but made space. Leo moved into the area they left and stopped, his fists curling. The view before him was almost as it had been on TV. Deyon was posing with the joker and the Queen. But this time he was viewing it up close and personal. Leo looked at the rest of the people in the room who were bustling around doing something or the other, then narrowed in on the small man who sat in what looked like a director's chair.

"More passion," the man called. "Kiss Deyon."

"The hell he will," Leo roared.

Everyone stopped and looked at him. Those in the doorway with him chuckled. Leo strode forward and when he got closer he was surprised to see Lis rise from where she had been crouching. There was a camera in her hands. She looked amused.

"Who is this man?" The photographer in the chair got down and came to him. "Get out. We agreed you locals can look from the doorway. Now shoo."

Leo glanced at Deyon. "Did he just say *shoo*?"

She nodded. Leo focused on him, looking down at the man who arched an eyebrow.

"You think you can intimidate me." He sneered and took a step toward Leo.

Leo was amused by his sputtering. "In case you missed it, I'm the police. So if you touch me, I will restrain you." He looked at Deyon. "He's a flighty little thing."

"Flighty. I'm going to kick you in your big cop ass," he roared.

Leo glanced at him, shocked, then laughed. The man growled and headed for him. Deyon got between them, pushing him back.

"Stop trying to act like the diva designer, René" — Deyon waved a warning finger — "or trying to piss of the McKingley residents. If you want your stay to be pleasant, I suggest you make nice with Leo."

René immediately brushed off his clothing then grinned. "Ah…you are Leo. The boyfriend. Nice to meet you." He put out his hand.

Leo shook it, watching the man who changed his attitude so quickly.

"I have an outfit I want you to model with Deyon then you can kiss her instead of Chandler." René patted his hand then walked away. "I'm sorry for being such a prick. Come, lunch is on me." René spoke to those in the doorway.

They surrounded René and so did most of those in the room. Leo watched after him as he chatted charmingly with the McKingley residents. Leo looked in disbelief as Miss Sadie put her hand in the crook of René's arm and let him lead her out as he flirted with her. In moments, the door was clear as the others left with them. Leo focused on Deyon.

"Wow." Was all he could come up with.

"Don't mind René, he gets hyper when working." Deyon chuckled then grabbed his hand. "Come meet Chandler and Kendrix."

Leo followed her reluctantly. He shook Chandler's hand, staring at him. When Chandler smiled, dimples appeared on either side of his mouth.

"I don't want Deyon. She's like a sister to me and you don't fuck your sister."

Leo grinned at his bluntness then shook his hand with more enthusiasm, "Great to meet you joker…um, Chandler."

"You've been calling me joker. I've been called worse." Chandler laughed. "We've heard a lot about you, boyfriend."

"Whatever she said is all lies." Leo shook his head.

"Then you're not sexy and kind even when you have assish tendencies?" someone with a throaty voice asked.

Leo focused on the beautiful woman who was known as Queen. She indeed seemed very regal and graceful. Her golden gaze studied him then she smiled, putting out her hand. From what Deyon had filled him in on this woman, she didn't stand on formality. Leo pulled her to him and hugged her.

"Welcome to McKingley, Kendrix."

"Oh…Deyon, I'm going to love living here if all men are as debonair as this one." Kendrix kissed his cheek then looked at him. "Is there any more like you in this town?"

"Ummm…"

"Don't mind her. She would run the other way. When she's not in Queen mode she's shy." Deyon pushed her away. "Unhand my boyfriend. I'll meet you all at the restaurant," Deyon said, leading him toward the door that led into the offices.

"You don't have time for anything. René will come and get you. He wants shots at the restaurant," Kendrix called.

"Shut up." Deyon waved.

Leo went behind her, trying not to laugh. Inside the secure area on the way to her office, Leo glanced at her.

"You didn't mention she was moving here."

"Oh…I didn't. Sorry. Yes, she and Chandler arrived this morning. She's staying in the apartment Rissa was using until she figures out where she wants to live. Chandler offered her his place, but we're working on making him stay for a bit."

"What? He has a place here?"

"For a number of years. His house is in the same area as mine. Kendrix is thinking of getting something out there too. I mentioned the Gomez place is for sale. She'd going to check it out and maybe buy it. She's longing for space so it will give her that." Deyon entered her office then stopped by her desk facing him. "You don't need to be jealous of Chandler, Leo."

Leo moved closer to her. "I know but, seeing him with his hands on you at the show—" Leo stopped, realizing what he'd admitted.

"I bet you watched it over and over again. You're cute when you're jealous." Deyon lips quirked.

"No man wants to be called cute." He kissed her gently. "I woke alone this morning. I was hoping we could talk then do other things."

"I had to meet René." Deyon pressed against him. "We'll make some time to talk, but I vote we have make up sex now."

Leo slid his hands down her sides as he kissed her hungrily. Deyon opened, shifting and widening her legs. He stepped forward then lifted her onto the edge of her desk. He stroked his hand down over the bare plane of her stomach then pushed the gauzy fabric out of the way.

Leo wrenched his lips away. "You're not wearing any underwear. Deyon, you were in a room full of people with no underwear and this bit of fabric." He rubbed it with his hand.

"Can't wear any with this. The lines show." Deyon gripped his shoulders. "Do we really need to talk about this now?"

Leo thought briefly then lust won out. He placed his hand back under her skirt then slid his finger along her slit and deep within. Deyon dug her nails into his shoulders and arched, pushing forward against his touch. Her slick wetness coated his fingers and Leo locked his knees as desire to be inside her hit him. He pumped in and out, rubbing his thumb over her clit before plunging in again.

"Leo," Deyon moaned.

"Yes…tighter on my fingers." Leo worked them in her.

Deyon made mewling sounds as she rolled her hips, clenching on his fingers. Leo quickly pulled his digits out then fumbled with his belt. She pushed his hands away and swiftly opened his pants, retrieving a condom from his pocket. Then pushed down his briefs, taking his cock in her hot hand. Leo pushed into her hold. Deyon squeezed his shaft and moved her hand, making him even harder. Leo gritted his teeth as she unrolled the condom over his erection. Deyon moved forward, opening her legs and bringing him to her. Leo sank into her wetness.

"Deyon." He grunted, setting a fast rhythm.

She held him tight, rocking in counter motion, her body rigid as she held him. Leo lifted her in his arms and grabbed her ass. Deyon wrapped her legs around him, moaning and gripping the back of his head for leverage as she sank up and down on his hardened member. Leo tightened his grip on her full ass, pulling her against him. He watched her eyes and the fierce expression on her face. His breath caught at how gorgeous she was. His woman. The woman who he wanted more than anything else. Deyon clenched her inner walls around him then whimpered, shuddering as she came. Leo groaned as he joined her in release. She exhaled harshly against his face then blew out a long, slow breath before grinning then kissing him gently. Leo met her kiss and lazily moved his tongue with hers. Deyon licked inside his mouth then withdrew.

"I've got to go to get changed then go to the restaurant. We'll pick this up later." She kissed him once more then said, "Can you do me a favor and take something Rissa for me? She's home off from work today. I was going by but can't make it."

"Sure." Leo lowered her to her feet kissing her.

Deyon pulled away sighing. "I want to just go home and go to bed with you."

Leo was seriously tempted. "I have to work."

"Me too. But later, my bed," Deyon said.

Leo straightened his clothing and took the bag she gave him for Rissa. He kissed her again before he left. In the hall, Leo paused recalling being called Deyon's boyfriend. He wanted to be so much more. He continued on his way out. Leo went to Rissa's before going back to work. Fifteen minutes later, he pulled into her driveway and parked before exiting his vehicle then heading for her front door. Leo slowed as the door opened and Rissa came into view then her fiancé. Leo was surprised—he hadn't known Deiter was back. The couple kissed passionately.

Leo scowled as he went closer. "Stop groping my sister."

They parted and Rissa glared. "He's going to be my husband soon."

"He isn't yet. It's not seemly to be kissing like that for everyone to see."

"Just like your acting like a caveman isn't seemly," Rissa returned.

"Close-knit communities are so nosy." Leo sighed.

"The phone has been ringing off the hook with people telling us about your spectacular way you claimed Deyon before she kissed someone else." Deiter laughed.

"You wouldn't let Rissa kiss someone else, either."

"That's true." Deiter inclined his head. "It's nice seeing you, Leo, but I've got to go to the university for a meeting. I'll see you later, Rissa." He kissed her again then went down the stairs.

"Don't get pulled into work. Just a meeting then home," Rissa called.

Leo leaned against the wall by the door watching between them with a smile.

Deiter turned walking backward toward his car. "I won't. I'm—"

A deafening boom exploded behind him and he went flying forward.

"Deiter," Rissa screamed.

Leo caught her before she could rush to the car. Rissa clawed at his arm.

"Rissa, I'll get him, but I need you to be calm. Get the first-aid kit," he stated calmly. "Don't argue. We can't both go and I'll be able to pull him from there."

Rissa turned her tear-filled gaze to him then he saw her doctor part kick in and she nodded. He released her and she headed inside. Leo spoke into his shoulder radio and ran down the steps. He grabbed Deiter under his arms, pulling him back from the fully engulfed vehicle. Deiter groaned. The sound relieved Leo—he was still alive. He quickly looked at him and noted there was blood in his hair, but he couldn't tell of any other injuries.

"Move, Leo." Rissa pushed him out of the way and started working on Deiter.

Leo rose, staring at the car, anger filling him. The sounds of emergency vehicles started coming toward them. Leo turned to look at Rissa. She was focused on Deiter so he glanced back at the car. He thought of something.

"Rissa have you been driving Deiter's car?"

"Yes, why?"

Leo didn't answer but filed the info away for him to tell Dimitri later. The car made a noise and instinct made Leo turn and push Rissa down on Deiter then cover them both the best he could. The second explosion was as loud as the first. Leo's hearing went for a moment then rushed back to him. Rissa gasped, shaking beneath him.

"Leo."

"Shhh...Rissa. It'll be okay." Leo cleared his throat, trying to not let the pain come through.

He could feel something had impaled in his shoulder and the wetness that he figured was blood. Soon he heard a voice call.

"Sheriff," Conner called.

"Stay back, Conner. I don't know if there is anot—"

"Shut up," another voice said calmly.

"James." Leo turned his head and blinked to clear his double vision.

"We're going to get you farther away from the car. Don't try to help me, you were speared really good in the shoulder. We don't want you to bleed anymore." James gripped him.

"Leo, you're hurt. Let me see," Rissa said below him.

"Rissa, shut up," James said firmly then focused on him. "Let me do the work."

"I can help," Leo protested going to move.

"Christ, I knew you'd say that." James smiled. "Don't arrest me later."

"For—"

James decked him.

* * * *

Leo woke moaning, then he sat up cursing. "I'm going to arrest that fucker."

"Now, now. Be nice. This James man got you away before the car exploded again. So you should thank him. I know we all want to, but he's suspiciously no place to be found. Probably hiding from your wrath," a cheerful voice said.

Leo flopped back, groaning and glaring at Dimitri. "He's not. More like gloating that he had an excuse to cold-cock me." He studied his brother. "How long have I been out? How's Deiter and Rissa?"

"A half hour—they just brought you in this room. He's fine. Has a knock in his head that needed stitches but fine. Rissa is fine too. Giving the staff hell to make sure the stitches are just so. Jackson put her out." Dimitri chuckled.

"Deyon," Leo said, not wanting her to hear about him being injured second-hand.

"Katiya and Warwick went to get her," Dimitri said.

Leo nodded. He remembered what Rissa had said. "Someone rigged the car. Rissa has been driving it."

"What?" Dimitri scowled. "First Deyon's brakes were cut and now Rissa's car. What the hell is going on?"

"I don't have any idea. I've been checking into Deyon's brakes being cut but have nothing to go by. Now Rissa's car. We don't need this with all the fires going on. There seems to be a run of bad luck going on in McKingley," Leo said.

"Deyon and Rissa's car, we'll figure out, but the fires…?"

At Dimitri's tone, Leo focused on him. "What?"

"I've been studying the data since the science lab blew. A few of the other fires, including the one at Deyon's store match. There is a signature to them. We have a serial arsonist on our hands." Dimitri looked grim.

Leo knew enough about fires to know what he meant. And what that meant for them too. They would be busy chasing this arsonist unless they could figure out what the connections were. Leo just hoped there wouldn't be more deaths before they found whoever was doing this.

"Do you have anything else?"

"I have some ideas…"

Leo listened as Dimitri filled him in.

* * * *

Deyon laughed as she exited the restaurant with Kendrix and Chandler.

"Deyon."

She glanced up at the sound of Katiya calling her name. Her smile faded as she saw the expression on her face and Warwick who was with her. Deyon took a step toward them.

"Leo."

"He's hurt but fine, Deyon. He's going to the hospital," Katiya said, gripping her hands.

Deyon knees went weak. Warwick held her up and she shook then stiffened and straightened.

"I'm fine. I'll go to h—"

"We're taking you," Warwick said firmly.

"I—" Deyon shook her head.

"No speeding or you could get arrested. Let us take you," Katiya said.

"You're joking at a time like this," Deyon demanded.

"It got you into the car."

Deyon glanced out of the door, startled she was sitting in the front seat of Warwick's Benz. She saw Chandler and Kendrix behind Katiya.

"We'll meet you at the hospital," Chandler said as he led Kendrix away.

Deyon sat back and barely heard the closing of the door. Distantly, she felt them driving but didn't really pay attention. *Leo, you'd better be okay so I can kill you.*

"What happened?"

"A car exploded at Rissa's. Deiter was hurt too," Katiya explained.

Deyon glanced into the back seat at her. "Deiter and Rissa. What the hell is going on?"

"I don't know." Katiya's expression was worried.

Deyon put her hand back and she gripped it. They sat that way for the rest of the trip. At the hospital, Deyon exited the car moving at a fast clip to the doors. Inside, she didn't spare the desk nurse a look as she pushed through the door into the back.

"Deyon," the nurse called.

"Where is he?" she asked.

The woman looked at her then gestured down the hall. Deyon glanced where she pointed then rushed forward.

"Jackie. Where is he? How are Deiter and Rissa?"

"I'll take you to him. Deiter is fine, but I'm going to kill Rissa if she doesn't calm the hell down." Jackson's cheerful tone reassured her slightly.

"She's usually so calm. I guess being in love makes her loony." Deyon walked with Jackson as he led her to a room at the back.

She stopped in the doorway, seeing Leo talking with his older brother. He looked fine, but there was a bandage on his shoulder. Leo glanced up and smiled when he spotted her.

"Deyon."

"It's good that you look fine because I'm going to kill you. How the hell did you end up getting hurt delivering chocolates to Rissa?"

"Come here, Deyon," Leo said softly.

She moved toward him, touching Dimitri briefly on the shoulder. He touched her hand then stood leaving the room. At the bed, Deyon didn't pause—she climbed in with Leo and put her head on his shoulder.

"Damn it."

She lifted her head. "What?"

"I want to touch you, but the shoulder hurts," Leo admitted.

Deyon looked the bandaged area on the other side of his body. She met his gaze then stroked her finger over his nose.

"You can't get hurt anymore."

"It happens sometimes, but the most important thing is, this time I'm fine."

Deyon knew with his job it could happen and she accepted that. She sighed then laid her head back against his chest.

"What happened, Leo?"

"I'll tell you, but you can't tell anyone else," Leo said.

Deyon looked up at him. "If it's work related then you don't have to if you can't."

"It is, but I want to share my job with you, not just the frustration."

Deyon heart raced then she smiled. "Go ahead."

She listened as he filled her in. "And Dimitri has no leads?"

"No and he's been checking but nothing. Sometimes you never find out why an arsonist does as they do. And your car—there is nothing we can find. Now the bombing of Rissa's car."

"Do you think my car and hers being bombed are related? Maybe even my store fire?"

"I don't think so." He frowned. "What was done to your car and your store are two different things. And the fire something else. We'll just have to figure out what is happening—in each case and why." Leo looked thoughtful.

Before she could ask anything else, Jackson came in.

"Deyon, you shouldn't be in bed with him," he said.

Deyon frowned. "Shut up, Jackie."

"Get down. I need to finished patching him up and then get him a room. Go keep Rissa out of my hair." Jackson pulled her up out of the bed.

"I—"

"Check on them for me," Leo said.

Deyon returned to his side and kissed him then left.

* * * *

Deyon helped Leo out of the car, scowling at his indrawn breath. "You should have stayed in the hospital."

"I'm fine. You'll take care of me," Leo said again, as he had when he'd argued with the doctors to let him out.

They had only agreed because she had said she would and Jackson was in the apartment at her house if they needed him. Deyon helped him inside.

"Thanks, Kendrix," she murmured as she opened the door.

Chandler followed them with the things they needed for Leo. He'd offered to help Leo in, but the stubborn man refused to let anyone but her to help him. She took him directly to the bedroom and got him settled. Leo grumbled a bit but went right to sleep. Deyon returned to the living room, spotting her friends in the kitchen, she told them where she was going before she slipped out the house to go to the building behind it. Inside she flipped on the lights then got ready. In moments she took her shooter's stance and fired at the target. In quick successions she emptied her gun. She pressed the button to bring the paper closer, noting it was dead center.

"When did you build this?"

Deyon turned, startled, and looked at Leo. The white bandage was a stark contrast against his shoulder.

"You should be in bed."

"And I will be as soon as you join me. Now answer me."

"Oh...I asked James to oversee it for me."

"James. How the hell do you know James?"

"From Shannon. I've been emailing with her while I was gone. Talking about weapons and so on. I mentioned your concern and she suggested I talk with James about setting up a place like this for using my weapons. There are places to sword fight and she's going to teach me to kick box."

"Oh, Lord. Like you need any help being more dangerous." Leo smiled then came close to her. He took the gun she held and placed it on the counter behind her before cupping her face. "Come to bed."

Deyon stared into his dear face. "I love you, Leo."

He smiled. "I know."

"Is that all you have to say?" she demanded.

"You know I love you too." Leo winked.

Deyon heart filled, but she wasn't letting him get away with that. "Tell me proper and I'll give you what I brought back for you from my trip."

"I thought we did that in your office earlier." He wiggled his eyebrows.

"Ass." Deyon smacked him gently in the chest. "Say it."

"I love you, Deyon." Leo stared into her eyes. "And I plan to keep telling you that every day. Now gimmie my gift."

Deyon laughed then pushed her hand into her pocket of her jeans. She pulled out the small bag there and handed it to him. "I was going to be all romantic and stuff, but I'm too impatient for that."

Leo looked at her curiously and opened the drawstring then shook the contents into his hand. He stared at the braided gold ring with gray stone in the center. Deyon loved how the masculine ring looked in the palm of his hand but wanted it on his finger. She took it, lifted his hand then slid it on herself.

"Ummm…Deyon, is there a reason you put it on my ring finger?" Leo sounded amused.

"You're marrying me, Leo."

"Is that a proposal?" He smiled.

"Nope. It's a 'I know you're marrying me because if you don't I will tranq you and take you before a preacher'." Deyon slid her arms around his waist. "Even when I was away and upset at you, when I saw the ring I knew what I wanted and you're it, Leonardo Wright."

"You know when a woman asks a man to marry her he likes to be romanced not threatened." Leo chuckled. "Then again, you wouldn't be my Deyon without it. I'll marry you, Deyon."

"I didn't have any doubt you would. Just so you know, I don't want a big wedding. I want to be married here in my backyard and come toward you barefoot in my wedding gown."

"With the way Mama is wedding crazy with the others, I'm going to leave talking with Mama to you," Leo said.

"I'll handle your mother. She's not going to tell me how I want my day." She wasn't too concerned about Mama Wright—she knew how to get her way with her. Deyon licked her lips. "Usually when you get engaged I think you would get naked and get wild, but you're hurt so that will have to wait."

"I'm not that hurt," Leo protested.

"For what I want to do, you need to be in optimum health." Deyon took her gun and put it away then led him out of her weapons' building.

"Come on, Deyon. How long is that going to take?"

"Two weeks if you don't push it and go back to work too soon." Deyon patted him on the chest. "It will be worth it."

Leo sighed. "Damn woman." Then he hugged her. "You know I'm going to enjoy telling our children how you proposed to me in your weapons' building. They are so going to think Mommy is strange."

Deyon loved the sound of that. "Being our kids, they'll understand."

Leo laughed, kissing her under the moonlight. Deyon hugged him around the waist, loving this man who had drawn her in with an irresistible force. She was going to enjoy seeing where their journey as a couple would lead them. Deyon already knew it would never be dull but certainly very unique. She tightened her grip and moaned, holding the man who would be by her side forever.

SEDUCTION'S DANCE

Dedication

To my sister thanks for passing on your love of
reading and your support. To Aliyah, thank you for
coming along for a fun-filled adventure with me. I
loved every second.
— McKenna Jeffries

To McKenna for taking the wild ride with me. It's
been a blast. To all those who sacrifice so much for
those who may never even realize it, thank you from
the bottom of my heart for all you do. God Bless.
— Aliyah Burke

Chapter One

Dimitri Wright rolled the cold bottle between his fingers, his thoughts not fully on what he was doing. He swore he was in the middle of an epidemic of relationships leading to marriage—all his siblings had paired off, one after the other, and their parents were happily planning the weddings. His mother had that gleam in her eye that put dread into every man who was single and enjoyed being so. Dimitri hoped she'd turn her attention to one of the cousins next—the Wright family was large, and they should keep her busy for a while. He was one of those men who liked his life the way it was. He didn't need a woman to change that—the thought of having to discuss feelings and all the other crap that came with being in a relationship made him want to lock himself in his house until people regained their senses. Hell, even the tentative, trying to figure out if you were even interested in each other was something he hated.

Give him an honest, blunt, straightforward woman and maybe he'd change his mind. The women who approached him were anything but that. They came at him with some excuse trying to capture his eye. But what they didn't realize was that he enjoyed the chase. The woman he wanted could be blunt, but he was old-fashioned and enjoyed being the one to make the first move. After that he didn't have a problem with her holding her own with him—he wanted her to. But *he* wanted to make the initial approach. Then if they discovered they had common interests, it was important for him to know she could share his silences as well as his conversations. He enjoyed those moments of being silent more than anything else. With his profession, he saw some of the most horrible things and just needed time to chill and be.

Dimitri rubbed the back of his neck as his thoughts turned to the fire he'd been sent to investigate earlier. There was no doubt that it was arson. The family in the home had died, all of them including the children—six, four, two and a baby. It was always so damn disheartening when there were kids involved. It was his job to find out who had eradicated the family from the face of the earth. Fire was a nasty business that didn't differentiate based on race, ethnicity or any other demographic. Once a fire was started, its hunger took all that was in its path. Arsonists lit them for many reasons, but sometimes it was someone who didn't even think, not knowing that fire isn't to be played with. These cases were the ones that made his gut burn. He loved his job—investigating fires, tracking down the source, gathering evidence and finding who did it. He didn't manage the last part all the time, but he damn well tried his best.

He thought of the open case of the serial arsonist he'd been trying to catch for the last few months. It had started with a fire in the science building at the university. There had been no fatalities, but there had been many other fires since then and in some of those, people had died. The fires seemed to be random — there was no pattern — which was making it harder to track him. Lately they had been quiet and there had been no fires with the signature Dimitri had found. Others in the community had assumed and even hoped that maybe the arsonist had stopped, but Dimitri felt in his gut they hadn't — there was something big coming. There was something about all the cases that bugged him, but he couldn't put his finger on what. That piece eluding him might be the one to solve the case.

The fire today hadn't been one of the serial fires. Dimitri lifted the bottle to his lips then drank his beer. He returned it to the top of the bar, rolling his shoulders. He'd been gathering evidence and was tight around his lower neck and back, but he hadn't felt like going home.

Absently, he glanced around the bar. It was frequented by cops, fire fighters and those like him who did business between the two places. He was actually based out of the firehouse but worked closely with the police force. The good thing was his younger brother Leonardo was the sheriff, and the cops knew him through Leo, making it easier for him to do his job. Not that he wouldn't go around them if he needed to in order to get his job done. But he'd rather not get in a pissing match, instead preferring to just get what he needed taken care of accomplished.

"It was a tough one," someone with a soft voice spoke beside him.

Dimitri turned his head then blinked, realizing that someone was sitting next to him. He noted the two empty beer bottles in front of the woman, which meant she had been there a bit. Probably had been when he came in, since he was still on his first. He hadn't even noticed her. Dimitri studied the woman. Her features blended in a face that he would call lovely but in an understated way. Wire-rimmed glasses covered dark brown eyes with thick lashes. Her hair was away from her face in a neat braid, the tail end resting over her shoulder. He glanced at her hand, noting she was rolling a bottle between her rich, caramel-colored hands as he had been. Her nails were short, neatly clipped, with their natural hue. Dimitri lifted his gaze to study her closer since he thought he recognized her. He tried to place where he knew her from. Suddenly it dawned on him.

"Deputy Conner. You were the cop at the fire with me."

The Sheriff's department had left a different cop there since they'd wanted to keep the area protected. The officer with him had been silent and efficient, and he had soon forgotten she was there. She hadn't tried to ask questions or engage him in conversation, for which he had been appreciative. Fire with kids hit him harder than most.

"Yes."

That was it, no other explanation. Intrigued, Dimitri watched the woman who he hadn't realized was by him. He remembered what she had said.

"Yes, it was a tough one."

She nodded and drank her beer. They fell into a comfortable silence. Dimitri noted a booth becoming available and slid off the bar stool, carrying his beer.

"Let's get the booth before someone takes it."

The woman blinked behind her wire frames but rose as he bid and followed him with her beer to the booth. Dimitri slid into it just in time. He lifted a shoulder at the fire fighter he worked with. The man inclined his head and went to the bar. Dimitri focused on the woman. She was sipping her beer and glancing around the packed bar. She finally put her gaze on him, her eyebrow rising as if asking what he was looking at. Dimitri lifted his bottle, using it to cover his smile — Deputy Conner seemed a little prickly. A waitress came over and Dimitri ordered some food. Conner ordered too then the waitress left.

"I don't remember seeing you before," Dimitri stated. He knew the cops who worked with his brother.

"Been here about six months." Her answer was succinct.

"O—"

A cell rang, interrupting them. Deputy Conner reached under the table and pulled out her phone.

"Excuse me." She studied the number and frowned before answering. "Conner… What are you doing in jail…? Christ, James, I've told you about that damn rooster." She listened then sighed. "I'll be right there to get you."

She hung up then glanced at him. "Gotta go. Just eat my food."

She rose, putting some bills on the table then turning away. Dimitri reached for her hand. She stopped, glancing at him questioningly.

"I don't even know your first name."

"Shannon," she replied.

Dimitri thought about her name. "Wait. Are you related to Conner from the ranch that has Sigmund?"

Dimitri smiled, thinking of the ornery bird that was a local legend. Like clockwork, Sigmund crowed incessantly from two-seventeen to six-seventeen a.m., every day. A new owner had bought the ranch not knowing about the bird, but they'd soon found out.

Now it was amusing for McKingley residents to see who would win the battle—man or bird. There was even a bet about it. Dimitri also recalled that James had helped out in the rescue of his brother Leo a few weeks ago. He'd meant to find him and thank him but had never gotten around to it.

"Yes. Cousins. We own the ranch together. Although I'm lucky enough to not live in the main ranch house, which Sigmund has a shine to. I'm at the foreman's house. Am I glad I decided to pick that one. James is cursing having the main house because of that 'damn singing fucker'." Shannon smiled.

Dimitri's breath caught. The smile changed her from lovely to beautiful. Shannon twisted her hand, pulling out of his hold. Dimitri drew back, realizing he'd been holding her.

"I need to get James out of jail."

"Leo really arrested him?" Dimitri asked in disbelief.

"No, a new deputy who thinks he has something to prove did." Shannon's face-hardened and her gaze became fierce.

Dimitri blinked, captivated by the woman who seemed to have a quicksilver personality. He'd first pegged her as reserved then funny and now she looked like a warrior ready for battle. Shannon inclined her head then turned and strode off. Dimitri watched her full-figured shape as she made her way through the tables to the door. Her stride was confident. Her loose purple T-shirt fell to mid-thigh, and she wore black jeans and sneakers. It was understated like herself. Her face, from what he'd been able to see, was sans makeup—it had looked soft and ready to be touched. Dimitri drummed his fingers on the table, unable to look away as she continued her trek. When she exited, he glanced at the tabletop, wondering what the hell had just happened.

You just met a woman who, for all intents, actually captured your attention with only a few words.

"I'll be damned," Dimitri said.

"Did you say something, Dimitri?" Carol the waitress slid their food onto the table.

He lifted his head and replied. "No. Wrap that to go."

He pointed at the food Shannon had ordered.

"She left you. Must be crazy." Carol smiled flirtatiously.

Dimitri didn't reply, his mind still on the woman who'd just left.

Exiting the bar, Shannon Conner resisted looking back at Dimitri. He had a similar look to his brother and her boss, Leonardo Wright. Rugged masculine features that weren't thought of as traditionally handsome but gave him more of a sexy, edgy look that made a woman wonder if she could tame him. His dark sienna skin made his light brown eyes even more compelling. Then again, it could be the intensity in his gaze. As he looked at her, it was as if he was seeing all her secrets. It was unnerving yet exhilarating. She'd heard of Dimitri from her fellow officers—heck, she knew about the whole Wright family—but hadn't worked with him until today.

In McKingley, their name was known along with the McKingleys as descendants from one of the founding families of the town. Both families were well respected. From what she'd heard, Dimitri was the oldest of his siblings and he was known as a loner. Many speculated he would be a hermit if not for his job, and said he only spent time with his family or friends and usually at private gatherings.

By the time Shannon had made it to her vehicle, she had already dismissed the meeting in the bar with Dimitri. With efficient motions, she headed to the station and to the door once she'd arrived. Her face remained composed, although inside she seethed and would let the deputy who had arrested her cousin know it. Shannon already knew why the jerk Mario had picked James up despite Leonardo telling them to not arrest him. Mario had been trying to get her to go out with him, and she'd refused on numerous occasions. Yesterday he'd gone too far and it had become physical. Shannon had only knocked him on his ass, though she could have hurt him very badly if she'd been so inclined. Hell, James could have too, but he hadn't out of respect for Leonardo. The men had become friends after all Leo's visits out to the ranch about James trying to kill the rooster. Even before their friendship, Leo had been more amused by James who had a tendency to run after the rooster naked. Not by choice but because James waited until it was so much on his nerves that he ran out of the house so focused on killing it that he forgot he didn't have clothing on. Shannon knew it hurt James' pride that one rooster was out-smarting him.

Mario was lucky James respected Leo or he'd be in a world of hurt. James was an ex-Navy SEAL and until recently, Shannon knew Leonardo hadn't known. Since he'd found out, James had told her they met often for some hand to hand. People saw James' open nature and mistook it for him being easy going. Shannon strode inside and slowed as she heard a familiar voice.

"Deputy Reed, why, after you've been informed not to arrest Mister Conner, did you?" Leo raised his hand, stopping Mario before he spoke. "Before you answer, be careful how you respond. Because I am already inclined to fire you."

"What...? I'm a good cop. You can't fire me over him," Mario sputtered.

"Not him. Over your lack of listening to commands, laziness and accosting a fellow deputy even though they have told you no to your unwanted advances more than once." Leo glared at Mario then shifted his gaze to Shannon.

She hadn't even thought he'd known what was going on. Leo focused back on Mario.

"Get out of my sight before I do fire you. One more thing and you *are* gone," Leo stated in a deadly voice.

Mario turned. He spotted her and glowered, fury on his face. Mario passed her and butted into her shoulder. Shannon controlled her reaction to pivot and knock him out.

Can't do that, Shannon.

Leo strode over then halted before her. His hands were behind his back. Shannon didn't need to see it to know the palms were over each other. She stifled a sigh. It was his lecture pose. Shannon didn't see him do it to anyone but her, his family and friends. She knew it was because he saw her as a friend since hanging out at the ranch with her and James. Although she was glad for his friendship, she could do without the lectures.

"How's Deyon?" She tried to forestall the lecture.

Leo scowled then said, "That reminds me, I need to talk with her."

"Lecture, you mean," Shannon muttered.

Leo frowned at her. "You've been spending too much time with Deyon."

Shannon smiled. She did enjoy the vivacious woman and her snappy attitude. The best part was that Deyon understood Shannon enjoyed her solitude and preferred staying in to going out, so Deyon often came over and they cooked, ate and chilled out together. Deyon had even made her a few outfits that fit her personality and wouldn't take payment for it. In turn, Shannon had taught her to kick-box. Leo was still peeved at that one, saying Deyon was enough trouble with her weapons. After seeing Deyon's weapons' room, Shannon actually liked her even more.

"I promise you can talk"—she made quotes with her fingers—"another time. This time I might even listen. But let me get James out of jail before he decides to let himself out."

"Too late." The cheerful voice of her cousin came just before he strode into the room. "You all really need better cells. The locks are useless."

"You broke out—" Leo turned to him. "Oh, for Christ's sake, he didn't even let you get pants at least."

"Nope. He had an ax to grind. You better handle it or I will." James strolled closer, seemingly unconcerned with his nakedness.

"I don't need either of you to handle it. I'll deal with it," Shannon stated.

Leo and James exchanged a look then focused on her. She didn't like it at all. Shannon crossed her arms over her chest, staring down James.

He smirked then said, "Uh-oh. The look. Come on, cuz, I need to get home." James headed for the door.

"Wait for some pants." Leo hurried to his office before returning and throwing him a pair.

James donned them, keeping a tight hold on the waistband so the pants didn't fall off his lean frame. He then left.

"Shannon. I know you can handle it, but I'm your boss. If you have any more trouble with Mario at work, come to me," Leo said firmly.

She nodded although she didn't plan to do any such thing. She followed James outside then stopped, putting her hands on her hips and watching him where he sat in the passenger seat of her black Wrangler Rubicon. Shannon got in the driver's side and poked him in the shoulder, pushing her thumb in.

"Quit it. You know I hate that." James swatted at her hand.

"Stop breaking into my jeep." She did it again.

"Spoilsport. It's my fun. You don't want to take it away from me." James crossed his arms over his bare chest.

"That face isn't going to work on me." Shannon started the jeep and drove out of the parking area, heading home.

James turned on the radio, tuning into the soft classic station they both enjoyed for the drive.

* * * *

Shannon frowned at the pot bubbling on her stove. James nudged her out of his way with his hip. Shannon took the hint and moved back to sit at the table by the window. She put her one leg under her and sat.

"I'm not in the mood for chili," Shannon said.

"I asked you what you wanted for dinner and you said chili. So we're having chili." James glared.

Shannon put her hand under her chin and her elbow on the table. He was right. She had stated it earlier this morning after he'd asked what she wanted. Although they lived in different houses, since it was just the two of them, they shared the cooking duties. At the times it was her turn to cook she went to James' place and made the meal then took some for herself if there was any left. And *vice versa*. A knock on the door made her glance up. Shannon frowned—they weren't expecting anyone. She put her hand on the table to rise.

"I've got it." James went to the door.

Shannon resettled, watching as James opened the door. From where she sat, she couldn't see who was there.

"Hello. I'm looking for Shannon."

She recognized the speaker. Curious, Shannon wondered what he was doing here.

"I'm James, her cousin. And from the look of you, you're a Wright. Hmmm…if I go by what Leo told me, you don't look neat as Jonathon would so you must be Dimitri, the oldest brother. Why are you looking for Shannon?"

"James," Shannon said warningly.

"The tone. Come on in then." James stepped back.

Dimitri entered the kitchen and paused by the door. "And you're Conner, the one who chases the rooster naked."

"Stick around long enough and you might see me do it." James chuckled and went back to his pot.

Dimitri focused on her then moved toward the table.

"What are you doing here?" Shannon asked.

Chapter Two

Dimitri waited a moment then continued to her. He stopped on the other side of the four set table and held up a bag she hadn't noticed he had.

"You left your dinner."

"My steak." Shannon smiled, going to rise.

"No need to move, you look comfortable. Where do you want me to put it?"

"In the microwave. I'm eating it now," Shannon said.

Dimitri smiled a sexy curl of his lips then turned. "James, can you show me where the plates are?"

"No t—"

"Hush. I've got it."

Shannon sat back surprised. Dimitri joined James and made himself at home getting the steak with garlic mash potatoes and asparagus heated up. He brought it back to her along with a bottle of cream soda, which was her favorite.

"Thanks," she stated as he placed the plate and drink on the table before her.

She lowered her head, said a prayer then picked up her fork and knife to cut into the steak. It was still tender. She made sure to get some sautéed onions and mashed potatoes on the fork then took a bite. Shannon moaned as the flavors burst over her tongue. A groan echoed hers. Shannon lifted her head, meeting light brown eyes. She stilled, watching him stare at her. The intensity of his gaze seemed stronger.

"Umm…thanks," she said, dismissing him.

Dimitri's smile widened.

Shannon put down her fork. "Why aren't you leaving?"

"He's trying to ask you out," James said.

Shannon glared at her cousin. "He is not."

"I am," Dimitri interjected quietly.

Shannon glanced at him in shock. "For God's sake, why?"

"She'd going to say no. Shannie doesn't date," James said.

Shannon ignored him focused on Dimitri.

"I asked around. You're a loner like I am. I find that intriguing." He shrugged.

Shannon stared at him then mimicked his motion. "Okay. Don't want to go out. Dinner here and a movie."

"Did you just agree to go out with him?" James asked in disbelief.

Shannon didn't answer him. Dimitri had already gotten her answer and he turned to leave.

"Stay for dinner, Dimitri. I really need to know more about you if you're going to date my cousin," James offered.

Dimitri glanced at her, waiting for an invite. Shannon lowered her head in a short nod then went back to eating.

Dimitri saw that small motion of her head then said to James, "Sure. Chili sounds good." He pulled out the chair across form Shannon, still studying her.

She had barely spoken to him last night, yet here he was today at her house having dinner. Dimitri hadn't been able to stop thinking about her all night. How she looked, her personality and mannerisms. It was as he'd stated—he was intrigued. In his gut, he felt that there was more to Shannon's calm, placid surface than what she portrayed to the world. Dimitri wanted to tap into whatever it was. He wanted to hear her speak and get excited about something. Hear her moan as she kissed him. The sound she'd made eating that first bite of her food had made him rock hard. And he wanted her to make it because of him.

Dimitri couldn't believe just last night he hadn't wanted a woman but now he wanted to unleash the woman he knew was inside Shannon. The fire in her gaze when she'd spoke of the man who had arrested James had shown him another side of her. There seemed to be many sides to Shannon—all of them he wanted to know and explore.

James served dinner and he enjoyed it, conversing with James while taking pleasure in each brief word Shannon spoke. After dinner he stayed and found himself taking part in their movie night, where they watched the three Transformers movies. Finally he rose to leave, seeing James push Shannon up and his way—he made a mental note to thank James later. Though she seemed reluctant, Shannon followed him. Dimitri opened the front door, stepping outside on the porch before facing her. She was framed in the low-lit entryway, and he couldn't take his eyes from her when Shannon cocked her head to the side, studying him, then moved. She kissed him, her tongue stroking against his lips. Dimitri opened, letting her in.

He slid his hands around her waist, pulling her into his body. She rested against him, fitting him perfectly. Shannon worked her tongue inside his mouth, setting off a sensation of need. Shannon released him as abruptly as she'd kissed him. She stepped back, crossing her arms over her chest and leaning against the doorjamb.

"I thought it best to get the first kiss out of the way. Now we won't have that to worry about. My next day off is Saturday. Come by about three, that way you can help me cook." She wasn't asking.

Dimitri nodded and made his way to his vehicle. Inside, he looked out of the windshield, noticing Shannon was still in doorway watching him leave. He started the engine then tooted his horn. She lifted a hand and Dimitri backed out then headed home. He was already anticipating their first date.

* * * *

Impatiently, Dimitri glared at the calendar. The days to their date were ticking away slowly. He pushed back in his chair, reading the report he had written. The case he had met Shannon at had wrapped up. The sad part was that it had been some fool teenager thinking it was fun to light rags and pitch them into trees. He'd done it in front of the Livingstons' house, which had led to the death of the whole family. The teenager was crying about how sorry he was, but it was too late for that—he was going to jail and would be there for a long time. Dimitri finished his report and emailed it.

"Heard you solved the case," Shannon spoke behind him.

Dimitri turned then stood, pleased to see her. She was in her uniform and held her hat in her hands.

"Yes, I did."

"Good"—Shannon studied him with her somber brown eyes as she spoke—"I usually bring my lunch and have it in the park near here. I packed extra since I decided to ask you to join me today. Would you like to?" She waited for his response, her movement minimal, just a thrum of fingers along her hat.

"Sure." Dimitri moved toward her.

Shannon stepped back and strode toward the exit. Dimitri followed her outside to her cruiser, noticing the other fire fighters watching them curiously on the way. She didn't pause to look at any of them but from her posture, Dimitri would bet she didn't miss anything. Shannon retrieved a medium-sized cooler bag from her car then they continued to the park. As they strolled, they passed various residents who waved at Dimitri and he returned their gesture. They didn't approach him to chat as would have happened to any of his siblings. People knew him and unless he stopped to visit, they wouldn't.

The bright New Mexico sun made the area seem surreal, like he was standing directly in a painting. He loved living in McKingley. A hand slid into his and Dimitri smiled, holding Shannon's hand as they strode through the park. She led him to a spot off the main path and sat at a bench, putting the bag next to her. Dimitri sat next to the bag as Shannon opened it and handed him a sandwich. He was surprised to find it was pastrami with Swiss cheese and condiments, as he liked it. He glanced at her in question.

"I asked around about you too."

He took a bite of his sandwich and they enjoyed their meal in the serenity of the park. Dimitri nibbled on white seedless grapes and drank his cranberry juice. Shannon had indeed found out about him—he figured she'd gotten her information from Leo. Shannon closed the lunch sack after handing him a bag. He opened it and saw it was filled with Snickerdoodles—his favorite cookie. Dimitri removed one then bit into it—it tasted better than any he'd ever eaten.

"What brand is this? It's delicious."

"I made it. Will make more for dessert for our date." Shannon smiled.

"If I didn't know better, I'd think you were trying to romance me." Dimitri pushed his shoulder against hers playfully.

"I am." Shannon turned her head, her dark brown eyes serious, then she winked.

Dimitri chuckled and finished the cookie—keeping the bag to save the rest for later. Shannon rose and he followed her, taking her hand in his as they retraced their steps back to her vehicle.

"I enjoyed lunch. Do you want to meet again tomorrow?"

He didn't even hesitate. "Yes. Same time." Dimitri kissed her gently.

Shannon pressed against him then moved away.

"Tomorrow." She got in her vehicle before honking her horn and driving away.

Dimitri stood on the curb and watched her leave. At least now Saturday didn't seem so far away.

* * * *

Over the following days, Shannon came by at the same time and met him for lunch each day. Each time she had something he enjoyed to eat and a dessert he loved. Dimitri felt himself being drawn even more to the enigmatic woman.

By the time Saturday arrived, he was awaiting their date even though he had seen her every day leading up to it. Dimitri drove toward the ranch with a sense of anticipation. He pulled into the driveway and exited his vehicle. Dimitri took the steps quickly and eagerly pressed the bell. The door opened after a few moments, but Shannon blocked the doorway

"Before you come in, I wanted to get it straight that we're not having sex. It's too soon. I'll let you know when I'm ready."

Dimitri's smile faded and he stared at her then demanded, "Is that all you think I want when I'm with you?"

"I don't know. Most men do. I'm just stating my position before there's a misunderstanding," Shannon replied in a cool tone.

"You know, Shannon, sometime you'll let go of that rigid control of yours and just feel."

"If you're waiting for me to get all gushy and moon over you, you're with the wrong woman."

"I don't want either of those things. What I want is Shannon, that passionate woman I know is in there, to let me in."

"I'm no—"

"Outside in the rest of the world you can keep yourself as rigid as you want to. But behind closed doors whenever it's just us, I expect you to be as blunt and honest in showing your reaction to me as you are when you speak." Dimitri crowded her into the doorjamb.

Shannon raised her head, staring him down then she nodded once. Having got to know her these last few days, Dimitri knew that was as much as he would get. He stepped back. Shannon gripped his shirt, pulling him to her.

"I didn't say anything about kissing." She kissed him hungrily.

Dimitri pressed against her, pushing her to the doorjamb and returning her kiss. Shannon opened up licking inside his mouth.

Shannon opened wide, sucking in Dimitri's tongue. She was already getting addicted to his taste. Since the first time she'd kissed him, she'd gotten more than she bargained for. Dimitri was one man she knew she would not be able to put in a neat compartment and keep him where she wanted him in her life. The thought both frightened her and made her want him even more. She'd gone back to have lunch with him every day because she hadn't been able to stay away from him. Each time and kiss had her longing to be with him. Dimitri had demanded she show her honest reaction to him—he didn't have any clue her coming to meet him for lunch was exactly what he demanded. She had asked about him—Deyon had teased her mercilessly, but she'd given her the information she'd sought. Shannon had found out the basics about him, the rest she would learn as she got to know him. Over the last week she'd gotten to know a few things about the man. Shannon gentled her kiss slowly before pulling away from him.

Dimitri's groan breezed along her lips and he seemed reluctant to release her from their kiss. Shannon thought of kissing him again but resisted.

She viewed his face and spoke bluntly, as he liked to hear from her.

"Lunch together each day is my way of letting you know I'm also intrigued by you, Dimitri."

"That's the first time you said my name." Dimitri's arms tightened where they rested on her waist.

Shannon thought about his statement, realizing he was correct. In her head, she'd called him by his name often, though never verbally.

"Come in." She took one of his hands off her waist, holding it as she waved him inside.

The sound of the door closing came behind her. Shannon led him to the living room and sat. Dimitri settled next to her, extending his legs and putting his hand behind her on the couch.

"We can wait a bit before starting dinner. Do you want to watch some movies or TV?" she offered.

"TV, we can find something that is on. I think there might be a *Criminal Intent* marathon." Dimitri shifted, picking up the remote.

"I enjoy that show."

He resettled against the couch, turning on the TV and flipping channels until he found the show he was referring to. Dimitri pulled her along his side, relaxing. Shannon moved closer, resting her head on his shoulder and putting her hand on his thigh. He tensed under her hand briefly, and they watched the show in companionable silence. The day was fun. They made dinner together, exchanging conversation about their jobs and other things they enjoyed then ate, continuing the easy-going atmosphere. After they'd eaten, they returned to the living room and watched movies late into the night.

Shannon blinked, looking at the screen without seeing it. Being around Dimitri was comfortable and she could get used to him hanging around.

* * * *

Shannon opened her lids, startled at the sensation of a body under her. She glanced down at Dimitri who she was lying on. In slumber, Dimitri's hard look softened, but she still got the feel of leashed strength from him. Shannon glanced at the clock on the mantle and grinned. Returning her attention to Dimitri, she shook him awake. His hand came up and held hers against his shoulder as he opened his eyes. A warm smile curled his lips as he watched her. Unable to resist, she kissed him gently then pulled away.

"We fell asleep."

"You did first then woke a little and seemed to think I was a bed. You pushed me over and lay on top of me. I was held hostage," Dimitri teased.

Shannon distantly remembered what he'd stated happening and snorted. "I'm sure you enjoyed being my mattress."

"I'll be your bed anytime you want one." Dimitri's gaze was filled with desire.

"I'll keep that in mind. Now come on, we don't want to miss the show." Shannon moved off him and stood, holding out her hand.

Dimitri stood, looking curious. He glanced at the time then a grin spread across his face. Shannon knew he understood and they walked to the front door, getting their shoes before heading outside and across the yard toward the main house. Once there, Shannon took a seat on the porch rail. Dimitri leaned next to her. A sound started, making them chuckle.

"Cock-a-doodle-doo," Sigmund crowed loudly.

He repeated it over and over, getting louder as time passed. Shannon waited then heard it.

"Mother fucking bird." Then the clomp of steps came from inside the house.

The door opened and the screen door slapped hard and a body flew out, barely touching the porch as he jumped off and ran across the yard. The sound of gunshots echoed the curses that came from James as he shot.

"He really is naked." Dimitri laughed, leaning against her.

Shannon joined him.

"Take that, you damn singing fucker." James shot a few times.

Then it was silent. James stopped, turning to them a wide grin on his face.

"I got him." He started to dance, his naked body moving in the moonlight.

Shannon averted her gaze, covering her mouth and pressing her face into Dimitri's shoulder. His shook with his mirth. James rushed toward them. Shannon raised her head and met James' gaze.

"He's spending the night already." James jerked his thumb toward Dimitri.

"Mind your business."

James studied them before addressing Dimitri. "You're making breakfast. I want blueberry pancakes."

"What if I can't cook?" Dimitri asked.

"Then you'd better learn quick. We share the cooking duties. We'll add you to the rotation." James wasn't even asking.

Shannon opened her mouth.

Dimitri spoke, stilling her words. "Fine, but you'd better come to the table with clothes on. I don't need to see your cock hanging out."

"You just wish you were as well-endowed as I am," James retorted, moving to the front door and opening the screen.

"Cock-a-doodle-doo!" Sigmund started again.

Shannon could swear she heard the glee in his voice. The sound of pounding made her glance at James.

He lifted his head and pounded it against the door, muttering, "Too damn mean to die. Damn singing fucker."

James straightened and returned to them. He held out the gun, butt first. Shannon took it, already knowing what was coming.

"No more Mr Nice Guy." James pivoted and went down the steps.

She watched him as he went into the yard. Sigmund was still happily crowing away. James pulled off his boots then took off into the inky darkness.

"Did you see that? He can move," Dimitri said.

Shannon had seen James do it before. She focused back on Dimitri and leaned closer, kissing him. Dimitri shifted his frame so they were pressed together. Shannon moaned and Dimitri groaned moving nearer to her. He stepped between her legs, kissing her, his hands on her ass.

Chapter Three

"Got him." James spoke by her hip.

Shannon wrenched her lips from Dimitri and looked down. She stared at James, who was covered from head to toe in mud. Under one arm he held Sigmund and the other hand clamped over his head, holding his beak closed. She was shocked he had actually caught the rooster.

"Did you roll around in mud?" Dimitri sounded shocked.

Shannon, knowing her cousin, didn't even have to ask.

"No. He ran, the bastard, but I was faster this time. Crow now, you fucking bird." James looked gleeful.

Shannon pushed Dimitri back then got off the rail and bent over to look at James.

"You caught him now, are you ready to make friends?" Shannon watched the pout appear on James face. "We both know you're not going to kill him. Admit it, you like the ornery bird. He reminds me of you."

James glanced at Sigmund then sighed and threw him. Sigmund dropped on the ground away from them. The bird glanced at them, shaking its feathers. As James went to get his boots, Sigmund rushed up behind him. James turned just before he reached him holding up a finger as if warning. Sigmund continued to him then pecked at him without connecting then dancing back. Then did it again.

"What are you doing, crazy bird?" James demanded.

"Sigmund. Call him by his name. I think he wants to play." Shannon watched as the bird did it again.

James stared at the bird, crouching before running to it, touching it then taking off again. Sigmund chased him. Shannon stared as her cousin ran around the yard, playing with the rooster.

"Oh, my God. He thinks he's playing with a dog," Dimitri said.

Shannon chuckled, agreeing with him as James picked up a stick and threw it. Sigmund did indeed run after the stick and bring it back.

"Your cousin is one strange man."

"Good thing he found a weird rooster. Come on. You can get some sleep on the couch while I get some shut eye in bed." Shannon headed toward the porch steps.

"So I'm spending the rest of the night?"

"Technically you already did. It's after two in the morning. And yep, on the couch alone. I want those blueberry pancakes. Can you cook?"

"Yep." Dimitri put his arm around her waist as they descended the stairs.

Sigmund ran up to them squawking.

"No, Sigmund, they are friends," James said then grinned. "I've got a guard rooster. How cool is that?

Come on, Dimitri, come play with us." James beckoned.

Dimitri hugged Shannon then ran toward James. Sigmund chased him. Shannon sat on the step watching her crazy cousin, his rooster and Dimitri. They were all laughing and having a fun time.

They are lunatics. She shook her head.

The men spotted her then whispered to each other. She was too far away to hear what they were saying.

They made a 'come on' gesture to her, chanting, "Shannon, Shannon."

There was no way was she going to play with them. James knelt saying something too low for her to hear to Sigmund then the rooster came toward her. Shannon eyed the ornery bird as it came closer to her. Sigmund cocked his head to the side as if studying her then opened his mouth.

"Cock-a-doodle-doo!" Sigmund pecked at her shoe.

"Ohhh… You're going to get it." She rose and chased the bird.

Shannon ignored the men who were leaning on each other laughing at her as she ran after the rooster. Soon they joined her and they all were playing with Sigmund. Later, after the sun rose, Dimitri made breakfast. James had finally put on some pants. Shannon glanced outside to her porch and spotted Sigmund perched on the rail. He'd followed James, not letting him out of his sight. It seemed as if James had indeed inherited a guard rooster.

Shannon peered across the table at Dimitri. She'd got a man who seemed to understand her. Only time would tell if he really did. It was going to be interesting finding out.

* * * *

Shannon entered the bar, checking around for Dimitri. She finally saw him sitting in a booth and her heart started to race. Shannon wiped her palms on her jeans knowing they were clammy. The way Dimitri affected her made her libido go nuts whenever she was in his vicinity. If she thought about him, or anything that reminded her of him, she got breathless and horny. Shannon made her way toward him. It was six weeks since she had first seen him here. Now they were dating and she was having a good time with him. They spent most of their time at her house, though on rare occasions they came to the bar.

Dimitri was just like her—he didn't like going out much. They had more fun at the ranch. James had taken his being around in stride and had even put Dimitri to work for the minimal chores they shared around the ranch. The ranch wasn't a working one, but they had a few horses they kept. Shannon remembered she wanted to ask Dimitri about going riding, as he'd mentioned he could ride. She arrived at the booth then he stood and kissed her gently then went to seat her.

"I need to clean up." She showed him her dirty hands. "My tire went out on me and I had to change it."

"Okay. Do you want me to order if the waitress comes by?"

"Get me a—"

"Steak with garlic mashed potatoes and asparagus. I know what you like." Dimitri smiled.

"You do, Mister Smarty Pants. What do I want to drink?"

"Give me hint. Alcoholic or not."

"Not." She waited, curious what he would say.

"A&W Cream Soda."

Shannon chuckled. "You do know me. Get me that." She kissed him.

"Okay. Oh, I found this place that makes cream soda. I heard it's the best. I'll tell you about it when you get back."

Shannon nodded then headed to the bathroom. She washed her hands then lifted her head meeting her gaze in the mirror. She wiped off her hands with a paper towel, still studying herself in the mirror. After throwing out the paper, she straightened her glasses. The sound of the door opening behind made her know she wasn't alone. Shannon didn't look, but knew from the sound of footsteps it was one woman who was in heels. Finished, she turned to leave. A woman was blocking the door while another leaned against the counter. Shannon realized she had been mistaken.

"I don't know what he sees in you." The first woman was beautiful and in red. The outfit showcased all her assets.

The second woman was dressed more casually in jeans, T-shirt and sneakers—she didn't look like she would be a friend with the other who was dressed so expensively. Shannon did note the one in red was indeed in heels. Personally she didn't see the use in wearing them. Give her flats or sneakers, she was good. Shannon calmly waited for them to speak again.

"What, are you mute?" the woman in red said.

"Just waiting for you all to get to the point." Shannon included the woman leaning against the counter in her glance.

"This is all her. I don't do the drama bullshit. Just waiting to see if you need help." The casually dressed lady studied her nails.

"Dimitri can do better than you." The expensively dressed woman spoke again.

Shannon studied the woman. "Are you an old girlfriend?"

"No we've never dated. B—"

"Ahh…so you wanted him and he didn't want you."

The woman's face changed, becoming furious. "You're rude."

"And you're acting like a scorned woman when you have no right to. He didn't want you so move on."

The woman stepped toward her. "I should deck you."

"What's stopping you? Because I'm a cop? Don't let that stop you. But just know I will retaliate. I can break your arm in three places with one blow. It hurts like a bitch," Shannon stated.

The woman glared. "You threatened me. I'm going to report you."

"Look, I have no patience for dumb or whiny people and you are coming across as both. You accosted me in the bathroom. Which really is beneath any woman to do to another. Get some pride. Dimitri didn't want you, and he is with me. Get over it and move on." Shannon gave her the facts not caring either way what the woman thought.

The woman sputtered then hissed. "You're a rude b—"

"Shut up, Fannie. You're whiny and dumb, now either apologize or hit the road." The woman straightened from where she had been leaning on the counter and jerked her thumb toward the door.

The perfectly made-up woman glared at the one she came in with. "I'm going to tell Simon that I couldn't get along with you." She sniffed.

"Please do." The woman tone was sarcastic.

Fannie turned and stormed out. Shannon studied the woman who was left.

"Why would you be with such a vapid woman?"

"Blunt. I like that. I'm Carmen Kincaid, by the way. And that wasn't my idea. My brother has atrocious taste in women. Fannie didn't think it through. Coming in the bathroom to confront a woman of a man you want with the sister of the man you are dating. Simon is going to hear about this. He's gonna get an earful for setting me up to have dinner with that woman. He was the one who I was supposed to be meeting here." Carmen moved toward the door, holding it open for Shannon.

"Are you trying to be friends? I don't like much people." Shannon exited.

Carmen laughed. "Oh, man, you tell it like it is. I wasn't, but you might not like much people, but I think we might become good friends. Give me your number and we can make plans to get together. Either at one of our residences, because I don't like going out too much."

Shannon stopped and studied the woman more closely. Carmen's black hair with honey highlights was at the top of her head in a messy ponytail. Her skin—the color of coffee with a hint of cream—was free of makeup. In Shannon's opinion, she was beautiful, especially with her hazel eyes and the teasing grin on her lips. Something about the woman was familiar.

"I know you from somewhere."

"I work at the same fire station as Dimitri. I'm a fire fighter. You can ask him about me if you want. Then let me know about hanging out." Carmen turned and started to walk away.

"Wait. I didn't say I wasn't going to give you my number." Shannon moved toward her.

Carmen turned to face her. "Just for the record, I don't much like people either. But you, I'm willing to make an exception for."

Shannon chuckled and they exchanged numbers.

* * * *

Dimitri glanced toward the ladies' room across the room, wondering what was taking Shannon so long. He finally saw her come out followed by Carmen Kincaid. She was a fire fighter at the station he worked in and he knew she was very good at what she did. At the firehouse, the men treated her like one of the guys. Carmen knew the job and they respected her for it. She and Shannon spoke for a few moments then Shannon headed toward him. The waitress arrived, putting the food down.

"Just in time," Shannon said sliding into the booth.

He lowered his head and she said a brief prayer then they started to eat.

"I saw you talking with Carmen."

"Yes. She was in the bathroom when I was accosted by a woman who wanted you." Shannon's reply was matter-of-fact.

Dimitri lowered his fork. "Excuse me?"

"Doesn't matter. I set her straight."

Dimitri was curious to hear the story. "About…?"

"That you're with me and she should have some pride instead of accosting me in the bathroom."

Dimitri snorted. He could imagine Shannon's face as she told the woman that. She continued to eat calmly. Watching her turned him on—it was amazing how every little thing she did turned him on. They had only kissed, nothing else. Dimitri knew he could have pushed for more, but he held back because he wanted her to take them to the next step of their relationship. That was how he viewed what they had—a relationship. Dimitri wondered if that was how she felt too. Shannon spoke her mind however, and up to this point she hadn't said anything. Dimitri scowled, imagining she wasn't thinking beyond their next date.

"We're in a relationship," he stated firmly.

Shannon looked startled at his abrupt words. Dimitri silently cursed himself. He was usually smoother with women, but Shannon wasn't like any other woman and that put him off how he usually acted.

Shannon smiled that teasing grin he'd gotten to know so well. "Is this a 'you man and me woman' declaration? Wanna drag me off to your cave?"

"Maybe." Dimitri resumed eating.

Shannon chuckled then stated, "Of course we're in a relationship. I don't just let any man play with our guard rooster."

Dimitri laughed, still amused by the way Sigmund had become so protective of James. The rooster seemed to think he owned James—he'd even heard James tell Sigmund he didn't. The rooster did still crow every night, but James had gotten earplugs—the two of them had come to a truce and bonded. Dimitri had also become fond of the ornery bird.

"Good to know." Dimitri touched Shannon's hand.

They chatted as they ate then after they'd finished, they left the bar and headed to their next destination. Half an hour later, Dimitri handed over their tickets and they entered the arena. They made their way to their seats.

"About time you two got here," Deyon said.

"We're just on time. Hey, Leo." Dimitri seated Shannon next to Deyon.

Leo waved and Dimitri took his seat on the end. He didn't pay any attention as the women spoke with each other. The lights flashed and they became silent along with the rest of the arena. Soon the contestants entered the ring.

"Harold is a great kick-boxer, but Kevin has more snap to his blows." Shannon sat forward.

Dimitri watched her instead of the competition. Shannon was moving and bobbing in her seat as she watched the contestants.

"Come on. You can do better, Harold!" she screamed.

Dimitri was enthralled. She was into the kickboxing competition. Shannon turned to Deyon and the women dissected what he was doing wrong. Suddenly they stood and hollered. Leo leaned over and Dimitri mimicked him.

"We've hooked up with some bloodthirsty women."

"And you love Deyon for it."

"Yeah, I do. The way she holds a gun or handles a sword, man, she knows what to do with it." Leo leered.

"I don't need to know about your kinky love life, little brother." Dimitri pushed at his shoulder playfully.

Leo moved back to his seat chuckling. The women sat looking between them questioningly. Dimitri wasn't saying a word.

"Knowing Leonardo, they are talking about sex. He has a one track mind," Deyon said.

Dimitri looked beyond the women to Leo. "Boy, does she know you."

"And she is grateful for it." Leo put his arm around Deyon.

"Really." Deyon sounded haughty.

Dimitri laughed, recognizing her tone. Leo was going to pay for that crack. He heard whispering but couldn't make out the words. He noted Leo was talking in Deyon's ear.

"Those two are a hoot. Leo and Deyon are a good match," Shannon stated.

Dimitri studied the side of her face as she watched the competition. They were too, if only Shannon would release that damn control and let her passion have free rein.

* * * *

Dimitri kicked the side of the horse and galloped after Shannon. Her joyous laughter came as she raced away from him. Shannon slowed, waiting for him to catch up. Dimitri pulled alongside of her horse and they cantered toward the ridge that had become their usual last stop every time they rode. They had taken one of the trails from the ranch and headed up to this place. They branched off and explored the areas around the ranch but always ended up at the spectacular view. At the ridge they stopped, gazing out over the beautiful New Mexico landscape.

"Every time we come here it gets more beautiful."

Dimitri glanced at Shannon who had spoken. She was facing forward, staring at the picturesque scenery.

"Shannon, instead of dinner at your house tomorrow, why don't you come to my place?"

"I have plans for us tomorrow." Shannon turned her head toward him.

This was the first time he'd heard about any plans different to their usual Saturday of dinner and movies at her place. Until this moment, he'd never asked Shannon to his house.

"Can't whatever plans you have be done at my house?" Dimitri didn't ask her what her plans were, knowing she wouldn't tell him. If she wanted him to know she would have out right told him instead of making it vague.

Shannon seemed to be thinking then she nodded. "It can."

A smile curled her lips. Dimitri didn't recognize that particular one. Shannon returned her attention to the view.

* * * *

Dimitri waited impatiently for Shannon to arrive, pacing in his entryway. She'd insisted she would drive herself to his place. At the sound of a car pulling in front of his house, Dimitri went by the door before peeking out of the window. Seeing her jeep, he opened the door and waited for her. Shannon strode up the walkway, her gaze locked with his as she moved up the steps to stop right before him. Dimitri hugged her then kissed her. Opening to him, she returned his kiss. Her arms curved around him holding him tight. Shannon slowly released their kiss, watching him.

"Show me your place."

Dimitri stepped back, holding her hand, then led her through his house. Shannon didn't say anything as he took her to see the various rooms of his home, then after they returned to the living room, where Dimitri flipped on the TV and sat. Shannon stood in front of him then headed toward the entryway.

"I've gotta get something from my jeep." She left before he could ask her what.

Shrugging, Dimitri settled back against the cushions of the couch. The sound of footsteps returning made him look up to see Shannon leaning against the doorjamb. Dimitri glanced down at the backpack she held in one hand then back to her.

"My overnight bag." Shannon straightened then headed down the hall.

Dimitri stood and followed her. She turned into his bedroom and his heart started to race as what she'd said actually registered. Dimitri moved faster toward the room. He entered and a body pushed him back against the wall. Dimitri grunted staring at Shannon. She burrowed her head in his neck then licked up the column of his throat. Dimitri lifted his head, a groan emerging. Shannon rocked her hips to rub against his rapidly hardening cock.

"I want you, Dimitri." She undulated against him.

Dimitri wanted them naked now. Shannon cupped his erection through his jeans and squeezed firmly, scattering his thoughts as she fondled him. Shannon released him then stepped back out of reach. Dimitri lowered his head, watching her. She reached for the bottom of her T-shirt.

"No," he stated firmly striding to her and removing her hand.

He gripped the hem himself. For a moment, Dimitri observed this woman who had figuratively knocked him off him his feet. He lifted her shirt, growling as he viewed her full bosom for the first time. He held her loosely then lowered his face, burying it between the plump breasts. Inhaling deeply, Dimitri kissed the satiny flesh then licked. Shannon's wanton moan echoed above him and he felt the vibration from her chest. Lifting her, he then carried her to his bed.

Chapter Four

Shannon wriggled in his arms and he held her tighter. Lord, she'd been waiting for this. Somehow, now, it just seemed so right. She liked being with him. A lot. He wasn't possessive or demanding. And he respected her as a cop, which was extremely important to her. Another plus was that he was very loyal to his family, and it didn't hurt that James got along with him.

Dimitri sucked her nipple in his mouth and she forgot everything except for how he made her feel. She arched her back, a moan slipping free as he continued to draw on the turgid tip. It didn't matter — to her it was almost as if they were skin on skin. Almost.

He removed her shirt and progressed to her other breast, brushing another teasing kiss over the exposed flesh. She wanted more. A quick flick of his fingers and her bra was unhooked. Staring into her eyes, he slowly dragged the strap from her shoulder down. Then he did the other one. Rising up, he removed the garment from her body.

"Beautiful," he muttered as his gaze touched her. "Simply beautiful."

She felt it. He watched her with such lust and desire all she could do was lie there and absorb it. Dimitri reached out and trailed a solitary finger down her sternum then over her breasts, circling them one at a time then moving up over her peaked nipples.

Her breaths became ragged and she bowed beneath his touch. Fire coursed through her veins and she wanted the experience to end, the burn was almost too much. And yet, at the same time, she wanted it to build even more.

Sure, she'd had sex before but hell, not a single man had ever come close to making her feel like this. And hell, she was half-dressed—him, completely. She clenched her fingers around the cool bedspread.

Holding her gaze, he lowered his head and lapped across one nipple. She gasped and whimpered. Another whimper followed a flick of his tongue. And another. She bit her lower lip and tried to keep quiet as waves of pleasure crashed over her.

"So responsive," he murmured, moving to the other breast and repeating his actions.

He moved his hands to her jeans and unbuttoned them. The sound of her zipper lowering was so loud it almost echoed in her ears. She kept her attention on the man before her. His expression was so intent, overflowing with hunger.

She lifted her hips slightly, assisting in the removal of her pants. He left the bed and pulled them off the rest of the way, dumping them on the floor. Now all she wore was a pair of high cut bikini panties—red plaid. His gaze burned as he stared at them then refocused on her.

"Never figured you for a plaid woman," he commented.

He hooked his fingers along the sides and she tensed at the touch of his skin there. Her belly clenched a few times, but he didn't move, just sat there and watched her. His handsome face was set in stone and she focused on his chest, which rose and fell with the rapid breaths he took.

"Never figured you for a man who seemed indecisive."

She wanted him to do something. To not sit there and stare at her. To touch, caress, lick, lave and bite. Something. *Anything.*

"So many options of what to do first," he said.

He moved one hand, trailing his fingers along the front of her panties then down to between her widespread thighs. She shuddered as he caressed the damp material, only to cry out when he slipped one under the edge and sank it between her lips.

"Yes. I think I made the right decision."

She arched her back, drawing him in closer. In and out, he moved his finger. Words escaped her and the control she was used to always having and maintaining in the bedroom had rapidly flown away.

Another finger joined the first and he growled low in his throat. "So tight and wet. Jesus, Shannon."

He withdrew and her panties were gone in mere seconds. Before she could speak, he ripped off his clothing and she found herself staring at a very naked, very aroused Dimitri Wright. He was fully erect and she licked her lips in anticipation. She wanted him. Wanted him deep inside her, stretching her. Filling her.

She shifted on the bed and watched him move toward her. Her pussy grew wetter and her nipples tightened to the point of being almost painful. He crawled up over her and pressed his weight into her as he joined their mouths for a kiss. His hard length rubbed along her slit and she instinctively tried to guide it in, though he didn't allow her much moving room.

He swept his tongue through her mouth as he ground against her. Planting her feet on the mattress, she lifted her hips. His cock slid along her wetness, gliding back and forth with his motions. She was damn near panting to have him inside her.

Tearing free from the kiss, she stared into his eyes. "Inside."

He reached past her head to the bedside table and opened a drawer. He drew out a condom and she was grateful for his caution yet unsure about why his having them there made a small voice in the back of her mind growl in jealousy.

It didn't take him long to open the foil packet and sheath his cock. She held her breath when he repositioned the head at her entrance.

He didn't slam into her. No, he slid in inch by inch. Her body trembled and she almost came just from him entering her. He stretched her and she moaned. A sound he echoed.

"Christ," he muttered. "You feel so damn good, Shannon. So damn good."

So did he. Dimitri positioned his hands on either side of her head and began to move. Back and forth, he stroked within her. She met him thrust for thrust and angled her hips to take him as deep as she could.

She dug her nails into his shoulders as he powered into her.

"More," she panted, needing the release that danced tantalizingly out of reach.

He listened. Faster, he drove into her and she kept up, asking for more with her garbled words and moans.

His head was by hers and she could hear his grunting. There was nothing soft and loving about this. It was primal. Raw. Precisely what she'd needed. What she craved more of. And, thankfully, what he was delivering to her.

"Uh, uh, uh." Her voice pitched higher and higher with each mewl she released. Eyes closed, she crested and clenched around him.

Dimitri swore gutturally and shuddered. Four more deep penetrating thrusts then she felt his cock pulse as he came. His body stiffened and a roar escaped his throat before he collapsed upon her.

They remained like that, intimately connected, limbs entangled until their heart rates slowed and breathing calmed. She pressed a gentle kiss along his clavicle and he returned the favor along the side of her neck where his face then stayed buried. Her fingers moved with a beat of their own as she drew idyllic patterns along his back.

He rose up and stared at her. Lowering his mouth, he brushed their lips together and began to move off her. She fought her instant reaction of tightening her legs and arms to keep him there as her own personal blanket. Instead, she allowed her arms to fall to the side as he climbed off.

Exhausted limbs didn't allow for much more movement than her rolling slightly to her side and watching him as he walked to the bathroom then returned moments later to rejoin her on the bed. This time, he tugged a corner of the coverlet over them and held her tight. His heartbeat in her ear soothed and relaxed her even more.

"You okay?" he whispered after they'd cuddled for a while.

"Mmm."

"I'll take that as a yes," he commented in a remarkably smug voice.

She shut her eyes and snuggled closer still. For once in her life, she would take advantage of a man holding her. There was no panic telling her to get out, or get him out. Over these weeks with Dimitri, she'd grown to enjoy his touch and she was in no rush for it to end.

* * * *

It was dark out—maybe around six or seven in the evening—by the time she stretched and yawned. Sitting up in bed, she clutched the sheet to her chest and worked through where she was and how she'd ended up there. *Dimitri*. She smiled at the memory and sighed. She reached for the bedside light and turned it on.

This was the first time she'd been to his house and now she took the opportunity to enjoy his bedroom. From the lamplight, she took in the dark, masculine colors, both for furniture as well as bedding. The major thing she noticed was it wasn't clean. She wouldn't put it as a pigsty, but it was far from orderly. Luckily, her clothes rested on a chair near the bed and she grabbed them then dashed into the bathroom.

After a quick shower, she dressed and left his room. She made her way to the living room where more lights were on. Still, no Dimitri.

"Are you hungry?"

His voice poured like dark velvet from the shadows and wrapped around her. She glanced over her shoulder to find him leaning against a wall. Hell, she'd not even seen him when she walked in.

"I could eat."

He flashed a grin, which turned her knees to mush. "So could I." Smoothly, he pushed from the wall and approached.

Good heavens, he moved like a man with a purpose. Powerful. Magnetic. She couldn't tear her eyes away. Her body thundered out its desire, as if he'd not sated her a short bit ago.

"So, are you telling me I have to cook something for you?"

Another heart-stopping smile. "Not at all. It's all ready, just waiting for you. Steaks and beer on the back deck."

Her stomach growled at the thought. "Sounds like my kind of meal."

He snagged her around the waist and drew her close. Nose to nose, he winked. "Personally, I'm anxious for some dessert."

She kissed him until he rumbled low in his chest and lifted her clear off the ground. Hooking her legs around his waist, she ended the kiss.

"Food first."

"Fine." He placed her back on her feet and popped her on the ass. She jumped then allowed him to take her hand as they went out the back door to the well-lit porch. The rich smells of cooking steak made her mouth water.

"Oh, that smells so good."

He went to get them a beer and handed it to her. "Thanks. Our dad made sure all of us could grill." A brief shrug. "The others try, but I'm just better at it."

She rolled her eyes and took a swig of her drink. "Modest, I see."

"Just calling the facts as we know them."

"I bet any of them would say they're better than the others."

A boyish smile. "Probably. But they'd be lying. Let's face it, I've had more practice. I'm the eldest."

"Wow. You think because you're the oldest you can grill better than the others." It wasn't a question.

"Not think. I know. Sure, they're good, but I'm a master. I'll have you know I'm known as the 'king of the grill' and that's by my family."

"Is that something you told them when they were babies they had to call you?" She rolled the bottle in her fingers.

"No. I earned this title and no one will take it from me."

"Is that a fact?"

He gave a perfunctory nod. "You can bank on it, baby."

She dragged her tongue over her lips. "Well, I hate to be the one who tells you this then." She shook her head. "Nope, not really. It actually gives me great pleasure. Your steaks are burning, oh wise n' all knowing 'king of the grill'."

* * * *

Dimitri watched Shannon as she worked on her kickboxing on a thick mat with her cousin James. They were outside, enjoying the cool day.

Shannon had dressed in some heather-gray boy shorts and a teal sports bra. Her feet were wrapped with white tape. It had been two days since they'd first slept together. And if he were honest with himself, he'd rather be home in bed—his or hers he wasn't picky—instead of out here with her cousin. But she'd told him she had plans with James and was coming here.

He knew it wasn't an ultimatum, from her, it was what it was. A statement. She wouldn't whine and make him try to feel bad if he didn't show up. She would be here and if he wanted to see her, he had to be as well.

Which explains why my ass is here watching her.

He settled back in the chair and waited for them to finish. He was impressed with her ability, yes. Still, he wanted her to himself. Right now, he was feeling a bit greedy. He had one more day off and wished to spend time with her, not share her with her cousin.

"You want a go?" James asked after helping Shannon up from the ground where he'd just put her.

"No, thanks. I will take your cousin though."

James walked off muttering to himself. *At least he's wearing clothes for the moment.* Dimitri got up from the chair and moved to where Shannon stood, hands on her hips and breathing hard.

"You okay?"

She looked up at him, sweaty and winded. "Sure. I love getting my ass kicked by him."

"Do you have to work today?"

She shook her head, still breathing hard.

"Come on," he said.

"Where are you taking me?"

"Just hush, Shannon." He took her hand and led her to his car. Once she was in the passenger seat, he got behind the wheel and started the engine.

She kept her silence as he drove back to his house. They walked inside after they parked. Down the hall, he escorted her to the bathroom and knelt by his sunken tub as he adjusted the water, and began to fill it.

Back on his feet, he went to the cabinet and withdrew a small pouch. He tipped some of the contents in the increasing water. Immediately the room filled with the combined smells of rosemary and spearmint.

"What's that?"

"Bath salts. Lis left them here a while ago. She uses this one after training for her triathlon. She claims this helps in removing mental and physical fatigue as well as restoring her energy and alertness."

Facing her, he took in the exhaustion upon her features. Without another word, he went to her and lowered the zipper on her bra. She stared at him as he slid it from her torso. Then he dropped to his knees and tugged down those damn enticing boy shorts, as well as her panties. After getting up, he found a pair of scissors and cut the wrappings off her feet.

Ignoring, or doing his best to, the fact she stood before him completely naked, he said, "Get in."

She climbed in and when it covered her up to her chin, he shut off the faucets. He placed a towel behind her head then brushed a kiss over her forehead before walking out of the room. A short time later, he returned with a shirt of his for her to wear and found her where he'd left her.

Standing over her, he looked down into the water at her firm breasts and bit back his groan. Christ, he wanted her so much. Her eyes remained closed and he allowed his gaze to linger along her toned legs and up to where they met.

"You planning on joining me or were you just going to stand there?"

He tore his stare from the juncture of her thighs and found her watching him, amusement and relaxation upon her face.

"Well, I do like what I see."

"As do I, but were you to climb in here, I could do more than just look at you clothed."

He needed no other encouragement. It didn't take him long to shuck his clothing and lower himself into the bath. The water, still hot, made him moan in pleasure. He settled beside her and she rested her hand on his thigh.

"Want the jets on?"

"Mmm."

He took it as a yes and reached out and around to press the button. The machine started up and soon the jets and the pulsing water they created were massaging them.

"You need a hot tub," she remarked.

"Do I?"

"Well, wouldn't it be nice to sit out in one and watch the sunset. Or sunrise?"

Her fingers moved closer to his cock yet still didn't touch.

"Yes," he said.

"See. It could be so nice."

Taking her hand, he placed it where he wanted it, on him—not near his shaft. "And this hot tub would make you happy?"

She readjusted herself so she straddled his lap, her pussy rubbing along his shaft before she took him deep. "I think it would be awesome to have you fuck me outside in a hot tub."

He palmed her breasts, struggling to stay focused on the conversation. It wasn't easy, not with her wet sheath cradling him. Tugging on her nipples, he watched her head drop back as she captured her lower lip in her teeth and began to slowly move.

"Do you now," he muttered.

"Oh yes." She undulated her hips and ground on him.

"How about me doing that right here?"

She stared at him, her eyes hazy with desire. "I think you should be doing instead of talking."

He rumbled deep in his throat and lifted her off him before slamming her back down.

"Oh shit!" she cried out.

He dug his fingers into her hips, working her hard on him. Up and down. He thrust deep and fast. Her lips were parted and her breaths came out in sharp pants and mewls. Water sloshed over the side and he didn't give a damn. All that mattered was the woman who sat upon his lap, gripping his cock in a vice-like hold.

There were no words to describe how it felt to be buried inside her. He just wasn't that articulate of a man. Either that or the word hadn't been created yet.

She came hard, back bowing, muscles tightening, and a scream ripped from her throat. The action shoved her breasts up to his mouth and he took the offered treat. Drawing one into his mouth, he sucked hard on it as she continued to work her muscles around his cock. With a nip, he moved to her other breast and did the same.

His balls had tightened and he knew he couldn't hold out anymore. She rolled her hips and kept moving even as she worked through the remnants of her orgasm. Releasing a low growl, he shot his seed deep into her.

It hit them both at the same time—her eyes flew open and they stared at one another, breathing hard and deep. He anticipated her move and countered it, keeping her where she was. On his cock. Where he wanted her.

Did he want her pregnant? No. Not at this moment. Was he sorry for coming inside her? Also a no. Being inside her without a condom had been heavenly.

"Stay," he muttered, flexing his fingers upon her hips.

She did and he smoothed some hair away from her face. Her features were flushed, lips parted. He reached into the water and came up with their hands joined, fingers intertwined. Brushing a kiss along the back of her hand, he continued to stare into her eyes.

"Let's go out to dinner," he said softly.

"Why?"

"Because I want to take you out."

"I don't have anything to wear."

He shook his head. "Bullshit. I know you, Shannon. You carry an extra set of clothes in your bag."

"So causal?"

"Yes." Although he would love to see her in a dress. Long or short, it didn't matter. Something tight that showed off her figure.

"Right now?" She tightened around him and he hardened inside her.

"Nope, not right now. We're taking a bath. Allowing the salts to revive us."

"Feels like someone is already revived," she teased with a lift of her lips.

He winked at her and began to move. "So I am."

They remained in the bath for a while before climbing out and drying off. She ignored his shirt and walked naked through to where her bag sat. He loved how unashamed she was of her body.

He observed her, tucking a towel around his waist, as she dug through and pulled out a pair of warm-up pants and a T-shirt. Followed by that were bra and panties. Five minutes later they were both dressed and in his kitchen.

"Come on," he said, closing the fridge and forgoing his attempt to find something to eat.

"Where are we going?"

"Miniature golf."

A smile lifted her lips, making him pleased with her reaction.

"Let's go."

He walked to the door with her only to stop on the porch then led her to his garage after making a decision. Opening the door, he smiled at her whistle of appreciation.

"Damn."

He stared with pride over his classic truck collection. Lately he'd not been able to spend as much time on them as he'd like.

"Which one are we taking?"

He loved the anticipation in her voice. "The '31 Ford AA."

"Awesome."

She hurried over to the medium-blue colored truck. Her fingers glossed over it as if she were touching a lover, gently and without hurry. He joined her and held the door for her. Soon they were on their way, traveling slowly along the back roads until they got in town where the speed limit was lower anyway.

At the golf course, he noticed all the looks they got when they climbed out. Well, to be fair, it wasn't them who got the looks, it was the truck. With his arm around Shannon's waist, they made their way to the front door.

He paid and they got their clubs then headed out to pick one of three options for courses. "Which one do you want?" he asked in her ear.

"Doesn't matter to me."

"Take number three."

She led the way and he followed, his eyes glued on the seductive sway of her hips. As she moved, he recalled how she moved on him. They played the course then stopped at the concession stand for a bite to eat. The sun had begun to set as he drove back to his place.

Shannon had just climbed out of the truck when her phone rang. She answered immediately. "Conner."

As she talked, the subtle changes that came over her took away the soft woman who was hell on his libido and replaced her with the consummate professional. By the time she hung up, he was already aware of what it meant.

"You can take my car," he said without preamble.

"You sure?"

"Yes. Grab your bag while I get my keys."

They split up in the house and met again at the front door. He grabbed her and planted a kiss on her lips. "Be careful."

"Always am," she retorted. "I had fun today, thanks."

He traced her lower lip with his thumb. "Thanks for coming with me."

She took the keys and dashed over to his sports car. Only after she'd whipped around and driven off, spitting gravel, did he realize he wasn't the least bit concerned with her handling one of his own cars.

Chapter Five

Shannon drove to the station, Dimitri falling from her thoughts the closer she got to her destination. Yes, the day had been fun, but work had called and that required all her attention. She wasn't going to become a statistic just because her attention was on someone else instead of the job.

She parked his car then jogged inside to change into her uniform. Buckling on her belt, she slammed her locker shut with a shoulder then engaged her lock once her hands were free.

"Thanks for coming in," the shift commander said when she walked up to his office.

"No problem, sir."

"You're going to be riding with Nick. I know, I know," he said cutting her off before she could comment. "He's a rookie. I don't want him out there alone, so you're going to have to sit on your desire to ride alone for the night."

"Yes, sir."

"Good. He's waiting for you by the car."

Grabbing the handles of her bag, she began the trek to her temporary vehicle.

"Hey, Conner. What are you doing here?"

She glanced over her shoulder to see Mario leaning there, his thumbs hooked in his duty belt, trying to look so much more impressive than he was.

"Working. Shouldn't you be doing that same thing?"

The man scowled at her and she walked off before she did something like kick him in the balls, just on principle.

Nick waited for her by the squad car. She sighed as she took in his face. Fresh from the academy, he looked like he was barely old enough to grow a beard, much less do the job.

"Deputy Conner," he said, straightening up.

"Evening, Nick. Call me Shannon. You're driving, let's get going. Have you gone through the checklist?"

He nodded. "Yes, ma'am."

She tossed her bag in the trunk next to his before climbing in the passenger seat. "Let's do this then."

Thankfully, the night went relatively smoothly. A few stops along the road, which she had to say he handled extremely well, and a couple of inside buildings. Around four in the morning, she fought off another yawn. She'd just not been expecting to be working tonight and hadn't gotten enough sleep.

"Need some coffee?" Nick asked as he stopped at a red light.

"Wouldn't say no to a tall cup of it, that's for sure."

"I'll pull in at the gas station."

"Wonderful."

True to his word, he pulled into the next one they came to. After parking, they got out and walked in. She nodded to the woman behind the counter and made a beeline for the coffee machine. As she filled the twenty-ounce cup with hot java, she peered around the store.

Nick was by the cooler doors grabbing himself a water. She shook her head. *Water? Really?* She figured if she were cut open she would bleed coffee, she drank so much of it. Only water on a shift would not fly.

Adding the sugar and flavored creamer—hazelnut this time—she stirred it until she was pleased all was perfectly mixed. Once she'd popped the top on, she took a sip and purred in pleasure as it raced down her throat, firing all the cylinders, which had been sputtering.

She walked to the counter, adding a candy bar to her purchase as well. As the clerk was ringing her up, the door opened again and in walked two men, baggy clothing and hats tugged down over their faces.

"Morning, gentlemen," she said, wanting them to know there was a cop in the store.

They seemed shocked to see her. *Odd, it's not like the car isn't right out front.* Holding the gaze of the one who'd looked up at her comment, she waited for him to acknowledge her. Finally it came, a brief nod of his head. Then they hurried off down the aisle where most of the candy was located.

She caught Nick's eye and he made his way up as well, stopping to say hello to the men then continuing. "Do you know them?" she asked the clerk.

"Yes. They're regulars in here."

"Any trouble?"

"Nawh. They just don't like cops much."

Addressing Nick this time she asked, "Did you smell alcohol on them?"

He shook his head. "No, ma'am."

She pocketed her change and waited for Nick to pay, all the while keeping an eye on the two men who were coming back up to the register.

"Have a good day," she said as they walked out.

Shannon paused outside the door and sipped her coffee. The men never looked at her, stayed focused on the woman taking their money. She slipped into the passenger seat and stilled Nick as he went to back out.

"Just wait a second."

"Why do we not trust them?"

"It's been my experience that when most people see a cop car sitting this close to the door they expect one to be around. Yet they were very surprised when they saw me. I just want to see where they go when they leave."

"And we follow them?"

"No. But if they get into a vehicle I want to run the plates, just to see who it is."

"This is a gut feeling?"

She drank some more. "You got it. You need to learn to trust your gut. It will point you in the right direction more often than not. So if something looks right but feels wrong, make sure you follow up until you're satisfied. And that works the other way too, just because someone looks like they did it but you're not sure and are having doubts, go with your instincts and dig further. Don't let the easy out stop you from spending a little extra time and walking a few more miles to get to the truth."

"I got it," he said.

She watched him drink his water. Nick Terray was your all-American kid. Tall and fit. Blond hair and blue eyes. Still, she looked at him and saw his innocence, though she was sure the naiveté would be gone in a few years.

The men walked out and she observed them. They had drinks and junk food in their hands. Again, the men didn't even seem to look or acknowledge the car there. They headed off down the street and she sighed.

"Let's get going."

"It's almost time for shift change. Do we go back now?"

"No. I know many officers want to rush back and get their paperwork done so they can leave immediately, but let me ask you a question. If everyone is back at the station, who is out here?"

Nick nodded and didn't ask about it again. They continued to drive until she directed him to head back. The night's paperwork took a while to fill out as she ensured Nick did his correctly. She showered and changed there before heading out to her borrowed car.

Mario was lingering near and she bit back her sound of distaste. Uncaring how rude she came off, she barely slowed and unlocked the vehicle.

"Hey, Conner," he said, sidling up to her.

"I'm working on very little sleep, Mario. Be careful I don't just tase your ass and leave you lying here convulsing."

"I like my women with fire."

Tossing her bag in the back, she faced him. His smarmy grin set her on edge and she bit back her snarl of escalating anger. "Congratulations. I hardly see what that line has to do with me. Since I am not, nor will I ever be, in that category."

His gaze hardened and he scowled, transforming his face from handsome to menacing. "Choosing me is not a bad way to go."

"Keep pushing me and we'll see just how bad your going will be. I don't know how to make this any plainer for you. I am not interested. Period. End of story. Finite. Fin."

"You haven't even given us a chance."

Like that would ever happen. Perhaps after an ice age coated hell it would be on her list of 'very unlikely but still possible' items.

"I don't need to. I don't like you in that way and never will. So leave me alone."

"You don't want to refuse me, Shannon," he said. His tone was low and ugly.

"Are you threatening me?" All senses went on alert and she straightened, no longer just annoyed, but also seriously angry.

He shook his head. "Just stating a point."

"She has a boyfriend." Another voice entered the discussion. "And I would suggest you step away from her before I do it for you."

Shannon jerked her gaze to the direction that familiar voice came from. She saw Dimitri standing there, arms crossed and fire blazing in his eyes. He had a tic in his jaw and she took a moment to just ogle him.

Damn, he was fine. Today Dimitri had donned a nice suit. One from the cut she knew had been made specifically for him—it accented his wide shoulders and narrow waist. Then he included her in his glare and she frowned. Why was he frowning at her? This wasn't her fault. She crossed her own arms and arched a brow in return.

"Dimitri, what are you doing here?"

"I came to see you and overheard this…person threatening you."

Mario blanched a bit. There was no mistaking that Dimitri and Leo were related and it didn't take a genius to figure out that Mario had just made the familial connection.

"I wasn't threatening her, man."

"It doesn't concern you, Dimitri," she said, part of her anger swinging to encompass him. She couldn't believe he'd assumed she needed him to come to her rescue.

"Doesn't concern the boyfriend when he comes across a man telling her that she needs to give them a chance?" Sarcasm dripped from his tone.

Mario slipped away and left her facing an angry Dimitri. "What is with you?" she snapped.

"He threatened you. You need to tell Leo. T—"

She lifted her hand to stop him. "Stay out of this, Dimitri. Mario is a pain in the ass, but I don't need you or Leo fighting my battles for me."

He walked up to stand in front of her. "Tell me something, Shannon."

She fought a yawn. "What?" Lord, she wanted to just make it home and curl up in her bed, cover her head and sleep for the day.

"Why didn't you tell him you had a boyfriend?"

She didn't miss a beat. "Because it wasn't any of his damn business."

"Maybe it would have stopped him from insisting."

"Mario needs to leave me alone regardless of if I am dating or not."

"But you're not dating just anyone. You're dating me."

She snorted at his arrogance. "So what, the Wright name should strike fear into his heart?"

"That fucker better stay away from you." His sentence was so low and gravelled she had a hard time understanding him.

"Your non-answer told me all I needed to know. I'm not stupid, Dimitri. I can handle Mario. And if you would think about it, sometimes the mention of a boyfriend is enough to send someone over the edge, so you may have just placed me in even more danger with your chest-pounding, Tarzan attitude." She shook her head. "Don't do that again. Ever."

She climbed in her loaner and drove away, cursing the meddling attitude of men who wanted to put all women into a category of being too weak or stupid to take care of themselves. She wasn't stupid and in all honesty, she'd not even thought of using Dimitri as an excuse they couldn't date. Her way had always been doing it on her own. Trusting herself. Besides, if she and Dimitri went their separate ways and Mario had thought that was the only reason, he would be back. With a vengeance.

That was something she didn't want. Ever. She blew out an exasperated breath and figured it would be something to deal with later. After she'd gotten some much needed sleep, she showered and dressed for another overnight shift. Dragging when she got home, she crawled back into bed. Later when she finally woke, she rolled from her bed and padded in bare feet out to her kitchen. She paused when she found the man seated at her kitchen table.

"We need to talk," he said.

* * * *

Dimitri had seethed as he watched Shannon leave the parking lot. He'd never been so close to ripping a man's head from his body before. Not until he'd heard him threaten Shannon. His woman.

Yes, he'd damn well said it. She was his. He liked it that way and had no intentions of that changing. Part of him had wondered why she didn't just tell that jackass she was dating. Then he'd confronted her on it and hell, he'd admit it, her words had given him a bit of a chill. Had he made things worse?

Officially, he'd been off work, but since he'd been there, he'd decided to go see his brother. He'd spun on his heel and headed inside the police department. After making his way to his brother's office, he'd knocked on the door.

"Come on in."

He'd pushed it open and stuck his head in. "Got a minute?"

Leo had looked at him and smiled causing the corners of his eyes to crinkle. "Sure thing."

He'd closed the door behind him and had made his way to one of the chairs across from his brother's desk.

"How are you?" Leo had asked.

"Been better."

"What's up?"

"I just overheard one of your cops threatening Shannon."

Leo's eyes had narrowed dangerously. "Mario?"

"Yes."

"Where's Shannon? Is she okay?"

"She's fine. Pissed, but fine."

"What happened?"

Dimitri had recounted what he'd been privy to, including the dressing down she'd given him.

Leo had been cursing as he finished. "I warned him." He'd smacked the top of his desk. "I told her to come to me if he refused to behave."

He'd felt better that his brother was as pissed about this as he was, however, he'd hated that it had been going on for a while now and hadn't been stopped.

"Did she leave?"

"Yes. Right before I came here to talk to you about it. What are you going to do about him? Because I'm telling you right now, he doesn't leave her alone, I'll handle it."

"Christ, Dimitri, do you think I want Conner to be bothered by that man? What good are you going to do to anyone being locked up? None. Then you also have to deal with Mom and Dad if you do that. And brother or not, if you do what I see written on your face to that man, I'll have no choice but to lock you up."

"She's been bothered and you've not done anything about it," he'd growled. "And can you sit there and tell me you wouldn't do the exact same thing if the guy who went after Deyon came back?"

Leo's expression had told him.

"Didn't think so."

"Deyon isn't the topic here. Not to mention, Conner is one hell of a cop."

"Topic or not, you'd do whatever necessary to protect your woman. Any of us would. So don't lecture me on what I shouldn't do. If she's in danger and you won't protect her, I'll do it."

"I'm not saying I won't do anything. Let me talk to her."

Dimitri had stood. "You do that."

The brothers had stared at one another before he'd given a crisp nod of his head then had walked out without another word. He'd still been seething when he'd made it to his car.

He'd woken this morning—following his chat with Leo—to find his car had been returned to him and the keys were inside his house. Only one would have done that. James. Part of him wanted her to still have his car and need to go back to his place.

Unfortunately, he'd had a full day ahead of him and thinking about Shannon and what he wanted to do to her wouldn't get it done any quicker. Tugging on his suit coat, he'd walked across the street and up the sidewalk to his first appointment.

The day had been long and frustrating but he'd gotten the information he needed in order to determine whether the case he was working was actually arson or not. He glanced at his wrist just as the alarm on his watch went off. Time to eat. He'd been intending on asking Shannon to join him as he went to his parents' house for dinner, but he figured she'd still be out cold.

He'd driven to his childhood home and smiled at the sight. He loved this house. Always had. After parking next to familiar vehicles, he'd climbed out and jogged up the steps. The smell of pork chops had filled the air and he'd smiled as his stomach had growled.

"Hey." Katiya welcomed him with a kiss and hug.

"Hey yourself."

He'd continued with the greetings as he hugged his siblings and parents. Everyone had been there and only he and Lis were without their significant others.

"Where's that lovely Shannon?" his mother had asked as they set the table.

"Probably getting ready to head into work. She worked an extra shift last night and is on again tonight."

"Girl needs to eat, doesn't she?"

"Yes, ma'am, but she also needs to be to work on time."

His had mother rolled her eyes and moved by him with piping-hot biscuits. He'd filled the water glasses as the others had pitched in and helped as well. After grace, they'd passed plates around and soon everyone was eating.

"So," Mama Wright had said, "tell me how the wedding plans are coming along for everyone."

He'd been able to feel the collective groan from all of his siblings. Katiya and Warrick had answered first, then Arissa and Deiter. Then it had fallen silent.

"Lis?"

She'd lifted her head. "Yes, ma'am?"

"Wedding plans. I've not seen your dress ideas. You know you have to let Deyon know with enough time, so she's not rushed to finish. Plus we need to know the date. How many times do I have to tell you this?"

On one side of Dimitri had been Harmony, Jonathon's fiancée, and Lis on his other. Both women had tensed at the same time.

"Apparently as many as I have to tell you to let it go, Mother."

"Mind your tone, young lady."

"I'm sorry, Mama, but I'm tired of going through this all the time. You're not listening to me."

His mother had put down her fork and knife before leveling a haughty stare at the baby of the family. "I have six children. Five of whom are engaged, and therefore five weddings to plan. That's not easy. So if I am asking for a bit of cooperation from you, I really don't see how that is so difficult for you to give."

"You're not asking, Mother. You're demanding. All the time. I'm busy. All of us are. If I wanted to spend what free time I have looking at dresses or sampling cakes then I would. But I don't. I don't want the fairytale wedding. Give it to Katiya and Arissa. I don't need it."

"All girls—"

Lis had shoved her chair back and bolted to her feet. "No. Not me. I'm never going to sit still and be a pretty dress-up girl for you, Mama. Not like your other daughters. And I'm sorry that's disappointing to you, but I'm not going to change." Tears had leaked down her cheeks and she'd bit her lower lip. "Let me make this as clear as I can. I'm not planning one. I don't have to. Archer and I are already married. I'm sorry, Daddy."

She'd whirled around and ran off. Harmony had slid her chair out then had gone after her, mumbling her excuse. He'd stared around the table at everyone. Looking at his brothers, he'd noticed the truth in their eyes. They'd known. He, on the other hand, couldn't have been more shocked.

Dinner had basically been over since that announcement. He'd helped clear the table after that and had finally made his way to the door after saying goodnight to his family. His mind had whirled with all that he'd heard at dinner. Despite his initial feeling of disappointment, he'd found himself grinning as he worked on his rock-climbing machine. For all her frailness as a child, it appeared his sister had guts and determination to do what he never would have believed she could do. He didn't know Archer that well, but all he cared about was how he treated Lis. And based on that, the man was just fine in his book.

After his workout, he'd showered and settled down on his couch with a file from work and a beer in his hand. He'd read deep into the night until his eyes screamed at him to allow them some rest. Frustrated for not being able to reach Shannon, he'd crawled between the sheets of his large bed, wishing she were there with him, her lush figure pressed against him.

He'd woken to not only his phone ringing but also his beeper. With a curse his mother would not even want to know he knew, he'd reached for the phone, already knowing the day was going to be a long one. He'd been right. Some days he loved being correct, however, this hadn't been one of them. A house fire this time. Deliberately set, and they'd lost two small children.

* * * *

He sat at the bar and nursed a drink. It was here he'd actually met Shannon Conner, after another house fire.

"You look like you had a rough day."

As if he'd conjured her up, a sultry voice commented from behind him. He smiled as he turned in his chair. Shannon stood there in a pair of jeans and a long-sleeved shirt with a wolf on the front. Her hair was braided and hung over one shoulder.

"Hey, beautiful," he said, taking a hand and drawing her close. "How are you doing?"

She leaned in and kissed him. Nothing but a light connection of lips, but it rocked him nonetheless.

"I'm okay. How are you? I heard about the fire." She moved around and sat next to him.

He readjusted so he could still stare at her. "I think it's the same person. The signature is the same."

"I'm so sorry."

"Me too, but not as sorry as that bastard will be once he's caught."

"Sure it's a male?"

Ever pragmatic, his Shannon. "No, but I would hate to think of a woman deliberately setting fires that take the lives of children."

She blinked. "Why? I would think you would hate anyone doing that, not just a woman."

"Women are supposed to be maternal. You know that whole mothering instinct. The bond which grows when they carry life."

Her expression remained skeptical. "And men paternal. It doesn't matter if it's a man or a woman. The fact they are doing this is still so horrific. I don't think a woman is more nurturing to a child than a man. I've arrested enough women to refute that claim some people make. Truthfully, in my experience, I've found women to be more vindictive and much more devious in what they do when they're pissed off."

He nodded in agreement. She made a very good point there.

"Enough about me," he said after she'd ordered a drink. "How are you doing? Has Mario left you alone?"

"I'm fine. Riding with a rookie for the week until his training officer comes back from his time off."

He frowned. "A rookie?"

"Yes. New kid. Smart and a fast learner."

He didn't like that. Rookies made mistakes. And that could cost Shannon her life. He kept his discontent to himself though, knowing full well it would not be appreciated. Her drink arrived and he looked at it, frowned and looked again.

"What are you drinking?"

"Ginger ale. I'm on my way in to work. Stopped in when I saw your vehicle." She drank it swiftly and put it down. "You have a good night, Dimitri. I have to get going." Shannon swung off the seat and pecked him quickly on the lips. "See you later."

He caught the back of her shirt before she could get very far and pulled her to him. "That's not a kiss."

"I know," she said, eyes sparkling. "But you've been drinking. I don't need to show up to work smelling like alcohol." Another cheek kiss. "Bye."

As she walked out, and after he'd finished staring after her like a hungry predator, Dimitri spied a man in the corner who had left his seat and gone after Shannon. Mario. Possessiveness welled up inside him and he tossed some money down then followed as well.

Chapter Six

Shannon rubbed the back of her neck and watched as her current partner left the convenience store with coffee. She grinned at him and he shook his head.

"This is your fault, Conner," he griped good-naturedly.

"That is a staple for all cops. And about time you started drinking it."

"I'm addicted. I didn't think we were supposed to have addictions."

She laughed and climbed into the driver's seat as he got in the passenger side, already sipping his hot beverage. Hers, from the start of the shift, was still there beside her. She had settled into working nights now and wasn't sucking it down as if it was air. Tonight was their last night working together.

"So, why are you so tired, Nick? Girlfriend keeping you up?"

He flushed as he buckled himself in. "Something like that."

"Something, huh? You do know that a mumbled response like that makes a good cop want to dig and find out the details."

He laughed as she backed out of the parking spot. "I had heard you were so quiet and serious."

"I am, but I like you."

She spoke the truth, she did like him. He reminded her a lot of her cousin, or rather, how James had been before he'd joined the Navy. Good outlook on life and a wonderful attitude. How long it would stay with him working the streets, she didn't know. Granted, McKingley, New Mexico wasn't anything like Los Angeles or New York City, but they did have their fair share of crime.

McKingley was growing and with growth, especially rapid growth, increase in crime occurred. She loved it here, though. She'd not been born here, but it felt almost like this was her hometown. It was definitely her town. She would do anything to protect it.

The radio squawked and she listened in as they got a call. Hitting the lights and siren, she gunned the powerful engine and raced off to the address.

After the shift was over, she headed out to her jeep, sliding her sunglasses on to block out the bright sun. She'd had fun with Nick but would be very glad to have her own car back. And the solitude she got riding alone.

She drove to the ranch and smiled at the sight of the vehicle before her house. On the porch was a man she had become very accustomed to seeing. Dimitri lounged against a post, presenting her with a picture that evaporated her exhaustion in seconds.

Climbing out, she swung her bag over her shoulder. "Morning," she called out.

"Morning."

"What are you doing here? Don't you have to be at work?"

"Day off. What about you?"

She grinned. "Well, I live here, so it's natural for me to arrive on occasion."

His smile made her knees weak. "Not what I meant, woman."

"Oh no? What did you mean then?"

He approached her. "You know what I meant."

She did. "I'm done with training. I get ninety-six hours and I'm back on days."

He nodded. "Ninety-six."

"Yes. Why, something you had in mind?"

The heat in his eyes told her just what that was. He took her bag from her shoulder and carried it inside. She trailed after him, mesmerized by his firm ass in his jeans. She gave a short bark of laughter.

"What's so funny?"

"Nothing, I was just thinking."

"About?" he prompted.

"How much alike you and Leo are and yet how very different."

He dropped her bag on the chair by the door. "What do you mean?"

"Have you two never looked at each other? I mean really looked?"

"He's my brother."

"Who you could be a twin with."

He frowned and she laughed. "Wow, from the look on your face it's like I just said I killed your dog. This isn't a bad thing. Just that the two of you look an awful lot alike despite your age difference."

"So you find him attractive?"

She shrugged. "Sure, I guess. I don't look at him in that light. He's my boss."

"And me?"

She sidled up to him, kicking the door closed behind her. "Are definitely not my boss. And you, I most definitely find attractive."

He wrapped his arms around her and tugged her until they were flush against one another. "Is that a fact?"

"It is."

"And what do you propose we do about it then, Deputy Conner?"

"I don't know about you, but I could use a shower."

"I could too," he said, his eyes burning her. "However, since we do live in the desert, I think we should get dirtier first and then clean up." He winked at her, his intention perfectly clear. "You know, with needing to conserve water and all that."

She went to work on his shirt immediately. Her breath caught in her throat at the sight of his exposed chest. Lord, help her, she just wanted to touch, lick and bite him. Delectable. All hardness and defined muscles. She spread her hands over him and smiled at his responding rumble.

* * * *

Two hours later they were sprawled in bed. Shannon lay upon his chest with nothing more than the robin's egg blue sheet covering their lower halves. Beneath her ear, his heart beat out a consistent thump and soothed her further. She had no intention of moving. For right now, this was her idea of heaven.

Still, he hadn't completely relaxed and so while she traced abstract patterns on his bare chest, she went against her nature to not pry.

"What's wrong?" she asked.

"Nothing," he replied after a moment's hesitation.

"You sure? Because you still seem quite a bit tense."

"It's just family stuff."

She got the hint—he didn't wish to discuss it. So she nodded and let it go. What else could she do?

"I found out that my baby sister is married."

Okay, apparently he did want to discuss it. "That's great isn't it?" She'd met Lis a few times at accidents and once at the annual police versus fire softball game.

"Well, I... Of course, it's just that, she didn't tell any of us." He moved and she waited until he stopped to resettle. "Not true, she told my brother, Jonathon, who a little bit ago told Leo."

"And you're hurt because she didn't tell you?"

"Of course, she's my baby sister. I saw the hurt look on my mom's face."

"No offense, Dimitri, but maybe she just didn't want the huge production."

He tensed. "What do you mean?"

"Don't be crazy. Anywhere around town here, you can hear a hum of gossip surrounding the upcoming Wright weddings. I hear it mentioned at least once a day, I can't imagine what it's like for the ones who are actually going through the act. I don't know her that well, but she is more subdued than her sisters. Look at it from her point of view. Every decision you try to make about what is supposed to be *your* day evaluated and possibly told how wrong you are. All these people in your business. It's not like your family is in obscurity here in McKingley."

"I'm her brother."

"And the oldest. James and I are close, but he can be an overprotective bear when he thinks he knows better than I do. She's the baby of your family. I remember the incident with your cousin Justin. And I saw the result. Noticed how often Leo was swinging by to check on her, how often he called to make sure she was okay. Hell, even how he tried to tell her she should take some time off work and recover. I felt smothered and it wasn't even for me."

He fell silent and she wondered if she had overstepped. Dimitri sighed heavily and tightened his hold on her, his hands stroking up and down her back.

"Point taken, Deputy Conner."

"You know she loves you, but cut her some slack. Archer seems like a perfectly nice guy. And we both know every single one of you Wright brothers had him checked out even though he grew up in this town with you."

His chest moved with his chuckle. "You have us figured out that well, do you?"

"Doesn't take much to figure out what brothers would do. You love your sister."

"You're pretty smart," he whispered into her hair.

"I have my moments."

"All the time."

She snuggled closer.

"What do you want to do tonight?"

Closing her eyes, she asked, "Do we have to do anything other than what we are right now?"

"Not at all," he rumbled. "We can stay in bed all night. I just thought you might want a bite to eat."

"Maybe later. I'm too content to move right now." It was true. Her bones and muscles felt like they had melted, leaving her just a limp pile upon the impressive man beneath her.

"Sounds good to me. Tell me something, now, Shannon."

"Hmm." She was close to falling asleep all over again.

"Has the thing with Mario been taken care of?"

There went her relaxed state. "You need to let that go. I can handle it."

"You're my girl. I'm not going to let it go."

"Listen to me," she said as she got off him and sat up, dragging the sheet over her chest. "I'll tell you like I told Leo. I can handle this. If, and I mean *if* I need any help on it, then I will ask. Until then, this is between the two of us. Myself and Mario. Not you. Not your brother. Not James. Myself and Mario."

He sat up as well and she bit back her groan at seeing his totally naked state. Dimitri didn't even bother hiding his thick cock and she had to tear her gaze from where it lay semi-hard against his thigh.

"A man like that is dangerous."

She ground her teeth and prayed for strength. "I know that, Dimitri. I'm not an idiot. I'm a cop. I also know how to handle a man like him. However, your and Leo's interference makes it harder. Trust me to know what I'm doing."

She held his gaze and watched the indecisiveness flash through it. His phone rang and their connection was lost as he strode over to his pants and pulled it out.

"Yeah?" he snapped.

The moment he watched her again, she licked her lips and lowered the sheet giving him a tantalizing peek at her breasts. Dragging her finger between them, she bit her lower lip. His cock hardened and rose from his leg.

"What, Leo? Uh, let me see if we can come for dinner."

She ripped the sheet to the side and continued with her finger, down her belly and between her legs to dip into her wet pussy.

His eyes flared with heat. "Nope. Sorry, Shannon and I can't join you and Deyon tonight. We're busy."

Dimitri tossed his phone down on the chair and was on her in a flash, pressing her back into the mattress.

She laughed for the sheer joy of being with this man. "Are you sure you don't want to go there for dinner?"

"I'm positive," he stated.

He rolled them over so she was on top. She reached for the pile of condoms on her bedside table, ripped one open then sheathed his turgid length. She rose up over him and sank down, taking him completely inside her with one movement.

Lord, he felt good inside her. Thick and long. She leant forward and splayed her hands on his chest then began to move. Up and down, back and forth, she set her own slow pace.

"Shannon," he croaked.

"Shh. No talking." She closed her eyes and reclaimed the rhythm she wanted. The burn grew, in him as well for he tensed beneath her, but she still maintained the same torturous speed. This wasn't something she wanted to end until she was good and ready. Her blood hummed and her skin tightened.

Dimitri gripped her hips and she opened her eyes just as he wrested control away from her. With a low growl, he began thrusting up into her, hard and fast. She dropped her head back and moaned as intense pleasure washed over her, sending her into a fierce orgasm. Inside her, she could feel his release as well.

Exhausted, she fell forward and lay on his sweaty chest, his thickness still buried deep within her.

Shannon had crashed immediately after they'd finished making love in bed, and he had taken that time to lie here and concentrate on her. He wasn't tired, rather he was perfectly content to stare at her. She lay sleeping against him, soft snores emanating from her. Even that didn't bother him. Dimitri stared at Shannon and felt that tug on his heart all over again. It'd been coming more and more often now, increasing with the time he spent with her.

It was two in the morning and he loved how the moonlight bathed her in a soft glow. Shannon gave her all when she did something. Lovemaking was no different. His cock stirred as he watched her, but he ignored it. She needed to get her sleep — she was exhausted having refused to sleep — she was adjusting back to days. She'd stayed up with him until tonight. Granted they'd been in bed, but there had been definitely no sleeping going on.

This woman had come to mean a lot to him and it scared him a bit. He'd never been this serious about anyone before. Part of him wanted to rush forward to deepen their relationship while the cautious part made him want to hesitate, slow it down. Protect himself. She and she alone had a power over him and he couldn't let her know it. He realized that she could seriously hurt him.

Rolling his eyes at himself, he sighed. *I shouldn't be so melodramatic.* Shannon didn't strike him as a woman who would do anything like that. It happened though, women hurt men and played them, he knew that, and he didn't want to be one of those men people talked about and whispered about how he'd been a fool.

Be honest, his subconscious chided.

If he were truly honest with himself, he would reveal that lately he'd been thinking in terms of something much more permanent every time he thought of Shannon. Something like his siblings had. The promise of forever. He could admit—reluctantly—he was jealous of what they had with their partners.

He wanted it too. Living in the same house. Coming home to that person in the evenings. Falling asleep together and waking the same way. Yes, that was what he wanted. He wanted what his parents had.

He ran a hand over his face. *I'm so pathetic. Mooning like this.* Blowing out a breath, he shifted then stilled as Shannon moved.

After she didn't wake, he breathed a bit easier. As sentimental as he was feeling at this moment, he didn't know what he might just spit out. He held her tighter and nuzzled her temple. She burrowed closer and he closed his eyes, enjoying the feel of her lushness against his form.

* * * *

The next morning they got up early then saddled the horses. After riding out to where they'd watched many a sunset, they faced the other direction and watched the sun come up over the horizon. The sunrise was beautiful, but he honestly had a hard time keeping his eyes off the woman who sat easily on the horse next to him. He loved watching her ride. Her motions were so fluid, so in tune with the animal.

"What's the plan for the day?" he asked as they slowly made their way back to the ranch.

"I don't know. I have to do some chores around here, but other than that, I have no plans." She readjusted in the saddle and looked at him. "Something you have planned there?"

"Not really. I was thinking we could grill out."

He studied her expression, waiting for her response.

"I take it you're planning on staying for my entire ninety-six?"

He blinked. *Is that a problem?* "Did you want me to go?" he questioned with reluctance.

"Didn't say that. Had I wanted you gone, I would have told you to leave."

That much was true, she would have done that. He gave a small smile. "Then what?"

"I wasn't expecting to have to have plans for my entire days off to tell you about."

He looked at it from her point of view. She'd pulled extra shifts at work on a totally different time so her sleeping schedule was messed up again and now he was expecting an itinerary from her on what she'd planned to do on her days off.

"Sorry."

"Nothing to apologize for. I had planned on catching up on some things around here that have been neglected. But grilling out sounds like fun."

He had been taking up a lot of her time and suddenly felt bad. Was he responsible for her falling behind on chores and work around here? Unlike at his house, this took a bit more work to keep up and running. It was older and as she pointed out, a ranch.

"How about you put me to work? I'll help you get caught up, then we can grill."

She nodded and gave her horse its head for the ride back to the ranch. Chatter was light and easy between them on the return ride. Once they'd arrived, she made a brief stop to wake her cousin then they went to the stable.

Not too much later, they were working, even James. However, Dimitri was having a hard time focusing on the job at hand. Continually distracted as he was by a pair of creamy brown legs in tight cut-off jeans, his painting was suffering.

"Thought you were here to work," James said.

Tearing his gaze from Shannon's ass for the umpteenth time, Dimitri looked at her cousin. James wore a pair of jeans and boots today while Sigmund, the demented rooster, walked around as if he hadn't a care in the world.

"I am working."

James stared at him, blinked, looked to the unpainted surface beside him then back to his face. "My mistake. I was under the impression you were painting. Hard to do that with a dry brush."

Flustered, Dimitri glanced down and found he hadn't even opened the can of paint yet. *Shit.* He shrugged. Really, what else could he do? He'd been caught and there was no excuse.

"You two are pathetic," James said in a tone that was more amused than anything as he walked away.

I don't run naked after a creature that likes to grab at dangly bits. He opened the can, stirred it then truly got to work. They continued in the sun until close to five in the afternoon.

"You joining us for dinner, James?" he asked as he rinsed out the brushes. "We're grilling out."

"No. I have something to do."

"Okay. Offer is there if you get back and we're still eating."

The man nodded and moved to Shannon's side. Dimitri watched as they chatted together. It wasn't hard to see the affection they had for one another. The other thing, which also wasn't hard to see, was that Shannon was worried.

After James had left, she walked to his side, all sweaty in her spaghetti-strap tank and those damn frayed jean shorts. There was no sign of the cop right now—all he was faced with was pure woman, with a body to die for and who wasn't afraid of some work. His groin stirred and he swallowed.

"Everything okay?" He shook the brushes to remove excess water.

"Yeah."

Her nose flared the way it did when she was lying to him. He wouldn't pry—it was family business and if she wanted to share with him, she would.

He pushed to his feet and smiled. "I'll start on the grill."

All thoughts about that vanished as she stepped flush to him and rested her palm on his bare chest. "Must have more of that water conservation first, don't you think?"

He rumbled his agreement and drew her up for a kiss. "I'm all for it."

She laid the brushes out before she jumped into his arms and latched her legs around him.

Kissing her as if it would satisfy the hunger he had for her, he carried her back inside her house straight to the bathroom where they shared a shower—one that didn't conserve all that much water. After they were sated did they get around to firing up the grill. And he didn't mind the delay in the least.

Chapter Seven

Shannon ran, feet pounding, after the perp who had decided it would be more fun to have her chase him, as opposed to doing the nice thing and stopping when she'd arrived on the scene. The other two had been cuffed and were by another squad car. But this wiry little bastard had opted to run.

He was fast, she'd give him that, but she'd be damned if she let him get away from her. Adding a bit more speed, she cursed her utility belt—always great to have, right up until she had to chase someone.

They hauled ass into an empty lot and she turned on even more speed, catching him and taking him down hard. She bit back her muttered curse as pain lanced through her right side.

"I told you not to run," she snapped off as she cuffed the man.

"I didn't do anything wrong," he cried.

"Of course not. What was I thinking? It must have been a different young man in his early twenties wearing cargo pants and a black Metallica shirt with a beanie on his head who robbed the store."

"Exactly. I was framed!"

Rolling her eyes, she climbed off him then jerked him up. "Tell it to the attorney I am going to advise you to get." As they walked, she recited his rights to him.

Mario and two other officers were back by her squad car where they'd all parked. Hers however, had the driver's door still open.

"Nice collar." Mario opened the back door of her cruiser for her. "We found the gun he dropped."

"Good." She guided the still muttering man into the backseat. "Sit and don't move."

The moment he was there, she slammed the door, content he'd be fine since the window was partially down. She moved and winced.

"You okay?"

Do I really want Mario to know I'm hurt? Not really, no. But the gasp that came from one of the others couldn't be ignored.

"Hell, Conner, you're bleeding."

Shit. She'd been afraid of that. "I'm fine."

"No, you need to get that looked at."

Over the radio, she heard them call for a medic. Dipping her head, she sighed heavily at the dark stain that spread out on the side her uniform shirt. There was a big tear in the middle of the new color.

"I'll take him back to the station for you while you get that cleaned up," Mario said.

She nodded, feeling grateful he wasn't being an ass at the moment. It didn't take long for the man to be moved from one car to the next. She kept her distance, what with her bleeding and all, there was no sense in taking unneeded risk.

She turned to view the ambulance pulling into the parking lot. The crowd, which had begun to gather earlier, had slowly faded bit by bit. Doors slammed and she caught sight of a tall man with bronze skin, chiseled features, black wavy hair and a firm body.

I know him. He was the one who partnered with the youngest sister of Dimitri Wright. Sure enough, she appeared as well, snapping on some gloves.

"Let's get you looked at," she said then looked up and paused. "Hey, Shannon."

"Lis."

"Come on."

She went to the back of the ambulance to sit on the stretcher while Lis helped her out of the uniform shirt and stared at the injury.

"How'd you do this?"

"Chasing some little bastard."

"Looks like you got caught on some metal. You also have some rash marks from like gravel."

"Figures, I took him down hard in a lot."

"I can clean it, but you need to get it stitched up."

"Can't you do it?"

"Well, yeah, I could."

"Do it. Just give me a local."

"You know they're going to want you checked out by a doctor."

Damn it, she was right. Especially since three other officers saw the injury. "Can't you do it quick and I can just say I cut myself a little bit?"

Lis held up the shirt. "That's a lot of blood for just a little cut." A short pause. "Come on, you know it's the smart thing."

She did know—problem was, she didn't like hospitals. A shadow blocked out the sun and they both looked up to find Leo there.

"What the hell happened? I got a call saying one of my deputies was bleeding badly and in the back of an ambulance."

"She's fine, Leo. Got cut, but we're on our way to the hospital." Lis spoke in an unhurried and unruffled way.

"You got her to go to the hospital?"

"Just make sure her car gets there. Let's go, Thom!" she added as she put a new gauze pad against the bleeding.

Shannon watched as her overly stubborn boss got shoved out of the way much like someone brushes away a gnat. The doors shut and Lis winked at her.

"He can be a bit over the top sometimes. I figured it would be nice to not have to listen to one of his famous lectures."

Shannon laughed and in the next moment sucked in a breath at the sharp pain.

"Lie back."

So she did. The trip flew by quickly and soon she was being helped out of the ambulance and walking inside with Thom. Lis waved goodbye from the back, where she immediately began stripping the cover off where she'd lain. Thom turned her over to a hospital staff member and left as well. A short time after that and she was getting her injury sewn up. Shannon was itchy, wanting out of there. She didn't like being in these places.

Later she entered the waiting room and spotted Leo leaning against a wall, watching the goings on in the emergency room. She figured he was waiting for her to finally be released. Shannon approached him and he straightened as she came to stand by his side.

"How are you?" he asked.

"Good as new."

The flare of his nose told her he didn't believe that.

"Honest. They wouldn't have let me go had I not been."

"I'm surprised you didn't try to get Lis to sew you up in the lot back there. I know you don't like hospitals."

There was no sense in telling him she had done so. She shrugged, then together they headed outside, her ruined and bloodied shirt balled up in one hand, leaving her clad in a black undershirt with a tear in the side.

"Mario took your guy back and booked him for you."

"Good. I have to head back anyway and change."

Leo moved to her passenger door and tossed her the keys. She looked at him, one eyebrow higher than the other in silent question.

"What? I drove your car here. I don't have a way back."

Great. Thankfully, he didn't press her on what had happened or on the issue with Mario. Of course, when he'd showed up unexpectedly at her house, he'd done enough pressing.

"Deyon wants to have another get-together," he said as she stopped at a light.

"When?"

"She was thinking next weekend. She wants it to be you and Dimitri, us and Arissa. Oh yeah, and Jackson."

She nodded and drove on. "Sure thing. I don't think I work."

"Thanks by the way for riding along with Nick."

"He's a good cop. Bright and learns quick."

"Yes, he is."

She pulled into the station and they got out before walking inside.

"I'll let Deyon know then that we're on."

"Sounds good."

Shannon headed to the ladies' locker room while Leo went wherever he had to go. She winced a bit while changing into her spare uniform. Next stop was to put in another shirt order. Once that was done, she made her way up to the squad room to see if she could locate her wayward prisoner.

Work ran over that night and normally she didn't mind but right now, she was tired. She wanted to just go home and put her feet up. All the work she'd been doing on the ranch had made her sore. Her recent injury compounded that but, since she was here, she figured she'd look in on her perp.

She and James had wanted to get a lot done before winter arrived and they'd been working hard and long hours to get their goals accomplished. Although her cousin was acting a bit stranger than normal. Which really said a lot.

Walking to her car, she pulled out her phone then dialed a number.

"Good evening, sexy."

Dimitri's baritone made her smile. "Evening."

"You coming over?"

"I'm sorry, I have to cancel. I'm on my way home now. I just need to crash right now."

"Everything okay?"

"Just been a long day." She knew he would have heard about her being injured but didn't mention it.

"Need me to come over?"

Part of her wanted to say yes. She didn't. Time alone had become a luxury. It seemed she and Dimitri were always together and for someone who had mostly been alone, it was tiring. Great, but tiring.

"No. I'm going to just get home and sleep."

"Oh." The one word was laced with disappointment.

"I'll see you this weekend at Deyon's thing. Good night, Dimitri." She hung up and got in her jeep.

'I'll see you this weekend'. Dimitri stared at his phone after she hung up. *Really? Not until this weekend?* He'd become so accustomed to seeing her almost daily, a week seemed like an eternity. She'd sounded exhausted. He got to his feet and walked to the door. There, he hesitated before toeing off his shoes and making his way back to the couch, where he plopped down. She didn't want him over there.

The frustration that hit him at that revelation caused him a great deal of disgruntlement. He paced and rubbed his hand over his head. Had something happened that she needed a bit of distance from him now? And there was the fact she'd never even mentioned being cut today.

She confused him. For so long he'd wanted a woman who wasn't clingy or needy. Now he had one and damn it, he wished she would cling a bit more. Or need him to come over after stressful days to help relax her. But no. His woman was perfectly content to keep him in the dark.

He got up and went for a beer. Standing in the kitchen, he drank about half of it before he moved again. *Who said being in a relationship was supposed to be easy?* Okay, so the logical side didn't help anything. He wanted it easy. He liked easy.

More than that, he liked things to work how he wished them to. And he would like a bit more from

Shannon now. But this most recent call made him wonder if she was on the same page as he was.

Hell, he didn't even know what page he was on himself. All he knew is he wanted to have her living with him. Fall asleep with her in his arms and wake in the morning, with their bodies curled together.

He finished off his beer then disposed of the container. Cripes, he had it bad. Pining over a woman. He went to the fridge and pulled out some leftovers to heat for dinner.

After he'd finished, he worked on a case then called it a night much earlier than usual. Come morning, he rolled over, reaching for Shannon before he remembered he was alone. He flopped onto his back with a muttered curse.

His cock was hard and with a frustrated groan, he sat up and climbed from the bed. He didn't want to find release alone and by himself, he longed to find release deep inside Shannon's body.

Instead, Dimitri worked out then took a short, cold shower. Padding around his house in his pants, he eventually went to fix some breakfast before going back to finish dressing. His phone rang as he was tying his shoes.

"Wright," he said into the receiver.

"Sorry to bother you, Dimitri. But there's been a fire and they want you out there to investigate."

Hell, he hadn't even been listening to the scanner. "Where?"

"The Oasis."

Shit! That was his sister Katiya's place. His heart plummeted. "On my way."

He dashed from the house then jumped into his sports car. He drove fast and after he arrived, he screeched to a halt by the numerous emergency response vehicles. Running toward the yellow tape, he flashed his badge then ducked under.

"Katiya!" he called out as he spied her.

She stood wrapped in her fiancé's arms. Warwick had a fierce scowl and Katiya's face was tearstained. Rhianna De'clare, the second in charge of the center, was also there. She looked composed, but Dimitri could see anger in her pale-gray gaze.

"Dimitri," Katiya said, moving to him for a hug before retreating to Warwick's arms.

"What the hell happened?" he demanded.

"I don't know," Katiya said between sniffles.

He frowned — she wasn't usually this emotional. Although it wasn't everyday one saw their pride and joy go up in flames.

"I closed the center today. There is nothing I could of think that could cause this." Rhianna shook her head. "We had to cancel our usual late classes for tonight."

"Dimitri!"

He turned at the muffled sound and sighed then hurried to the person who'd yelled for him. "Carmen. What the hell is going on?"

She took off her helmet and shook her head, which remained clad in her Nomex flash hood and facemask. "Not sure, Chief's in the back looking for you though."

"How bad is it?"

"It will take a bit to repair, luckily there wasn't anyone inside. From what I remember last time I was here for the breakfast thing, it was empty rooms that went up."

"Thanks."

She nodded then slapped the heavy helmet back on her head after fixing the flash hood. With a single touch to her helmet as a salute, she jogged back in to where the flames had begun to fall under control.

"I'll be back," he told his sister before jogging around to where Carmen had said Chief wanted to see him.

He had to wait a while since the flames were much stronger in the back. Finally, the man approached him. He looked tired and more than a bit stressed.

"What's up, Chief?"

He coughed then reached into his pocket and pulled out a cigarette. Lighting it, he sighed then crossed his arms. "Damn, I needed that."

"Carmen said you wanted to see me."

"Yes." Chief took another puff. "You can't run this investigation."

"Excuse me?"

"This is your sister's place. You know how this is."

"Fuck that. I'm not being pulled from this case, Chief. You're right, it's my sister. And I'll work damn hard to make sure whoever did this is brought to light."

"See, you're already assuming it was arson. It may not have been."

Dimitri blew out a breath and tried to control himself. Nope, it wasn't working. "I'm on this case."

"There's no way I can keep you from looking into this, is there?"

"Nope. You may as well allow me to stick with it. Even if you pull me, we both know I'll be looking into it and following up my own leads."

"I was afraid of that."

He waited. Chief was correct—he was assuming it was arson. Mainly because he knew how strict his sister was and to what extent she vetted the contractors who came in and worked on her building.

"Very well, this is what's going to happen then. And this, Dimitri, isn't up for negotiation. You will do it this way or you will be barred from all information."

"You can't…"

"I can and I will. You're too close to this and if something turns up, I know damn well the DA isn't going to want your connection to the victim as a potential problem for their case."

"What's the stipulation?"

"You'll be working with another investigator."

All his instincts rebelled and he had to forcibly keep the refusal inside his mouth. Chief must have been waiting for it — his eyebrows rose as he watched.

"Who?"

"Someone from the FBI field office."

Great. Someone who worked a desk. Not what he needed. He needed a person who worked fires. Understood them and how people who set them thought. "Why the feds?"

"Because they're really not doing anything else on this case yet it has finally *occurred* to them you may be onto something with a serial arsonist and offered to help out. It's not like it was a secret who's building this was, you know. Your family knows some big people."

"Wonderful. Do I get to meet this person?"

"Right now," Chief said, gesturing with his chin. "Meet Agent Gahlau."

The name sounded familiar to him. He turned to find himself looking at a tall woman. She was beautiful — her black hair was drawn back in a severe, no nonsense bun, her golden skin shined healthily and she had vibrant green eyes. Nope, he'd never met her before — he would have remembered.

"Inspector Wright," she said, holding out her hand. "I'm sorry we had to meet under these circumstances."

He took her hand, surprised by the strength in her grip. "Dimitri."

"Shayla."

"And how much experience do you have investigating actual fires, Shayla, versus sitting behind a desk at the local FBI office?" He knew his tone was sharp, but damn it all, he didn't want some rookie trying to figure this out.

Her green eyes narrowed slightly. She spoke, but, her tone had none of the welcoming warmth from before. Hell, it should have put out all the flames here and in hell.

"I get that I'm encroaching on you. We just thought you'd appreciate the help in ensuring this went smoothly and you didn't have any results tossed out in court because of your relationship with the victim. And as for your question, I've been in the FBI for all of six months. Before that, I worked in Los Angeles since I was eighteen as a fire fighter. So I'm very confident in my skills as I've been learning about fire and reading its signatures since I could walk. More than that, though, my father was the top arson investigator in two major cities before we moved to the West Coast." She turned and walked off, calling over her shoulder, "I'll be at your office at six."

"Good move, Dimitri. Piss off the woman who you'll be working with." Chief laughed and puffed on his smoke.

"I had to make sure she knew fires."

"Don't you remember Albert Gahlau?"

"Yes, that's where I remember the name." He paused. "Oh shit, that's…"

"His daughter."

Dimitri blew out a breath. This was not a good day. He'd insulted the daughter of a legend when it came to solving fires and his sister's center was currently in flames, although they were thankfully being pulled under control.

Chief walked off, talking into his radio. He stopped and looked back. "Do us a favor, Dimitri. Be nice to her. I think she'll be good enough."

Dimitri went back to where his sister stood and explained the situation to her. When she nodded, he let it go and he continued to stand beside her, offering silent support. Tomorrow morning he would be back to start getting to the bottom of this. It hit him that Shayla knew what time he would want to start collecting information at the site of the fire. Had he just been managed? He would want to be here about six-thirty, which would give them a bit of time before to talk.

Katiya and Warwick finally left. He remained off to the side, alone watching as the fire fighters doused the final flames.

Chapter Eight

Dimitri rose from where he was crouched in the wreckage at The Oasis. He glanced to his left and spotted Shayla working her way toward him. Before they'd met earlier in his office, he'd found out more about her, from before she'd become an agent. He'd heard nothing but good things about her. Dimitri had even contacted his cousin, who was also in the FBI, and she'd provided some insights into Agent Gahlau. Their discussion had solidified what he'd come to find out about Shayla—she was meticulous and driven to do her best. He wouldn't have expected anything less from someone whose dad was so well known.

They had agreed they would work the scene together, overlapping, then would share their findings with each other. Dimitri went back to work studying the scene.

He hadn't spoken to Shannon last night although he'd been tempted to call to see how she was. But her dismissal yesterday had been clear and he was not going to push. Dimitri's gaze narrowed when he spotted a familiar pattern he'd seen in other fires. It was as he'd thought—the serial arsonist wasn't done. That he was back and going after the center showed he was planning to take many lives. Usually The Oasis would have been running a late night class at the time it was hit, but he'd learned from Katiya that they'd had to cancel yesterday because of a pipe bursting. If it wasn't for that, there could have been a massive amount of casualties. The arsonist had to have known of The Oasis' late class on that one night a month to hit at the time he had.

Dimitri thought of the other cases and again over this one then it finally dawned on him what was bothering him. He needed to go back to his office and files.

"Shayla, I'm heading back to the station." He glanced at her.

Shayla lifted her head, her green eyes curious. "What's up?"

"I think I figured out the link between all these cases, but I need to confirm some things first." Dimitri beckoned to her and headed toward the door.

He nodded at the officer there, thinking of the scene when he'd first seen Shannon. While the center was closed since it was still a crime scene so it was empty, he knew Rhianna and Katiya would be in today to handle center business and in case those handling the case and clean up needed access to any other rooms that needed security clearance for them to get in.

In moments he and Shayla were in his SUV and he headed to the station. Shayla didn't speak, just made notes while he drove. Dimitri used the time to think over the scene and what was happening. After they reached the station, he lifted his hand to acknowledge the greeting from the fire fighters, but he didn't stop. Inside he shrugged out of his windbreaker before hanging it up then grabbing the files, a notepad, his laptop and going to the conference table. He dropped the files on the table by the chair then gestured to Shayla to sit. Dimitri took a seat, booting up his laptop.

"Read me the names and addresses of all the places fires were set. If they are businesses, give me the listed officers of company." He paused. "Once you are done, read through it all and give me your thoughts on it. Including the scene we worked today." He put up his hand as she opened her mouth. "I know you haven't had a chance to write it up or think too much on it, but I want your impressions. Profile the arsonist and why they would light a fire at The Oasis."

Shayla nodded then gave him what he'd requested. Dimitri wrote them on his notepad as she did. Once he had the list, he went to work on his computer searching the internet to get the info he needed. He stood, reaching for his desk phone then called places he couldn't access when he searched online. Dimitri slammed down the phone on the last contact then stretched. He glanced at the time—they had been working for hours.

"Lunch? There's a shop that makes sandwiches we can order from."

"Sure." Shayla didn't lift her head from the file as she told him what she wanted.

Dimitri placed the order then refocused his attention on his list. Now it was there for him to see clearly, it clicked. He lifted his head and saw Shayla was watching him.

"The fires all have a rage to them. For some it was like they were playing. But those with a body count...those were to create the most damage. These are all very personal." Shayla paused. "The Oasis, from what you told me, would have been filled with people. They were deliberately going to create havoc. Hurt the most they could. Yes, this is a bubbling rage…someone is out to hurt who they are targeting." Her brow furrowed. "But there is no link between all these fires. No common one person. So who is the target?"

"That I have the answer for." Dimitri stood and went to his file cabinet where he pulled out another open case then handed it to her.

There was a knock on the door and he went to get it. He paid the deliveryman for their lunch then went back to Shayla where Dimitri placed her sandwich and drink within reach. Shayla didn't stop her reading of the file. Dimitri didn't touch his sandwich either, having lost his appetite with the knowledge of what she read. What he had found made the idea of eating impossible. Shayla closed the last file.

"This is a car bombing." Shayla shook her head. "This couldn't possibly be linked to the arsonist."

Dimitri didn't say a word as he slid the notepad toward her. Shayla read what he had written, flipping through the pages for over twenty-five fires. She sat back and stared at him.

"I think I see some of it, but explain." Shayla tapped the notepad.

"You can clearly see the places that are linked to my family. They work there, part of boards of directors or partially own some of the places. But the others without any of them listed affect someone my siblings have become involved with"—Dimitri ticked those off—"Deiter and Harmony work at the university. But Harmony—my brother's fiancée—walks through the science building to get to the bus. My brother Jon was beside himself the day of the fire, not sure where she was. She'd been delayed and that possibly is why she wasn't there. Deyon—a friend of the family and who was dating my brother Leo, but they recently became engaged—her store was lit on fire, but because of the system she had, it was minor and the fire was contained quickly. Deiter's car was bombed, but Arissa would have been the one driving it and so she would have been the one to get killed." Dimitri didn't let his mind imagine such a thing happening. "The rest of the buildings, my sister Katiya's fiancé Warwick, or his company, has a part in or serves on the board of directors." Dimitri tapped his finger on the table. "Each and every one is linked to my family or someone they are involved with or engaged to."

"You state a good case, but from what I've heard of your family, there are officially six of you but there is also another man who is family although he wasn't officially adopted." Shayla put her arms on the table. "There has not been a direct attempt on you…" She paused as if thinking. "Your younger sister Delicia, or Tarak Brady."

Dimitri was surprised and impressed she knew so much about them.

"Just as I'm sure you checked up on me, I did the same with you." Shayla grinned. "Your family would make an interesting case study." She sobered. "If the arsonist holds to what they are doing then one of you not directly attacked will be next. Can you think of who would be targeting your family?"

"That is the problem. I have no clue. There are so many people we all deal with, but I can't think of anyone we pissed off that much." Dimitri shook his head. "I just don't know who it could be, or what, to warn anyone to look out for. Hell, he did a fire then car bombed Deiter and Arissa." Dimitri sat forward.

"Son of a bitch. Deyon's brakes were cut the same day her store was hit. We didn't think they were connected at the time, but maybe they were."

"We need everything they have on that. Then we go over the files, videos we have of the scenes. There is a common denominator there we are missing." Shayla picked up her sandwich. "Call the sheriff and bring him in on this." She stopped, eyes widened. "Sorry, it was made clear we are only here to help, not take over."

"It's okay." Dimitri said. "I'll call Leo."

"We've got a lot to do figure out who this is before…"

Shayla didn't finish her statement. Dimitri didn't need her to. Because he knew that if they didn't find was doing this, eventually they would kill someone he cared about. His thoughts filled with Shannon. He'd have to protect her and knew she would fight him on it. Dimitri didn't care. He would not let her being in a relationship with him put her in danger.

* * * *

Shannon frowned at the knock on her door for she wasn't expecting anyone. Rising from where she was lounging on the couch, she went to her front door, checked first to see who it was then opened it.

"What are you doing here?" She stared at the woman in her doorway.

"You invited me." Carmen looked more amused than offended.

Shannon remembered that she had invited her over to barbeque. "I forgot. I made special arrangements with my mechanic to take my car into the garage to get fixed." Shannon blew out a breath. "Come in then."

"Such a warm welcome." Carmen entered. "We can go drop off your car to the mechanic and then come back to eat."

They had met a few times on scenes that overlapped and they had talked briefly and Shannon had decided to invite her—this was the first time she'd been here.

"Okay. Let's see if I have anything in my freezer first in case we need to buy something." Shannon led the way to her kitchen then quickly checked the freezer.

"We'll have to get something. Give me a sec while I check with my cousin to see if he wants to join us." Shannon turned then said, "Get a water if you like."

She opened the back door then jogged down the steps and strode across the yard toward James' house. As she walked, she realized she hadn't heard Sigmund this morning. That was strange. Shannon stopped, looking around the yard for him. Usually the bird wasn't too far from the house or, if James was about, him. Shannon continued to the house before noting James' truck was missing. She halted, putting her hands on her hips. James was being very erratic and secretive lately—she made a mental note to ask him what was happening with him. With spending all the time she had with Dimitri, she hadn't pushed James on what was going on.

Shannon retraced her steps, thinking of Dimitri. She knew he'd probably heard of her injury, but he hadn't said anything and she was glad for that—she didn't need anyone hovering over her.

Inside she collected Carmen and they got in their respective vehicles and headed to town. At Bennett's Towing she exited her car and looked at the building. Archer Bennett, the owner, had told her to bring in her car anytime today, informing her he'd be working in the shop even though the auto body part was closed today and the towing was for emergencies. Carmen parked next to her and got out.

"You don't need to come in," Shannon stated.

"I am." Carmen shrugged. "I'll just stay in the waiting area while you talk."

Shannon headed to the door and pressed the bell as Archer had told her to do.

"Come to the door by the garage," a scratchy voice said over the intercom.

Shannon frowned — the voice didn't sound like Archer's deep baritone. She dismissed it, thinking the intercom had probably altered it. With Carmen by her side, they went to the door and it buzzed. She pulled it open and entered. The area beyond where they entered was dark, making Shannon frown again. Instinctively, she moved to the other side of Carmen to protect her if needed. Her off duty weapon was in a holster at her ankle, but she didn't reach for it. There was nothing odd she could see, but something was bothering her. She placed her hand on Carmen's, stilling her. Carmen looked at her curiously.

"Now, now, Shannon, don't ruin the party," a voice called out from the darkened part of the garage.

Shannon stiffened as she recognized the voice and the reason the intercom had bothered her. She blanked her mind and focused.

"This is getting really tiresome, Mario."

His laugh was ugly before the light flashed on, temporarily blinding her. When her vision cleared, Shannon took in what she was seeing in one glance. Mario was smiling, pressing his gun against Archer's head — Archer was tied up and kneeling at Mario's side. Carmen gasped. Shannon gripped her arm in warning, not taking her gaze off Mario and his hostage. Carmen gripped her hand and squeezed twice. Shannon remembered that Carmen had said that was her signal with her partner when they couldn't communicate in fires. It was the signal for 'I'm okay'. Shannon returned it then released her, knowing she would be fine.

"There's no need to keep them here. It's me you want… Let them go," Shannon stated walking toward him, her hands held up.

"You are really an arrogant cunt." Mario laughed again, the sound nasty. "You're the prelude" — he pushed the gun at Archer — "but he is the main event." Mario pulled out another gun and leveled it at her. "Stop moving."

Shannon stopped, continuing to keep an eye on him. There was a madness about him. A sound dinged then the scent of smoke filled her nose. Shannon stared behind him in horror as fire engulfed the walls beyond them.

"Fire!" she called.

"Isn't it beautiful?" Mario laughed manically. "My creation."

Shannon stared at him in shock. "Why?"

"You all are so stupid." Mario waved a gun at her. "All those fires I set and none of you knew I did them. Bombed that Wright bitch fiancé's car too. Too bad she didn't die, or him. Hell, the sheriff. I want them all to die." Mario focused on Archer. "But especially him. He took what was mine." Mario hit Archer across the head with the gun. "Lis is mine." He lifted the gun which used to be against Archer, leveling it at the back of Archer's head.

"Why would you do all this?" Shannon spoke, hoping to get his full attention.

"Lis—she's mine. Did you know we met when we were children? We were both in the same hospital in New York when she was rushed there while her family was on vacation. She was so beautiful and we played, but then her family came and they took her away." Mario paused, a sick smile twisted his face. "I never forgot about her. Then, to my surprise, when I was working on the force in New York I met a family member of hers. There she was in a photo, after all those years. I recognized her right away, even told him about her. He kept me informed on her life." Mario frowned. "Justin said I could have her. But then they killed him and I knew nothing of what was happening. So I got a job here to be close to her. It wasn't until I was here I found this one with her. He thinks he can have her." Mario lifted his head.

In his eyes, she read his intentions to kill them all.

"She's going to be a widow."

Shannon was surprised he knew they were married. As far as she understood, no one in town did.

"They aren't married," she lied. *I need to stop this by any means necessary.*

"Liar. I heard it on the bugs I have in their house. The one thing I liked about you was your refreshing honesty"—Mario cocked the gun he held on her—"it figures being with a Wright would taint you."

"I'm confused, Mario. You want Lis, but you kept coming on to me." Shannon shifted, debating if she could make it to her gun. "Why would you do that?"

"You were a pleasant distraction," Mario snarled. "But you felt you're too good for me. Hooking up with that Wright. Some arson investigator. He couldn't find shit."

Shannon eyed the fire filling the area, coming toward Archer and Mario.

"The fire. You need to move forward."

"Oh…that's not necessary. We're all going to burn. Just hope you're dead before the bombs go off." Mario laughed again then sobered abruptly. "You think talking will keep me from shooting him"—he smiled—"you're wrong."

He pulled the trigger. Shannon stepped up as Archer fell, slumping to the floor. Mario turned both guns on her.

"Uh-uh. Give me your piece," he said.

Shannon didn't want to. Mario's smile widened then he looked behind her briefly.

"Come up here, Carmen," Mario said. "It's bad luck you're with Shannon today."

Shannon moved in front of Carmen. "It's me you want, so no."

She glanced at Archer and noted the stain spreading on his shoulder—thank God Mario hadn't shot him in the head. She lifted her gaze to Mario.

"I want him to burn. Feel it as it takes his skin." Mario spat on Archer then kicked him.

Shannon went for her gun. Mario lifted his and fired by her feet. She stopped then looked at him.

"You're not faster than a bullet." Mario shifted one of his guns. "Come here, Carmen. *Now.*"

"No." Shannon whispered low so only Carmen could possibly hear.

"I have to," Carmen said as softly. "Save us."

Carmen came into Shannon's view, her hands up. "Mario, you were always such a fucking weasel."

Shannon stifled a chuckle. When Carmen was close enough, Mario backhanded her with the gun. Carmen spun then fell to her knees by Archer, lip split from the hit. Carmen spat, the blood staining the floor, then shook her head, making her hair frame her face.

"Is that the best you've got?"

Mario didn't reply. He turned his gun on Archer. Carmen dropped forward over him, gasping as she took the bullet. Shannon moved her hand behind her and pulled her knife from her back sheath, thanking God for her cousin who had taught her to always have a backup. Shannon flung her knife as Mario lifted his head. As it struck home in his throat, Mario gurgled and moved his hand, grasping at air. Shannon pulled out her gun and fired repeatedly, heading for him.

"I hate fucking whiners." She lifted her hand and shot him in the center of his forehead.

Mario fell back then became engulfed in flames. Shannon ran to Carmen. She was out and a blooming stain of red had formed on her upper right shoulder. Mario hadn't killed her. *Thank God.* The heat of the flames made Shannon sweat and she looked up to see they were almost upon them. There was no way she could get them both out. Shannon glanced around then noted the open bin. She moved Carmen off Archer. Carmen groaned and opened her eyes before blinking.

"I've been shot."

"Yes," Shannon snapped.

"You could fucking be nicer. I'm shot, damn it." Carmen turned her head and saw the flames.

Shannon could tell the moment the firefighter kicked in. Carmen got to her knees and watched her coolly.

"Time to go."

"We're not going to make it." The whoosh made Shannon look up. The fire rose, coming greedily toward them.

"Son of a bitch accelerant."

"The bin," Shannon said as she grabbed Carmen and lifted her arm over her shoulder then yanked her up.

"Archer—"

"Shut up. I can get him quicker, I need you in the bin to help me get him in." Shannon led her to the bin. "Help me move it."

She propped Carmen beside her then put her shoulder against the side.

"Fuck," Carmen swore as she helped her.

"There. That's good." Shannon turned to Carmen.

She was sweating and swaying. Shannon grabbed her then pushed Carmen up and inside, not waiting to see what happened when she landed. Shannon rushed back to Archer. She grabbed him and began pulling him across the floor. He groaned then glanced at her from glazed eyes before passing out again. Shannon puffed, dragging his dead weight across the floor. Archer was a tall, muscular man and she felt each step in her back and shoulders. But she would not let him go. She hit the bin and Shannon worked to try to lift him.

"Come on, Shannon. Put your back into it." Carmen screamed hanging out the bin to help.

"I am." She finally slid under his shoulder and pushed him partially up.

"Got his hands," Carmen said.

Shannon felt him moving. "I don't need commentary."

Carmen laughed then commanded, "Get under lower in his back and push."

She did and he moved farther. Carmen yelled orders and Shannon pushed until he was up and over into the bin. Archer groaned after he dropped in. Shannon glanced behind her, eyes widening as she saw the flames almost at her—the heat was nearly unbearable. She grabbed the side of the garbage bin and pulled herself in. Shannon grabbed the top and closed it.

"We should have run for the door," Carmen said in the darkness.

"You could get out and go try," Shannon said.

"Such a bitch," Carmen muttered.

"Ladies, why are we in the garbage instead of running like hell from the fire?" Archer's deep, strained sounding voice came.

Shannon was glad to hear it. A bright light flared and Shannon stared at Carmen holding the flashlight.

"What? It's good to be prepared," Carmen said. "We're going to bake in here."

"Not if the bomb gets us first," Shannon said absently, thinking of what she'd viewed and why she had got them in the bin.

"Then we need to go," Archer groaned. "Untie me."

Shannon slid her hand down the waist of her pants and pulled out another small blade. She paused, noticing Archer and Carmen watching her.

"What?"

"Talk about prepared." Carmen peered at her clothing. "What else you got hidden under there?"

She cut off Archer's bindings. "A switch blade under my breast and another knife on the outside of my right thigh." Shannon listed what she had, still reviewing in her head what she had seen.

"Jesus, Shannon. You're a walking arsenal." Carmen breathed a bit shakily then laughed.

"Christ, what does Dimitri think of you having all those weapons on you?" Archer asked. "And why do you even have them?"

"When we've been together I'd already removed them. James, my cousin, taught me to always be armed, just in case." Shannon anxiously thought of all contingencies.

"God, I need to meet him," Carmen said. "That is if we live."

"We're going to live," Shannon replied. *I hope.*

"How do you know?" Carmen asked.

"The situation of the bombs he had placed that I could see." After she contemplated their position, Shannon nodded. "This is the optimum spot."

"For what?" Archer groaned.

Archer was sweating and she knew it wasn't just from the heat of the fire bearing down upon them.

"The blast. With the way he placed the bombs, with us in this spot this could propel us out the bay doors." *There's a lot of shit that could go wrong.* "Or if there are others then we'll just roast."

"You're so cheery," Carmen said.

"How do you even know if it will work?" Archer shifted closer.

"I have a feeling it's this James," Carmen said. "If this works, I'm going to kiss you. Then hump James' leg in gratitude."

"Unless he wants you near him, I suggest you don't try," Shannon warned.

"I'm a wily woman and I'll get around him." Carmen chuckled then sobered again. "What happens if the fire reaches us before the bombs go off?"

Shannon didn't answer her question since it was obvious.

"Too bad we don't have a cell phone to call for help," Archer said.

"Well shit." Carmen slid her hand into her pocket.

"You had this all the time." Shannon snatched the phone out of her hand. "We could have called for help already."

"I was a little distracted getting shot," Carmen growled.

"Stop your whining. You're talking, so it can't be that bad." Shannon dialed.

After the dispatcher picked up, she filled them in then closed the phone and sat to wait. Shannon moved closer to Archer and Carmen as they sat in the garbage and waited for help to arrive. Time crawled at a slow pace and she didn't know how much time passed. There was a rumble then a whoosh. They clung to each other, not sure if it was the fire or a bomb.

Chapter Nine

Dimitri rubbed his eyes, tired of looking at videotapes. He glanced at Shayla who looked as cross-eyed as he did. His office door burst open. Dimitri went to rise then stopped as he spotted James. He sat back down and paused the tape. Leo shifted his hand off his gun then crossed his arms over his chest.

"What are—?"

James cut off Leo. "Someone tried to burn down Shannon's house."

Dimitri stood quickly. "Is she okay?"

"She doesn't even know." James scowled and paced. "They tried. Sigmund caught them and they hurt him." James cupped the sling around his body. I had to take him to the vet. The bastard drugged him."

Dimitri stared at the sling then at James. "Tell me you don't have Sigmund in there."

"Of course I do. The vet said the sedation will wear off soon. Then we're going around town until Sigmund identifies this fucker." James stomped away then back. "I knew something was off at the ranch."

"Stop pacing and explain, James," Dimitri said sharply.

James stood before him. "For months, someone has been spying on the ranch. I've been trying to catch them, but when I get close they vanish. I got a license plate one time, but it was from a stolen car."

"How did you know it was stolen?" Leo asked.

"I had your dispatcher run it for me," James stated.

"Damn it, stop charming my dispatchers." Leo scowled.

"I can't help if they like me." James smiled then his expression went fierce. "This morning, Sigmund didn't start his cackling as he does."

"Who is Sigmund?" Shayla asked.

"Who are you?" James demanded.

Shayla eyes narrowed. "Agent Gahlau. I've heard about you, Mister Conner."

"Have you?" James' face blanked and his eyes went cold. "I would believe what I heard."

Shayla didn't back down. "I do. Just as you should believe I can't be intimidated."

James kept his gaze locked on hers as he continued his story. "Sigmund is a rooster and he is better than a clock. He crows incessantly from two-seventeen to six-seventeen a.m. every day."

Shayla nodded then averted her gaze. James smiled coldly then focused on Dimitri. His expression became more human—that was the only way Dimitri could describe it.

"He didn't and I noticed and got up. I went outside, I saw someone running from Shannon's place. I chased them, but they got away again. This time they were on a dirt bike. I checked Shannon's to see what they were up to and found what they were going to set the fire with. They hit Sigmund with a dart and knocked him out cold. But this time they screwed up and left a witness." James patted the sling. "Sigmund."

"You really can't believe that a rooster will be able to identify a person who tried to set a fire," Shayla said in disbelief.

"James, you can't go around with Sigmund to find this person," Dimitri replied.

"Who's going to stop me?" James smiled.

Dimitri looked at Leo for help.

"I'd love to arrest him, but there is no law against taking around your rooster." Leo shook his head. "Although people will wonder why." Leo paused then said, "Then again, they think James is weird anyway."

"At least someone should go to keep him out of trouble," Dimitri said.

"I can't assign one of my officers to loony and rooster sit," Leo said.

Dimitri sighed then put up his finger. "I have someone who can go with them."

"I don't need protection," James protested.

"This isn't for you. It's for everyone else. And to make sure if you did find anyone with your asinine plan, you don't kill them," Dimitri said.

Leo sat up looking startled.

"Yeah, you didn't think of that did you? We're dealing with James," Dimitri stated and he dialed.

"If you do anything, I will arrest you, James," Leo stated. "And don't you dare think to break out."

"You're still just mad I decked you." James sat at the table. "You'd think you'd be grateful that I saved you sorry hide."

Dimitri ignored them as they bickered. When the phone was answered he said, "I'm at the station and I need you."

He hung up, knowing he didn't need to wait for an answer or a response. Dimitri sat and started the tape again. He wasn't worried about James seeing it. They watched the one they were on then another.

Dimitri had put in the next one in as James asked, "What are you all looking for?"

Dimitri hesitated then said, "A common face at the fires we are watching."

"You mean the serial arsonist," James said.

"How do you know? We haven't revealed this to more than a few people in the department." Dimitri stared.

"I've seen the scenes after you were through. I was curious." James shrugged. "It was obvious" — James gestured to the tape—"just as obvious is the common denominator."

Dimitri looked Leo and Shayla then at James. "We watched the same tape, there is no common yet."

"Because you are thinking as a firefighter" — James looked at Leo then Shayla—"and a cop or law enforcement."

Dimitri sat forward, realizing what he was inferring. "You're saying it's one of us?"

"I can't believe none of you saw that idiot Mario." James sneered. "He looked smug on each tape and even those he wasn't working, he was there in the crowd."

Dimitri thought of the tapes he'd viewed and did remember seeing Mario working but didn't remember him in the crowd. "You're biased."

"But I'm not and if the man I saw too is Mario then he's right," someone with a deep voice said.

Dimitri glanced at Tarak. None of them had even heard him enter, yet he was sitting quietly behind his desk across the room.

"I wondered how long you'd sit there before saying something," James said.

Dimitri looked at him and realized he had heard him. He also noted James had moved so his back, which had been to the desk before, no longer was. Dimitri had noticed that about James and Tarak—they didn't like anyone they didn't know at their back. Tarak rose and strolled toward them. Although he had a slight limp, he didn't look to be in pain, which meant he was taking care of his leg. Tarak picked up the remote then started the new tape. Silent, they watched the next video. Tarak paused the tape.

"That's the man on each tape."

Dimitri stared, stunned at seeing Mario in the crowd as The Oasis burned. He wasn't in uniform and the look on his face was gleeful.

"Son of a bitch." Leo rose. "I'm go—"

The bells rang loud and were followed by the code then the details of the location.

Dimitri stood staring and Leo then Tarak.

"Archer's."

Leo's radio crackled and he moved away, speaking into it.

Dimitri followed, barely aware of the others coming too. Leo suddenly stopped and turned to him.

"We have an officer who needs assistance." Leo grabbed his shoulder. "It's Shannon."

Dimitri grabbed him. "Where?"

"She's at Archer's."

Dimitri ran for his vehicle. The door slammed by his side and he barely spared Shayla a glance as he drove, following the fire trucks. Even before they got close, he could see the fire. Parking a distance away, he then hustled to the scene and stood by the captain. He didn't ask anything, only listening as the man issued commands. From where he stood, he could see the blaze was fully engaged. Suddenly there was a boom that shook the area. There was yelling as those approaching the fire ran back.

"Shannon," Dimitri whispered, knowing they would not be able to save her.

The garage door blew off and something flew out, making firefighters dive for cover to get out of the way. Dimitri's knees weakened as the flames engulfed the building. Even if she was still alive inside, he knew that the fire would get her. They would not go in and risk anymore lives until they were sure there were no more explosives.

Numb, he turned and spotted Lis in her uniform standing behind him. The same look of anguish he was sure that was on his face was on hers. Dimitri was confused why. Tears rained down her face and she dropped to the ground, screaming.

"Archer."

It was then he knew her husband was in the fire. Dimitri hurried to her. He dropped beside her, pulling her into his arms and rocking her. He blinked, trying to still his own tears, but they fell anyway.

I didn't even get to tell Shannon I love her. The thought resonated in his mind. Dimitri felt a hand touch his shoulder and looked up helplessly at Leo. He averted his gaze from the pity he saw there. Dimitri frowned as he viewed James and Tarak striding through the cops and fire personnel as if they belonged there. He craned his neck past Leo's leg to see what the hell they were doing. Tarak stopped along with James at a misshapen object. Dimitri realized it was what had blown out of the garage. He watched, confused as the men lifted the lid. Suddenly three figures stood, leaning over the lip. Dimitri jerked away from Lis and stood.

"Shannon!" he roared.

"Archer!" Lis yelled.

Dimitri ran toward them. The three people in the bin were laughing, leaning over the edge. At the bin he stared at her lovely face.

"By damn, it worked." Carmen laughed loudly then groaned. "Christ, I'm shot. Medic."

"Whiner," Shannon said then focused on Dimitri, touching his face. "Why are you crying?"

"For you."

"Silly man," she said softly.

Dimitri lifted her out into his arms.

"Oh, my, you all are really strong. What's your names?"

Carmen's breathless voice caught his attention. James and Tarak held her up, leading her away.

"Shannon, I told you I would hump his leg," Carmen called then said, "Two for the price of one."

Dimitri looked at Shannon in question.

"Long story," Shannon said. "Put me down. I'm fine. Archer and Carmen are the ones in—" She passed out.

Dimitri lifted her. "Help!"

"Chill, Dimitri," Thom said coming up to him. "Probably a concussion."

"There's blood on her," he said, not appreciating his attitude.

"And on Archer and Carmen." Thom tried to take her out of his arms. "Let go, Dimitri."

A hand squeezed his shoulder and he looked at Leo then released his hold. Thom laid her down then started to check her over. He and another EMT put her on stretcher and took her away. Dimitri followed them to the ambulance. He spotted James and grabbed him.

"Go with her."

"I don—" He breathed out. "Okay, I know you have to stay here. I'll go."

Dimitri knew it was hard for James—he hated hospitals and didn't go near them no matter what. James went into the ambulance and the doors closed moments before they left. They were quickly followed by two more ambulances.

"Shit—Archer. How is he?" Dimitri asked.

"He was shot, but he's talking." Leo sighed. "And laughing. What the hell happened here?"

Dimitri looked away from the departing ambulance and back at the still blazing fire. "I don't know. But we'll get the story from them later."

They both headed to do their jobs.

* * * *

Shannon woke in pain. She figured that was a good thing and she was alive. The power they had flown out the garage with had deafened and stunned her. When the lid of the can had opened, and she'd seen James, she'd wanted to laugh. So she had. They had all stood and laughed like loons. They had lived and she had to remember to thank James for his paranoia which had made him teach her all sorts of things. Things that until today she hadn't thought she would have to use.

She opened her eyes and saw Dimitri sitting in a chair by her bedside. Then she realized he held her hand. Shannon smiled, looking at the large man slumped in the chair, asleep. His face was all she'd been able to think about as she'd knelt in the trash, praying to see him again. As if he'd felt her scrutiny, his lids fluttered open and his light brown eyes met hers. A smile curled his lips and he sat forward, leaning his elbow on the bed then brushing her hair from her face.

"Hey, how're you feeling?"

"That's an obvious answer."

"True. I imagine being flung by a bomb would make you ache. You have a concussion and some abrasions. And you'll be hurting like hell tomorrow from the knock you all took when the bin flew out of the garage." Dimitri smiled then studied her. "I love you, Shannon."

She drew in a breath then rolled her eyes. "Duh. I knew that even if you didn't say so."

"That's not an appropriate response." Dimitri scowled.

"I'm not going to go all weepy, Dimitri, and fawn because you said you love me."

"I know that's not your way." He gripped her hand, kissing it. "I just needed to tell you."

Shannon ran her fingers along the side of his face into his hair, pulling him closer. "Just as I need to tell you I love you too."

Dimitri grinned.

"That doesn't mean I want you to get all caveman. I can solve my own problems," Shannon said.

"I know. But Mario is the arsonist and until we catch him—"

"Didn't you all find a body in the fire?"

"We did. They haven't identified it yet." Dimitri looked confused. "What's that have to do with Mario?"

"Didn't Carmen or Archer tell you?"

"They were sedated from surgery by the time we got here."

"Oh yeah. They were shot." Shannon nodded. "They were so chatty I wouldn't have known. They are strong."

"From what I heard, Carmen was flirting with James and Tarak. James was trying to not leave the hospital because I asked him to stay. Tarak told him to wait outside and he'd let him know if anything happened. He was outside in the parking lot when I arrived."

Shannon imagined James was probably halfway through a bottle of liquor by now. He had a hard time being in hospitals. She went back to the original topic. "The body is Mario."

"What? What happened?" Dimitri asked.

"Get Leo and I'll fill you all in at once," Shannon said.

Dimitri stood then opened the door, sticking his head out. "Leo, she's awake."

The sound of footsteps came toward them. Dimitri retook his seat then Leo filled the doorway. He came to her bedside and patted her hand.

"Good to have you back with us, Conner."

"Sheriff." She thought about telling them what she knew. "Do I have a roommate? I don't want what I have to tell you to get out."

"You have a roommate. It's Carmen and she's out cold. Warwick pulled some strings and got you all into a room together. Archer is across the hall. The family is in the waiting room, waiting to see you all," Dimitri said.

Shannon nodded then filled them in on what had happened in the garage. She answered their questions the best she could.

"Archer will have to tell you how Mario got into the garage," she said, blinking as she fought sleep. *I could use a good twelve to fourteen hours of nothing but eyes shut, dead to the world, sleep. Should have slept first then told them later, but that wouldn't be me. I'm a cop first. My own needs come second.*

"We'll talk to him and Carmen after they wake," Leo said. "Get some rest, Conner, and you're going to get an award for your heroism."

"Keep the award. I was doing my job." She glared at him.

"Suck it up, you whiner. You know it's what's going to happen. You foiled an arsonist and saved two people." Leo grinned. "There will probably be a ceremony too."

"You're enjoying saying that too much."

"I know. We do our job and don't want the fanfare, but they will do it. For the public," Leo said.

Shannon snorted but didn't say anything further.

"How'd you know the bin would fly out like it did? Or if you'd even survive the impact?" Dimitri asked.

"James," she mumbled closing her eyes.

"Damn man, we'll have to thank him again," Leo said.

"I'm even afraid to know the details on why he would know something like what Shannon did," Dimitri replied.

"It's classified," she said sleepily.

"Get some rest, Shannon."

"I want to go home." She shifted on the bed.

"As soon as the doctors release you, I'll take you home." A hand stroked along the side of her face. "Now sleep."

* * * *

Shannon stretched, wincing as her aches made themselves known. They were better after a few days but still enough to make her know what she'd been through.

"God, stop moving damn it." A voice mumbled beside her. "It's the ass crack before dawn. Let me sleep."

"Why are you in bed with me again?" Shannon glared at Carmen beside her. "When are you going home, by the way?"

"When I went to sleep I was in the guest room. It's probably your man who put me in bed with you, again." Carmen didn't even open her eyes. "I would go if *your man* would let me go. It's his fault I'm still here. He confiscated my keys and no one will come get me to take me to my apartment. I can't walk, it's too far." Carmen lifted one lid and glared at her. "So you're stuck with me until he stops hovering like a damn nurse from hell."

"God, he's a pain in the ass." Shannon nodded. "Not letting us do anything. Ordering us around to rest."

"Bullying us if we think of doing anything he deems not acceptable for our recovery." Carmen glared at her. "It's all your fault I'm here. You shouldn't have told him my family was out of town and I didn't have anyone to take care of me."

"He asked what you would do when you went to your apartment." Shannon scowled. "I didn't know my telling the truth would result in this. I really would rather be sleeping with Dimitri."

"I'd rather be sleeping with James. Or maybe Tarak. I can't decide which one I prefer." Carmen smacked her lips. "Maybe a sandwich with me in the middle."

"I don't want to hear it," Shannon warned.

"You're the one who woke me up." Carmen harrumphed. "Shut up so I can sleep."

"You'd have better luck with Tarak. Maybe. James is…" She trailed off, trying to figure out a good word to describe James.

"Strange. Hell, the whole town knows that already. But there is something about him." Carmen pursed her lips. "And Tarak is just…"

Shannon waited for her to continue, but Carmen started to snore softly. She sat up, opened the bedside table to retrieve an item then slid out of the bed. In the hall, she went left in search of the man who kept putting Carmen in bed with her and sleeping elsewhere. She knew he did it because he was concerned of hurting her while she slept. No matter how often she told him she was fine, he wouldn't listen. Since she was still working on the other rooms of the house, only one of the guestrooms was habitable. Shannon pushed open the door then stood in the doorway, looking at Dimitri who was sprawled in the center of the bed. The moonlight bathed him in a soft glow, letting her clearly see his masculine features and broad chest. Shannon closed and locked the door behind her then walked to the end of the bed and yanked the covers off. Dimitri jerked awake, startled.

"Shannon, do you —"

She crawled up the bed and cupped his erection. Dimitri's eyes widened and he shook his head.

"I'm not broken." Shannon opened her mouth and sucked in his cock.

Dimitri shuddered then groaned. She suckled his member greedily, enjoying the sweet taste of him. He touched her hair, but he didn't grab on as he usually would. Frustrated, Shannon swirled her tongue over the head of his cock then pulled back. She slid the condom from her nightstand on his straining member then rose over him. She held his cock and lowered herself onto his erection. Dimitri's fingers flexed on her hips, but again he was gentle.

"Stop holding back," Shannon growled.

"You were hurt." Dimitri looked at her.

"Were. I'm fine now." Shannon lifted up then slid down.

Shannon moved, rocking on him. She squeezed tight on his erection and finally Dimitri broke. He gripped her ass, turning her under him then plowed into her in fast demanding thrusts. Shannon moaned, taking him in and rotating her hips. She held his ass, pulling him into her. They gasped as they came together.

"Shannon," Dimitri grunted as he came.

Shannon quivered, clenching and coming with him. Dimitri's harsh breaths sounded in her ear. Shannon kissed the side of his neck.

"If you ask me to marry you, I'll say yes," Shannon stated.

Dimitri stiffened then turned to meet her gaze. Shannon didn't expect a proposal, but she wanted to let him know where she stood, just as she had when they'd started getting involved.

"But when we get married, I won't have a big wedding. You have to tell your mother that." Shannon closed her eyes.

Dimitri moved off her then cuddled into her. "I will."

It wasn't a proposal, but she already knew it would be coming.

* * * *

Shannon glanced at Dimitri at the aisle surrounded by flowers for the wedding. He looked so dapper standing beside his brothers in his suit. She couldn't wait to muss him up. Dimitri was watching her with a grin on his face. He winked then turned his attention to the minister. Shannon relaxed in the family section on the bride's side.

Katiya and Warwick looked like they were part of a fairytale as they took their vows. This event was a big splashy affair and his mother was in her glory. Mama Wright was having a ball planning the wedding for all her children. Shannon glanced at Tarak who was to Dimitri's left then amended the thought. Well almost all. She had her sights set on pairing Tarak off too. Shannon peeked at James sitting on her left then Jackson as well and wondered if she should warn them that Mama Wright had plans for them too. She decided she wouldn't—let them deal with the matchmaking mama on their own. That would pay them back for laughing at her.

Shannon glanced down at her hand, still not used to seeing the engagement ring on her finger. The ring was the reason they laughed at her—she kept playing with the ring without knowing it, and the men took joy in pointing it out to her. Hell, it was Dimitri's fault, since he'd started it. Two months after she'd said she'd say yes, he'd proposed. They'd been engaged a month already, but it was still new to her.

Shannon focused back on the proceedings in front of her. When they'd announced their engagement, Dimitri's mother hadn't been surprised and hadn't tried to take over or get her to have a big weeding. Shannon suspected that Deyon had something to do with that. Since Leo's engagement, Mama Wright had calmed a bit in her wedding fervor for them. Instead, she'd turned her attention to hoping the rest of what she felt was her family would get married. Heck,

Shannon had heard people in McKingley thought it was an epidemic that was spreading to the single people in town. They would have to wait and see if it was.

Shannon studied Dimitri again. For herself, she didn't mind one bit being engaged. She clenched her legs together remembering Dimitri's promise before he left her to go take part in his sister's wedding — they had plans to ditch the reception early and go home. She was thinking they could forgo the reception and go home to bed. Now she'd just have convince Dimitri. That, she knew, wouldn't take too much effort.

"I now pronounce you man and wife," the minister said. "You may now kiss the bride."

Shannon stood with the rest of the church and cheered as Warwick kissed Katiya, his bride. Shannon's gaze locked with Dimitri's and she imagined all the years they would be together in a seduction's dance.

About the Authors

McKenna Jeffries

McKenna Jeffries has loved the written word from time she picked up her first book. Soon she was creating tales of love and family.

Although McKenna used to make up stories she never thought to put them on paper until…she realized the stories would keep filling her head until they were written. Since then she's been writing and sharing her books.

There is always some new story floating around her head. An itchy feeling in her fingers fills her until she can get a piece of paper to write it down.

She writes because it's a love affair. Writing is in her blood and she enjoys taking readers on a journey.

Aliyah Burke

Aliyah Burke is an avid reader and is never far from pen and paper (or the computer). She is married to a career military man, and they have a German Shepherd, two Borzois, and a DSH cat. Her days are spent sharing her time between work, writing, and dog training.

You can find their contact information, website details and author profile pages at http://www.totallybound.com.

Totally Bound Publishing